Impending Justice

By

Debby Dickerson and *Judi Candela*

PublishAmerica
Baltimore

© 2008 by Debby Dickerson and Judi Candela.
All rights reserved. No part of this book may be reproduced, stored in a retrieval system or transmitted in any form or by any means without the prior written permission of the publishers, except by a reviewer who may quote brief passages in a review to be printed in a newspaper, magazine or journal.

First printing

PublishAmerica has allowed this work to remain exactly as the author intended, verbatim, without editorial input.

All characters in this book are fictitious, and any resemblance to real persons, living or dead, is coincidental.

ISBN: 1-60610-161-7
PUBLISHED BY PUBLISHAMERICA, LLLP
www.publishamerica.com
Baltimore

Printed in the United States of America

Dedication

To my much loved family:
Mom, Dad, my children and their spouses Mike and Chris, Lynn and Keith, and Laura and Jason. To my grandchildren Ashley, April, Mikey, Kyle, Brooke, Brett, Danielle, and soon-to-be great-grand-child.
Love big, smile often, and be safe.
Love you all, Mom (Judi)

and

To my family:
Husband Steve, children Brad and Lori, and Grandchildren. Also, my parents Helen and Albert Sinclair.
The grandchildren to keep you young.
The children to tear at your heart.
The husband to drive you crazy.
The parents to set you straight.
Thanks to all of you for the magic of love. Take care of each other; and have a loving life.

Love you all, Mom (Debby)

1

What a time to run out of gas. Susan should have paid more attention to the gas gauge. Instead she was focused on driving through the thick fog surrounding her. She concentrated on getting to her grandpa's house, wondering what had prompted him to request she come home this particular weekend. Between driving in the unrelenting fog and thinking about her grandpa, she ignored the warning signs on the gauges. It was too late to worry about the gas light coming on now. The bright orange warning light lit up the entire car. Susan realized this meant there was only a trace of gas left. She only hoped it was enough to coast to the side of the road out of traffic's way.

As the vehicle sputtered and died, Susan chuckled to herself. Who was she kidding? She was on a desolate road, so it was highly unlikely there would be any other traffic to worry about.

She sat in her car a few minutes trying to decide what to do next.

For such a smart attorney, how could she be so irresponsible to end up in this predicament? She, of all people, had to be organized and detailed when she faced judges, juries, and clients. Susan would be the first one to criticize a colleague if they didn't have a case well planned and ready for court. And yet, here she was sitting in the middle of the woods because she didn't plan ahead for this journey.

If nothing else, she was going to have to formulate a plan to get out of this situation. Susan had to rely on her survival instincts to get her out of the woods and to her grandpa's house without a car. Her first idea was to call her grandpa from her cell phone. As she dialed his phone number she realized the cell phone didn't work. There was no service, probably due to being too far away from any cell phone tower. Now she had to come up with an alternate plan.

Thinking it would be no problem to walk the rest of the way, she gathered up her purse and jacket. She grew up in the area, so there was no reason to believe she couldn't find her way on foot. Yet, it had been a long time since she romped through these woods. Of course, Susan's days of romping were long gone. As a child she had no fears strolling in the woods. As a little girl she enjoyed the sounds of leaves rustling, the birds cooing, and the occasional squirrel running up a tree. Now she was a stranded adult in a hurry to find her grandpa's house. Susan wasn't in the mood to smell the roses or appreciate her surroundings. She was smart enough to realize she could easily get lost if she took the wrong direction. Susan was not happy with the situation.

Then she remembered her Grandma Nora had given her an Emergency Kit to carry in her car. Susan had no idea what was in the Kit; but decided it was as good a time as any to find out.

She climbed in the back of her SUV, rummaging through the boxes of legal documents she kept in her car. Susan finally found the Emergency Kit buried underneath mounds of boxes and clothing. It was difficult to reach, but luckily she was a petite woman that could crawl through small spaces to retrieve it. With the kit in hand, she exited the vehicle. It was a good thing there were no mirrors available because Susan would be alarmed seeing herself so disheveled. Her long blonde hair was a matted mess after crawling through the vehicle. Her grandpa would be surprised to see his beautiful granddaughter in such disarray. Of course, that was the least of her worries.

Susan found a flashlight, but realized it had been sitting in her car for over two years. Now she wondered if the batteries were still strong. Naturally, it was still better to have a dim light than no light at all. Susan began walking as she muttered to herself about what an idiot she was to run out of gas. The further she walked, the wetter her clothes got from the damp fog. She was getting chilled, so she stopped long enough to put her jacket on. While she was standing there she heard strange noises in the area. Susan had to remind herself that after living in the city for five years, all country sounds were strange. There was no reason to be afraid.

To help keep her mind off her predicament, Susan decided to play a game with herself. She would listen to the various noises; and then try to identify what they were. It was a game she used to play when she was a child growing up at her grandparents' house. As she thought about the game, she reflected about when she moved in with her maternal Grandparents. Her father had gone to prison and her mother died shortly after that. Susan was young so she didn't have a lot of memories of her parents; but she would always remember being raised by Charlie and Nora, her two wonderful Grandparents.

Susan had many happy memories with her grandparents. At the time she didn't realize how much knowledge she would gain from them. A simple game of identifying sounds was actually a learning experience. Grandpa Charlie made it fun, so it didn't seem like it was educational at the same time. It's a game she continued to play as an adult. Was she hearing a Tree Frog or Whippoorwill? A few seconds later she heard that weird noise again. This time it sounded closer, she thought. Yet, her sense of direction was out of kilter so she couldn't be really be sure where it the noise was coming from.

Suddenly Susan heard a terrifying scream that sent a chill down her back. She quickly shined her fading flashlight around, trying to locate the source of the sound. Out of the corner of her eye she caught sight of something. To her relief, it was just an owl swooping down by the side of a road. Just as quickly as it swooped downward, it soared back up to the trees. Susan wondered if it was a Screech Owl. Her grandpa used to say Screech Owls could scream and make sounds like a person in distress. Susan had never heard one the whole time she had lived with her grandparents; but her grandpa mentioned he had seen a few recently.

Susan looked at her watch to see how long she had been walking. It felt like she had been walking hours, but it had only been minutes. Time seemed to drag by while she was trying to keep her wits about her as she walked alone in unfamiliar territory. She was hoping to see the porch light shining at grandpa's house very soon. The flashlight batteries were extremely weak now; and she was losing light quickly. Between the fog and useless flashlight, she could barely see two feet in front of her.

Not wanting to waste any time, Susan continued walking. She concentrated on every step she took, trying to avoid any holes or rocks that might cause her to trip. The last thing she needed was to get injured and have to wait to be rescued. She was more determined than ever to speed up her pace to reach Charlie's house soon.

The strange sounds continued to get closer. Susan thought she heard a clopping sound, but didn't recognize what was causing it. Just as Susan wondered about her wisdom in choosing to walk, she heard something in the bushes to the side of her. With a quick turn she shined the light in the direction of the sound. It was a scared rabbit running away, just as frightened as Susan was.

By this time, Susan's nerves were frayed. She was so distracted by the unusual noises; she accidentally strayed away from the road she was originally on. Now she found herself in the woods with no path to follow. Between the strange sounds and the rabbit darting out of the bushes, she was a bundle of nerves. The flashlight was no longer working. She tapped the light on the side of her hands, hoping it would bring some life to the batteries. Nothing worked. The flashlight was of no use anymore. She was going to have to guide her way through the woods without light.

Feeling very afraid, Susan was ready to give up. She even considered going back to the car but knew she wouldn't be able to find her way back where it was parked. She considered curling up by a tree until daylight; but admitted to herself that she was too frightened to do that. As she dwelled on the dilemma she was in, Susan could tell the clopping noise was even closer than before. She tried forcing herself to be brave, but it wasn't working. She had no choice but to keep moving. Susan remembered her grandmother singing out loud when she was stressed over something. Maybe it was time to sing. In reality all she wanted to do was cry.

Finally Susan was at the crest of a hill. She thought she could see lights flickering at the bottom of the hill. Unfortunately, she still needed light to guide her down the hill or she might stumble and roll the whole way down. With the fog clouding her vision, she couldn't be certain what she was seeing. It could be her eyes just playing tricks on her. Then she remembered bringing the flares. Now she hoped she could figure out the instructions on lighting it. Susan had read the directions when her grandmother gave them to her, but that was a long time ago. She remembered something about pulling a cord and then striking it. Finally, with trial and error, Susan managed to get the flare lit.

Holding the flare out and to her side she had enough light to help find a path. It burned so brightly it was difficult for her eyes to adjust to the light. Everything looked three-dimensional with the flare burning so intensely. She couldn't focus properly. While Susan was trying to deal with this new problem, she stumbled over something lying in the pathway. She aimed the flare toward the object to see what she tripped over. With that, Susan screamed! She had tripped over a man lying on the ground.

The man did not respond to Susan's scream, nor did he move after she tripped over him. Susan realized he was either dead or seriously injured. It was obvious he needed help. With a shaky hand she reached down for his wrist to check his pulse. She felt nothing. Because Susan was shaking so hard, she didn't know if she checked his pulse accurately. She took his pulse a second time, but there was still nothing.

Susan started running down the hill, screaming all the way. She slipped again, almost losing her balance. Pulling herself together she took a deep breath and began running again. She realized the last tumble caused her to lose the flare. Once again, she had no light to guide her through the unfamiliar area. She heard the clopping sound again.

Just then, out of the fog, she saw a massive object coming toward her. To avoid getting hurt, she threw herself down on the ground for protection. She heard very loud clopping sounds as an animal whizzed past her. In that brief glance, Susan recognized the animal to be a huge horse. The running horse would have knocked her over if she had stayed standing. She was relieved to know it was a horse that caused the clopping sounds rather than some unknown beast. Yet, she was still shaken knowing she could have been trampled to death if she hadn't thrown herself out of its path.

Even though she was dazed, Susan could see that someone was climbing off the massive horse. She could make out that the person was dressed in black; but the fog was so heavy she couldn't tell whether the person was male or female. Susan got the impression that the person was tall and thin, but wasn't sure. Everyone looks tall when you're looking up at them from the ground.

A young woman ran over to Susan to make sure she was alright. She asked Susan if she was injured and offered to help her stand up. Susan took the woman's arm and got back on her feet. As she was helping Susan get up, she introduced herself as Paula White. She explained that she lived a few miles down the road; and was out taking her horse for a ride. Susan then introduced herself as Susan Mitchell, Charlie Fletcher's Granddaughter. She explained how she was on her way to her grandpa's house when she ran out of gas, then got lost trying to walk the rest of the way. They both agreed it was a good thing Paula found her.

As Susan's nerves settled down, anger set in. Susan surprised Paula with her outburst. She wanted to know why the heck somebody was riding a monster horse at full speed in the middle of the dark woods! And how dare she use the horse as a ramrod to plow everything down in its path! Paula was taken aback by the angry questions, but understood why somebody who almost got ran over by her horse could be upset.

Paula regained some of her composure. She explained why she was out riding her horse in the middle of the woods. She was feeling claustrophobic and needed to get out of the house for a while; and her horse, Casey, needed the exercise. Paula told Susan she heard somebody scream, so she was trying to find where the scream came from. She further explained the reason she was riding so fast was so she could get to the person who was screaming for help. With that, Susan apologized for being so impolite.

She explained to Paula that she isn't normally this uptight and rude. With a perplexed look on her face, Paula waited to hear what Susan had to say next. Susan went on to describe how she discovered a dead body as she was trying to find her way out of the woods. Seeing that Susan was clearly shaken, Paula put her arms around her. While she tried comforting her, Susan broke down and sobbed. Susan described how she ran out of gas, heard strange noises, got lost, and then tripped over a dead body. She admitted she's never been this frightened in her entire life. Paula didn't know what to say. It was obvious that Susan was traumatized.

Paula grabbed Casey's reins and swung herself back up in the saddle. She told Susan to climb up behind her. Paula offered to take Susan back to her house so she could get her brother, John. She said her brother would know what to do. Susan looked at Casey, realizing there was no way she was going to climb on his back with no saddle. Yet, Susan was afraid to stay in the woods alone. As she attempted to climb on the massive horse, it was clear that she was not going to succeed. Casey was beginning to get jumpy with a stranger trying to climb on him. Paula was afraid Casey might buck Susan off, so she asked Susan to stay right where she was and promised to come back with help. Paula told her the house wasn't far away, so she could be back within half an hour. Susan decided she could handle staying in the woods alone for that short of a time, even though she didn't like the idea. The alternative of getting bit or thrown off the huge horse wasn't appealing either, so Susan told Paula to go without her.

Susan watched the horse and rider leave. She started thinking about the clopping sound she had heard earlier. Then she thought about the poor dead man laying somewhere in the woods. Susan began wondering if there was any connection to Paula and the dead man. Susan's mind was going in several directions. For a brief moment she wondered if Paula had anything to do with the death of the man in the woods. Instead of acting like a woman lost in the woods, she was reacting like the lawyer she is.

Ever since she passed the Bar Exam, Susan tended to view every negative situation as a legal case. She always has her lawyer cap on, ready to solve a case or convict a bad guy. Susan was an excellent lawyer in the court room; but her thinking was distorted in the middle of the woods. She was glad Paula was getting help and couldn't read Susan's mind right now. Susan realized she was grasping for answers, letting her mind wonder so she wouldn't dwell on her personal predicament of being lost. Even so, she was cognitive enough to know she could not depend on a stranger rescuing her. What if Paula didn't come back? She needed to get to Grandpa's fast. Susan wanted to get as far away from the dead body as possible. She started jogging as fast as she dare with the fog still too thick to see more than a few feet away.

Finally, she saw the familiar farm house only yards away! Thank goodness Grandpa had the lights on. It actually made the old house look rather eerie with the fog so thick around it; but at the same time looked like a safe haven. As she approached the house, she kept her fingers crossed that Charlie would be at home. Surely he'd be there knowing she was coming. As she was half way down the lane to his house, she saw her grandpa come out on the porch. Susan yelled his name, causing him to look up.

As she reached the porch she fell into her grandfather's arms. Susan was so happy to see Charlie; she didn't want to let him go. They stood on the porch a long time, hugging. Finally, he escorted Susan inside the house. The first thing he asked her was why she was on foot. Where was her car? Susan explained how she ran out of gas; and then got lost in the woods. Charlie asked why she didn't call him so he could have picked her up. She told him her cell phone didn't work amongst all the trees in the woods; so she had no choice but to start walking.

After she sat down Charlie could see she was exhausted. He offered to get her some hot tea or cocoa; but Susan insisted she didn't want anything. She only wanted her grandpa to sit next to her. She wanted to tell him all about her horrible nightmare of being lost in the woods. Susan was trying to tell Charlie about the dead man she discovered. She was so out of breath that he was unable to understand what she was saying. Charlie told her to take it easy and catch her breath first. While she was trying to recover, the sound of sirens could be heard in the distance. Her grandpa looked at her with concern. He realized something was seriously wrong. He told her to take her time and tell him what happened tonight.

Susan told him everything. She began with how she ran out of gas, decided to walk the rest of the way, tripping over a dead body, and almost getting run down by a horse. Charlie was numb as he listened to the events of her journey. He couldn't believe what he was hearing.

He immediately thought about the sirens they heard only moments ago. Charlie wondered if it had anything to do with the body his granddaughter just discovered. His instinct was to hold her in his arms to protect her from this nightmare. Susan felt like a little girl again, secure in her grandpa's arms.

IMPENDING JUSTICE

From the moment she walked into Charlie's house, Susan felt an overwhelming feeling of safety and warmth. In spite of the blaring sirens in the distance, the house was full of great memories of love, laughter and happy times. It was always a safe place for Susan. As she looked around the room her eyes filled with tears. There in the corner of the living room was her old stuffed animal, Pluto, sitting on the stool her grandpa made her when she was a child. She suddenly remembered leaving Pluto behind when she moved to the city…knowing Pluto would remain safe with her grandparents, just like she always felt protected when she was there.

While Susan sat on the old lumpy sofa absorbing the smells and sights of her favorite place to be, Charlie fixed her a hot cup of cocoa with marshmallows. Charlie never forgot how Susan loved to drink her hot chocolate when she was frightened or sad. After a few sips of her yummy drink and her grandpa sitting by her side, Susan was finally able to relax. The sounds of the siren faded, but she couldn't get rid of the fear she experienced in the woods.

Seeing that she had calmed down, Charlie asked her to tell him again everything that happened. She told him again how she ran out of gas, found a dead body, and almost got hit by a horse. Charlie let her speak without interrupting. When she finished explaining the series of events, Charlie told her he was going to call the police to make an official report. Unfortunately, when he attempted to make the phone call, the lines were dead. Charlie suggested Susan get some sleep; they would try to call again in the morning. He was concerned about Susan's state of mind. Charlie felt his granddaughter was too exhausted to hold up under the inquisition she'd have to endure at the sheriff's office. He thought Susan would be more clear-minded to answer the police questions tomorrow, after she's had some sleep. Charlie assured her that there was probably a reasonable explanation for what happened. They would both feel better waiting until tomorrow.

2

The next morning Susan woke up to the sun shining through the window, offering another beautiful day. She knew it was going to be a good day, but wasn't as confident about feeling well herself. The pain in her arms and legs reminded her how she threw herself on the ground to avoid getting knocked down by a horse. Bruises were popping up everywhere! She was very stiff and sore, taking each step slowly. Just what she needed! Charlie was still sleeping so she tip-toed carefully as she shuffled into the kitchen to make some hot buttered toast.

She was ready to put the bread in the toaster when she noticed Grandpa Charlie standing at the doorway laughing. He told Susan she was a breath of fresh air to see sitting in his lonely kitchen. Charlie missed the old days when his wife, Nora, was busy cooking in the morning. He kissed Susan on the top of her head and thanked her for coming to stay with him. Charlie offered to make Susan a nice country breakfast. He was sure she hadn't been eating well by the looks of her.

After a good night's sleep, waking up to the sounds of birds chirping, the thought of eating a home-cooked breakfast sounded wonderful. Unlike her cold, lonely apartment, Charlie's home was inviting and warm. She looked forward to joining her grandpa for a country breakfast and reminiscing about the good times. It was a short-lived sentiment though. The reality of the last night's excitement overtook her happy thoughts. She remembered her grandpa saying they needed to call the sheriff's office to report the dead body she found. Charlie didn't forget they needed to call the sheriff's office; but when he tried to call the phone was still dead. He told Susan they would have to drive to the sheriff's office after breakfast. Without saying, that chore sure put a damper on the visit.

After her grandma passed away, Susan had considered moving in with Charlie; but realized it was too far for her to commute to work. Susan worked in Springfield, which was at least a two hour drive from Charlie's house. Plus, she often worked late preparing cases for trial. It would not be in her best interest to live so far away from work, so she opted to move into a small apartment near the court house instead.

Susan's boyfriend, Mike Hayes, also lived in Springfield. As a police officer, he worked various shifts, so their schedules made it difficult to maintain a good relationship. If Susan moved to the country to stay with her grandpa, she'd hardly ever get to see Mike. Between her job and her boyfriend, it seemed best to remain in Springfield for the time being. So when she did visit her grandpa, it was extra special because she didn't get to see him as often as she would like.

After a wonderful breakfast together, they discussed their plans for the day. Susan hated wasting her visit playing detective, but she couldn't ignore the scary events of last night. As soon as she showered and dressed, Charlie agreed to drive her to the police station so they could make their report. Afterwards they would drive to where her car was stranded. Charlie suggested they take a gas can with them to put some gas in the tank. Then Susan would be able to drive it to a gas station to fill up.

As they entered the police station they noticed it was a full-house. There were the standard community drunks, lawyers yelling at officers, people handcuffed to a wooden bench, and a variety of other unseemly characters. They found their way to an officer who took their report. Charlie and Susan both hoped the dead body might have been found by now. Maybe the officer could enlighten them to what happened or whose body it was. Instead, the officer just thanked them for reporting the incident and bid them farewell. Stunned, Charlie and Susan quickly left the building.

On the way to find Susan's car, Charlie stopped at the phone company while Susan waited in the car. To his surprise, when they checked the lines they told him his line was broken. They didn't have an explanation for it, but they could tell through their computer system that the actual wires had been destroyed. The clerk stated that it was possible an animal had gnawed on it, breaking the line and causing the phone not to work. Charlie was suspicious about the clerk's explanation. He had never heard of an animal destroying telephone wires. The clerk said a repair man could be sent out tomorrow to inspect the line. Charlie had no choice but to accept the fact his phone wasn't going to be fixed right away; but he didn't have to like it.

Because Susan was already stressed from the previous night's events, Charlie decided not to mention the phone lines had been destroyed. He didn't want her to worry about it and besides, it was going to be fixed by tomorrow anyway. Right now the important thing was to get gas for Susan's car. As they drove along they were laughing and reminiscing about old times. Charlie would tell her what silly stunts she used to do as a little kid; and Susan would tell him how she remembered Grandma yelling at him for eating pie before dinner.

With Susan's directions, they finally approached the area her car ran out of gas. They reached the spot she left her car, but discovered there was no car to be found. The vehicle was missing. Susan clearly remembered being in this general area when her car died, but now she wondered if maybe the fog had her more disoriented than she realized. They walked around looking for tire tracks but found none. Could she have been this lost, she wondered? She's driven to Charlie's house many times and knew the roads pretty well. Susan didn't understand how she could be this wrong about where she left her car.

Susan wondered how far she had walked last night when she came upon the dead man's body. Charlie showed Susan the path she probably followed when she left her car. They decided to walk a little ways to see if maybe somebody moved her car. Without discussing it verbally, Charlie and Susan were also looking for the body she had found. No matter where they looked, they found nothing. In addition to not finding the car or the dead body, there was no evidence or indication that a horse had run through the area. No hoof prints, no tire prints, no body. Susan couldn't help but think maybe the horsewoman, Paula, might have some answers…but who is she? Charlie said he was unaware of any neighbor named Paula. Charlie also stated he was unaware of any neighbors that had horses. They were both baffled.

When they got back to Charlie's car they had to figure out what the next step should be. They already reported the dead man to the police, but they forgot to mention Susan's car was missing. In fact, Susan didn't want to report it missing if Paula or her brother might have put gas in her car and then drove it back to their house for Susan to pick up. Then she remembered locking the car doors, so it wouldn't be possible for anyone to drive it away. Yet, since she didn't know Paula or her brother, maybe it was better to be safe than sorry. Charlie and Susan drove back to the sheriff's office to report the car missing.

After they made the second police report, Charlie suggested they drive to the café in town to have lunch. Afterwards they could go back to the house. Each was trying to humor the other. Neither one wanted to dwell on the negative events of the day. Susan was worried but didn't want Charlie to know. Charlie was scared too, but didn't want Susan to know. They were both anxious to keep each other protected from concern over everything that happened.

Charlie was anxious to get home so he could look at the telephone wires, but didn't want to rush through lunch. He wanted to know if the lines had been cut by an intruder or just chewed by some critter in the night. He hoped it was an animal and not somebody evil cutting his wires. The phone was Charlie's only way to maintain contact with the outside world. It would be awful to think somebody could be so mean to cut the wires making Charlie unsafe in his own home.

Relaxing at the café, they started looking over the menu. Charlie told Susan the café had a reputation for serving the best home cooked meals in the state. Susan said she was anxious to find out because she was starving. They both decided to order the special of the day. The special that day was meatloaf, mashed potatoes, green beans and rolls. In addition, there was iced tea to quench their thirst. The waitress noticed they had made up their minds so she prepared to take their order.

The waitress was Lois Williams, a long time resident of Monroe County. Susan observed Ms. Williams looked to be about the same age as her grandpa. She mentally noted she had a "grandmotherly appearance" and probably should be retired by now. When Lois approached the table she called Charlie by name. She asked him what he was doing in town on a Saturday night. Apparently her grandpa didn't come to town often on a weekend, as she was learning from the waitress. Lois chatted more about how the town always goes crazy on the weekends with so many kids hanging around. The town kids would spend the weekends trying to make money with car washes or selling items people didn't need or want. In between their activities they would come to the café for a Coke or Milkshake, which kept Lois hustling trying to keep up with them.

As she was writing their lunch order, Charlie asked Lois if she remembered his granddaughter Susan. He mentioned that Susan didn't come to town often, but he wanted to make sure she got to eat at the finest diner around. With that, he winked at Lois and she blushed. Susan just looked back and forth at them wondering how well they really knew each other. She was going to have some questions for Grandpa later. Susan found it fascinating to observe two people their age flirting with each other.

While Lois was bussing the other tables, Charlie and Susan settled in their chairs. They both started talking at once, and then began laughing. Susan could feel some of the tension leave her body. It felt good to be with her grandpa. Nobody else could make her feel this relaxed after such a traumatic ordeal on her journey here. They agreed to enjoy their lunch and avoid talking about dead bodies or missing cars. Later they could discuss all the things that have happened; but for now they were going to just enjoy each other's company.

Smiling his boyish grin, Charlie asked Susan to tell him all about her boyfriend Mike Hayes. He said he wanted to know everything about him. He wondered when he was going to get to meet this special guy. Susan squirmed in her chair. This was not a subject she wanted to discuss right now. She was having difficulty dealing with her relationship with Mike; and wasn't ready to talk about it. Susan looked her grandpa in the eye and told him there would be no meeting Mike during this visit. She explained that her relationship with Mike had gone sour recently. Susan felt that Mike was too controlling. She had the impression Mike expected her to jump when he wanted something. She wasn't pleased with his attitude at all.

Of course, Susan admitted that Mike had a lot of good qualities as well. After all, she was attracted to him in the beginning. She began describing Mike as a Brad Pitt Look-Alike. Realizing Charlie didn't have a clue who Brad Pitt was, she chuckled to herself. She clarified what Mike actually looked like by describing him the way Charlie would better understand. Susan described Mike as tall, dark, and a very attractive man. He was in his mid-thirties; and had been a police officer for eleven years. Mike was a "Big Brother" to two boys from the inner-city. She summarized her former boyfriend as a good man overall; but too secretive for her liking.

The other thing that bothered her about Mike was how he was always asking questions about her father. Susan stated she had made it very clear from the beginning that the subject of her father was off limits. Of course she didn't tell Mike how little she knew about her own father. Because her father was never in her life, Susan labeled him as her "DNA donor" instead of thinking of him as a dad. She continued telling her grandpa that she wasn't willing to talk about her father to Mike or anyone else until she learned more about him herself. After blurting that out, she told her grandpa she was sorry for being so blunt. Susan knew it hurt Charlie to talk about her father, so it was a subject they generally avoided when they were together. This visit was going to be different though. She had questions regarding her father; and her grandpa was the only one with the answers.

Charlie was disappointed to learn how unhappy Susan was with her boyfriend. He was looking forward to meeting him; and assumed she was going to bring Mike with her to announce their engagement. Instead he was saddened to learn Susan was unhappy with her relationship with Mike. He always hoped he'd walk her down the aisle some day in the near future.

An engagement was obviously not going to be happening after all. Charlie was even more shocked to hear Susan talk about her dad. In all of her 30 years she never asked many questions about her father. He knew one day she would be curious and want to know all about her dad;

and he was prepared to discuss it when she was ready. It just didn't occur to Charlie that this visit was going to be the time.

Lois brought their dinners out and asked if they needed anything else. She'd come back to check on them shortly. With forks in hand, they started digging into their delicious feast. They settled into a comfortable silence, each having their own thoughts. As they enjoyed their lunch, Charlie's mind drifted to thoughts of Susan's missing car, the dead body she found, and the recent problems with the downed telephone wires. He remembered Susan mentioning the woman on the horse. In such a small town everyone knows their neighbors; but he had never met or heard of a woman named Paula White. He wondered where she lived and who she was. Charlie always made it a point to know his neighbors, so he wanted to find out who this mysterious woman was.

While Charlie was lost in his own thoughts, Susan was thinking of Mike. She thought back to how weird he had acted when she told him she was breaking up with him. Susan knew she was vague when she tried to explain why she felt their relationship wasn't working. She felt she couldn't give him a specific reason, because even she couldn't put her finger on what exactly bothered her. What she was certain of is that she was unhappy. There was something about Mike's attitude that made her feel uncomfortable; so she wanted to end the relationship before they got too serious. When she left Springfield to visit her grandpa, she told Mike she didn't want to see him anymore.

Instead of arguing or becoming emotional about breaking up, he acted very cool and calm. Mike didn't debate the break up whatsoever. Instead, he voiced his disappointment that he wasn't going to get to meet her grandpa. It didn't take a Rocket Scientist to figure out how strange Mike's comment was. He was more concerned he couldn't meet her grandpa; and less disturbed that Susan was breaking up with him. After all that, Mike still insisted he wanted to ride along with her so he could meet Charlie. She made it clear that Mike was not going with her to visit her grandpa. Susan wanted to go alone and leave their rocky relationship behind. She didn't need somebody like Mike in her life.

After their meal Lois walked back to their table with the check and a huge piece of chocolate cream pie. She also had a sly looking smile on her face as she placed the luscious dessert in front of Charlie. Lois then asked Susan if she wanted any dessert, but she declined. When Lois walked away Susan turned to her grandpa. There he sat with a sheepish grin on his face. He told Susan he "thought" Lois has a soft spot for him. He explained that since his wife died, Lois had been treating him extremely nice. Susan couldn't help but giggle. Her grandpa has a girlfriend! How sweet!

As happy as she was for her grandpa, Susan felt it was time to deal with the problems that surrounded them. She suggested Charlie eat his pie while she summarized the situation. She started talking about how she found a body, then the body was gone; she heard a horse, then there was no horse around; she met a girl named Paula White, then discovered nobody knows a girl named Paula; she left her car stranded, then it was gone. Susan summarized by thinking she must be completely crazy! The one thing she was sure of though is she could not have walked all that way from her apartment in the city to her grandpa's house in the country. She had to have driven, so where was her car? She can't be totally crazy!

Charlie listened and watched the expression on Susan's face. He could see how stressed she was from the ordeal she just experienced. He didn't want to upset her any further, so he chose not to mention the phone lines being cut. He would keep that to himself for the time being. He assured Susan she wasn't losing her mind. He agreed the events were bizarre, but refused to believe Susan was going crazy. Charlie was sure they could get to the bottom of this soon.

On the way home, they decided to stop at the neighbor's house right up the road from where Susan thought she left her car. As they pulled into the drive, Grandpa spotted Grady outside working on his tractor. Grady could have posed for any Farm Magazine. He was the perfect candidate that looked like what the public expected a farmer to look like. He wore his shirt sleeves rolled up with a pack of cigarettes nestled in the cuff. His face was weathered and sunburned. Grady could be found on his tractor most every day, until late in the evening. Charlie drove the car closer to where Grady was. He rolled down the window and asked if he had seen a stray car or horse around any time last night or today. Grady told him he wasn't aware of any car or horse anywhere. Then with a second thought Grady suggested that maybe the new neighbors had horses. He said somebody bought the old Maddock place, so it was possible those folks had horses.

Grady glanced over to Charlie's car and noticed Susan sitting there. With a big grin he ran over to her window and asks if she came back to pay him for stealing that old hat of his years ago. They all laughed at that comment. When Susan was little, Grady's wife gave Susan his old hat and told her to get the ragged thing out of her sight. Susan used it for her snowman and Grady had looked for his hat for days. When he finally found it, he agreed the snowman needed it more than he did. They continued exchanging chitchat about the old days, had a few more laughs, and then decided it was time to head home.

3

When they pulled up in front of the house, Grandpa made no move to get out. He had been dreading having to tell Susan her father was getting ready to be released from prison. Her father, Mark Mitchell, was going to be out on parole. He had been in prison for the last twenty-eight years for armed robbery and shooting a guard. Even though Mark was his son-in-law, he had only visited the prison twice to see him.

The first time Charlie went to the prison was to tell Mark he was the proud father of a beautiful baby girl. Mark's wife, Sarah, gave birth to a healthy little girl, named Susan. Charlie explained why his daughter couldn't bring the news to him herself. Sarah had a difficult pregnancy and was still recovering from an even more difficult birthing experience. She physically wasn't able to make the drive to the prison, so Sarah wanted her father to bring Mark the news. Charlie told Mark that Sarah would come visit him as soon as she was back on her feet. He assured Mark that they would take good care of Sarah and the baby in the meantime. After all, Charlie and Nora were now the proud Grandparents of little Susan…and they would make sure their daughter and grandchild were well taken care of. He also told Mark that Sarah and Susan would continue living with them as long as they needed to.

The next time Charlie visited the prison was to bring Mark sad news. He had the unpleasant duty to inform Mark that Sarah was killed in a car accident. Without having time to grieve for the loss of his daughter, he felt obligated to tell Mark what happened. Charlie always felt that his daughter had given up on life and became careless after Mark went to prison. Although she loved Mark with all her heart, she was embarrassed that her husband had committed such an awful crime, causing a guard to be killed. When he went to prison, Sarah felt she lost a part of herself. Mark not only left a wife behind, but a baby daughter as well. It seemed as if the wreck was Sarah's way of giving up. Charlie always blamed Mark for causing his lovely daughter to lose her life so needlessly.

When Sara died, Charlie and his wife Nora adopted Susan. They took over total responsibility, getting her through the usual scrapes, broken arm, teenage years, puppy love, and finally law school. Now she is a full fledged lawyer and adult. They stood by Susan all those years of her fighting off bullies that made comments to her about having a murdering father. She never got to know him; yet she was always put in a position to defend him. Now Charlie only wished his wife Nora could have lived to see how successful and beautiful Susan turned out. She would have been proud.

Susan was aware her father wanted to meet her. A few months ago her grandpa mentioned Mark would be getting out of prison soon; and wanted a chance to know his daughter. She just wasn't prepared that this reunion was going to be so soon. Apparently she was going to have to do some serious thinking about how she would deal with their first meeting. Susan reflected how her life was good in spite of not having a father or a mother. Her mother died, so she couldn't help that she wasn't there to raise Susan. But her father, on the other hand, made bad choices causing him to be taken away from her. He was never there for her or anyone else in his life. Susan resented that she was connected to this man at all.

From what she knew about her dad's life, it was anything but pleasant. That didn't give him the right to do illegal things though. It certainly didn't give him the right to kill somebody. To make matters worse, her dad would never even admit to the burglary, much less the murder. He wouldn't tell the police if he had partners or where the stolen money was.

Charlie broke her train of thought by telling her his real reason for inviting her to visit. On one hand he was hoping the visit would be Susan announcing her engagement. On the other hand, Charlie wanted to have the opportunity to tell Susan in person that her father was being released from prison. He didn't want to tell her on the phone that her dad wanted to meet her after all these years. Susan deserved to hear this news from her grandpa first. If she was willing to meet her father, then Charlie wanted to make sure he could be with her. He didn't want her having to deal with this by herself. She was grateful to hear that.

Just staring off in space she was thinking about what the meeting would be like. Her grandpa told her Mark was being released in three weeks. This gave Susan very little time to think about it before deciding what to do. She always knew one day this was going to happen, but wondered why it had to be now…with her world completely turned upside down from the past few days, she didn't know if she was ready for an additional problem. For so many years she tried to block her father out of her mind. She never knew him, so it was easy to keep him at a distance. Yet, it always loomed over her head that there was a man out there that shared her DNA. He never seemed like a real person. He was more like an ancestor that was gone long before you can remember.

When her grandpa first invited her to stay with him a few days, she was delighted. For Susan the timing was perfect. She had just finished a very lengthy trial that took all her stamina and energy. After four months of deliberation, she finally won the case. Instead of celebrating though, she was in the process of ending her long relationship with Mike Hayes. She was ready for a breath of fresh air, so staying with her grandpa was the well-deserved break she needed.

Unfortunately, the breath of fresh air she was looking forward to was now turning into a foul smell instead. There were too many unanswered questions developing on this journey. This was not at all what she had anticipated during this visit. Susan didn't know which problem should be addressed first. Even though she knew her father would eventually get out of prison, it hadn't occurred to her that it was going to be this soon. Add that to the bizarre events since she arrived in town, Susan was beginning to wonder if it was a mistake accepting Grandpa's invitation. Maybe she should go home instead. Of course, that would be running away from the problems. Sooner or later she'd have to face everything anyway, so she might as well stay.

Susan loved her grandpa too much to even remotely consider leaving now. She would never leave him alone to deal with all the mysteries surrounding her visit. Susan could never leave him without clearing everything up. As much as she dreaded meeting her father, that had to be taken care of too. Now that she realized this visit could last a lot longer than planned she decided to call her boss, Matt, to request a leave of absence. If she were on official leave from her job she wouldn't feel pressured to hurry back.

Once she made up her mind to take an undetermined amount of leave, she felt accomplished. At least she had taken the first step towards making this visit a productive one. Grandpa would be pleased to know she was staying longer than originally planned. This made Susan anxious to tell Charlie her decision. But first she needed to call her boss and make if official. She dialed Matt's number and got the recording. She started to leave a message but Matt heard her voice and picked up the phone. Susan explained she was going to need to be gone longer than planned. She hoped Matt would readily agree, but he didn't make it that easy. He had to tease her a little and tell her the law firm would never survive without their star attorney. After his silliness, he told her to take as much time as she needed. Matt felt like she deserved some time off. He did mention; however, that her boyfriend kept calling the office demanding to know when she was coming back to work. Matt promised nobody would tell Mike where she was coming back. It was up to Susan whether or not to tell Mike how long she intended to be gone.

While she was relaxing on the front porch, Susan began thinking about her father again. She had a very difficult time picturing what he looked like. She hadn't seen him since she was a little girl. His image had faded over the years. Her recollection of her dad was a big, strong man. She thinks he had facial hair and a deep voice too. Susan believed they laughed a lot when they were together. It made her wonder if that was a selective memory or if it was true. Were those memories wishful thinking? Susan wasn't sure anymore.

She did remember the taunting she took in school when the kids made fun of her for having a "bad daddy". That was an awful time in her life. She often came home crying because of the ugly comments she had to endure. The pleasant memory was that her grandpa was always there for her during those miserable times. It was her grandpa that comforted her and made her happy again.

As Susan recalled, when she heard her mother was killed in a car accident her world shattered. Susan's mother was her "rock". Sarah was full of life, full of fun, and the best mother anyone could have. She cherished that memory of her mother. When her mother was gone, she continued to live with her grandparents. They were two of the most wonderful people in the world.

It could still never be the same without her mom; yet, she knew how lucky she was to have Charlie and Nora. They were warm, loving, and represented everything her mother was about. For this she would be forever indebted. As an adult Susan realized how much her grandparents sacrificed to raise a child at that time of their lives. It was an awesome gift her grandparents bestowed on her.

Now Susan was faced with her father stepping back into her life. It was a confusing feeling. If anyone, she wished her mother and grandma could come back in her life. Of course, that could never happen. Instead she was going to have to deal with this situation. Her dad was a blurry memory at best. She wasn't sure how she should feel about him returning. With mixed emotions she knew she would accept the challenge. The next step was to schedule a date and time to meet with him. At least this would keep her mind off the other mysteries going on since she arrived.

4

Susan's cell phone rang, startling her from her far away thoughts. She checked caller ID to see who was calling. It was Mike, the boyfriend she left behind. After a few seconds she decided to answer the call. Otherwise he would just keep calling and wasting her minutes. Susan was polite but not overly friendly when she answered the phone. Instead of asking Susan how things were going, he tells her that he wants to come visit her at her grandpa's house. Susan broke out in laughter, wondering what else could happen during this visit! The last thing she needed was a whiny ex-boyfriend following her around town.

Her first instinct was to remind him that she didn't want him coming the first time he asked...prior to her leaving the city. He ignored her statement, telling her he could be there by morning. With hesitation she started thinking it might not be a bad idea to have him around. Right now she could use a little friendly emotional support. It might be helpful having Mike at her side. If nothing else, Mike was an excellent police officer; and had the reputation of being helpful more often than not.

Maybe this was a good time to explain to Mike everything she knows about her dad. It might be the ideal time to uncover all the secrets she's held in all her life. If she opens up about her dad, maybe it will help her in future relationships. Right or wrong, as long as Mike would accept his role as her friend instead of lover, she wanted him to be with her. He agreed to do whatever she asked.

While Susan continued chatting with Mike on the phone, her grandpa was busy scouting around the backyard to check the telephone wires. Sure enough, his worst fears came true. The wires had been cut, not chewed. Somebody had tampered with his property. The question is, "why?" Is it a coincidence his granddaughter happened to be here when these bizarre events began? Who could possibly want his phone lines cut? Who would steal Susan's car? Charlie couldn't help but wonder if any of these things had to do with his son-in-law being released soon.

Charlie told Susan he was going to ride into town to get grass seed and fertilizer. He told her there were patches of mud that needed to be filled while the weather was still decent. Charlie asked Susan if she'd bake him a sweet apple pie while he was gone. He told her it would be wonderful to come home to the aroma of a homemade pie, just like when his Nora was alive. Maybe the yummy smell would release their happy memories of grandma baking and making the whole house smell like some fancy bakery. When Charlie returns from the fertilizer store they can indulge in the aromas and talk about the many happy memories they share.

Charlie didn't like lying to Susan, but wanted to keep her from worrying. He made up the story about buying seed and fertilizer.

He was really going to the sheriff's office to make an official report about the telephone wire bandit. He thought it might be beneficial to make a report just in case anything else happened. At least then it would be on record.

While her grandpa was gone, Susan dug out her grandma's favorite apple pie recipe. She was having fun playing in the kitchen, just like the old days when her grandma used to let her help. Looking back she realizes she was probably more of a nuisance than help; but her grandma never let on. Those were fun days indeed.

While she was waiting for the pie to bake, she leisurely strolled through the house. Susan was enjoying the opportunity to absorb every happy memory this house held for her. Each room offered something good to remember. She glanced over to the stool her little stuffed animal, Pluto, always sat on. To her surprise Pluto was not in his normal resting spot. For as long as she could remember Pluto was always on the stool. In fact, she knew it was there just yesterday. Susan guessed her grandpa must have moved it when he cleaned, then forgot to put him back. She knew it had to be somewhere because her grandpa would never throw Pluto away. He knew it was Susan's favorite toy.

On the way to town, Charlie looked for anything out of the ordinary. After all the years of driving up and down this road he no longer paid much attention to the way it looked anymore. He decided he would be more observant this trip and really notice his environment. As he drove along he thought he saw unusual tracks in the dirt. He didn't recognize what kind of tracks they were other than it appeared to be that of a large animal. He stopped his car to take a closer look. Not only were there horse hoof prints, there were tire tracks as well.

Charlie noticed someone had taken the time to attempt covering up the tracks. He was really curious now. The tracks were on his own property, but he hadn't given anyone permission to drive on the grounds. He knew neighbors some times went hunting on his land; but they never drove or rode a horse through his property. In fact, he didn't know any neighbors that owned a horse. Glancing at his watch he realized he had to hurry. The sheriff was waiting for him.

When he arrived at the sheriff's office he was anxious to see Frank, the town's sheriff. They had been friends for years, so he would be honest with Charlie about anything he might know regarding the problems going on. First thing Charlie noticed was how tired Frank looked. He probably needed a long vacation because he had been working hard recently. When Frank looked up and saw Charlie, he thought his friend had just come in to visit. Frank relaxed thinking they could just kick back and have a friendly chat; but Charlie wanted to talk business.

Charlie asked Frank if he had a chance to read the police report he filed. Frank admitted that it had been so hectic in the office the past two weeks he didn't read any recent police reports. He told Charlie he's been so busy arresting teenagers for drugs and drinking that he's hardly had time to be with his wife Judy. In fact, he was considering an early retirement just so he could have more family time. Charlie was surprised at that comment because he knew how dedicated Frank was to his job. He couldn't imagine Frank being serious about retiring. Frank could tell his friend was worried about something, so he told Charlie to tell him about the police report.

He began by giving Frank some background of recent events. He told him about Susan's trip, the stalled car that is now missing, the dead body in the road, the girl on horseback, and the cut phone lines. Of course Frank was well aware of the dead body being found. That was the urgent case he was working on. He had heard about some of the phone lines being down but didn't give that too much thought considering there were so many wild animals that probably caused that predicament. What he wasn't sure about is why Susan's car was missing.

Charlie added that Susan's stuffed animal, Pluto, was also missing. With that Frank had to chuckle. He certainly didn't see the importance of an old stuffed animal being a problem compared to a dead body in the road. He quit laughing when he saw that Charlie was serious about this toy missing. Frank realized if this toy was missing it might mean somebody had broken into Charlie's house and stole it. Taking the toy didn't seem like a big deal, but the fact that somebody broke in his friend's house was truly a problem. Then Charlie explained the connection of that toy and his son-in-law being released from prison. Pluto was the only toy Susan's father ever gave her. The day he was arrested, Mark gave Pluto to Susan's mother to give to Susan later. Finally, he added that Mark was being released in three weeks and wanted to meet Susan.

Frank agreed there seemed to be too many coincidences lately. It was all worth checking into. Knowing Mark, Frank thought there could be a connection to the missing toy and Mark being released. He jotted down a few notes as Charlie talked, then suddenly looked up with a puzzled look on his face. Charlie asked what was wrong. Frank stopped writing to ask Charlie to repeat what he just said about Mark being released. Charlie restated that Mark was being released in three weeks.

Frank seemed surprised by this statement, so Charlie stated he thought it was normal procedure for the sheriff to be notified any time a local was being released from prison. He assumed Frank would have already been notified of the release date. To Charlie's surprise, Frank had already been notified. Frank explained that Mark had been released over a week ago. He's been staying at the local hotel in town. Charlie turned pale. He couldn't believe what he was hearing. The only reason Charlie knew when Mark was getting out is because Mark wrote him a letter telling him. Charlie had no reason to believe Mark would lie to him about the release date; but obviously he did.

In Charlie's mind, this new information verified Mark was still dishonest. Why he would give him a false release date he didn't know. What he did know was that he had to overcome his anger with Mark for now. He had Susan to think of; and she didn't need to hear anymore bad news right now. Let Susan make up her own mind about her father. She's a bright woman and will be able to see right through his dishonesty. No point in burdening her with his opinion about his son-in-law.

Charlie requested that Frank send out one of his detectives to look around his property. Maybe they could make sense of the tire tracks and/or the horse hoof tracks. With their training they might be able to pick up some clues that Charlie would otherwise overlook. He would let the professionals handle it. His energy had to be in protecting his granddaughter right now. If Mark hurts or upsets Susan in any way, he would be sorry he ever got out of prison. That much he could promise.

Before he left, Charlie had one more question for Frank. He wanted to know if the guard that was killed in the robbery had a family. It had always bothered him that the man his son-in-law killed might have left behind a family. He felt guilty for not finding this out sooner; but in his defense, he was more concerned for his own pregnant daughter at the time.

When Mark was arrested for the murder, his wife was nine months pregnant. She was very distraught knowing what her husband had done; and turned to her parents for comfort. Charlie and Nora were glad to be there for their daughter, but they were all overwhelmed with the situation. His daughter's needs were the priority at the time; so not a lot of time was spent thinking about the guard that was killed or the family he might have had. Frank told him not to beat himself up over it. It was only human that he worried about his own family at that time. They had all been through Hell and back. After a few moments Frank answered Charlie's original question. He acknowledged the guard did indeed have a wife and young son.

Charlie left Frank's office with a heavy weight on his shoulders.

He learned a lot during his brief visit with Frank. His intention was to find out if Frank had read his police report. Instead he learned about Mark being released already. That was shocking news. Secondly, he learned the guard had a family. That saddened Charlie. He thought that might be the case, but knowing it for fact made it more of a reality. His son-in-law caused a lot of pain for a lot of people. He was ashamed to claim Mark was related to his family. More importantly, Charlie felt bad for Susan.

As he drove home he couldn't help but wish his wife was still alive. She always had a special knack to put things in perspective. No matter what the situation, Nora could make it seem less evil. She used to give Mark the benefit of doubt. Even after he was in trouble with the law, Nora pointed out the positive aspects of having Mark in their lives. She reminded Charlie that if it weren't for Mark, they wouldn't have their precious Susan. He could never argue with that logic.

Charlie wasn't sure what to do next. Susan was a grown woman; she could make her own decisions. In fact, she was probably a lot tougher than he gave her credit for. The problem was Charlie still thought of Susan as that defenseless little girl being bullied. She would come running to him for comfort during those dreadful times. He guessed deep down he expected her to run to him when she had problems. Charlie realized the most he could do is stand by her side. He would be there when she wanted comfort.

When he got home he smelled the aroma from Susan's apple pie. Charlie was ready to skip dinner and have a piece of her delicious pastry. Susan warned him it may not be Grandma's apple pie, but it was the closest she could get. Charlie just laughed. They decided to sit on the porch while indulged in their dessert. As they ate every last morsel, they told stories of Nora. Charlie mentioned how much he loved when Nora would put whipped cream on every dessert she made. When Susan asked why he loved that memory so much, he blushed. Charlie said, "I loved the way your grandma plopped it on." Susan knew there must be an underlying meaning to that statement, but she wasn't going to ask. It was really wonderful reminiscing about old times with Grandpa.

It seemed like the right time to bring up the subject of Mike. She asked Charlie if it would still be alright if Mike came down for a few days. He told Susan it was okay with him providing they both agreed to follow house rules. He reminded her of the rule grandma had in effect when their daughter started dating. No boys allowed in the bedroom! Susan tried to retain a straight face and reminded him those rules were made in the dark ages and surely didn't apply anymore. Charlie burst out laughing. He was just teasing, but added that his rules still applied. His rule was the woman better start rustling up some real food for their supper. Susan laughed and gave Charlie an affectionate squeeze as she went in the kitchen.

As she got up to enter the house, she turned around and asked her grandpa if minded her staying a little longer than the original plan. Charlie told her she knew better than to ask such a silly question. Susan was always welcome in his home. The door would never be locked to her. He couldn't help but wonder what caused Susan to have a change of heart about Mike coming. Charlie decided it was none of his business, so he wouldn't ask. Whatever made her change her mind was okay with him.

Relaxing on the couch with their nightly cup of hot cocoa, they were each lost in their own thoughts. Charlie was thinking about how much to tell Susan about her father. Susan was thinking about Michael coming to visit. She was pretty sure she did the right thing in agreeing for him to come. Yet, there was a little part of her that had her doubts. Too late now. She had already told Mike he could come.

She glanced over at her grandpa and saw a worried look on his face. Susan confronted him about the expression, letting him know she could tell when he was worried. She didn't like him bottling up his feelings. That couldn't be good for his blood pressure. If something was wrong, she hoped he trusted her enough to talk to her about it. She reached over to take the cup out of his hand. She gently put her hand over his, waiting for him to talk about whatever it was that was bugging him.

With a slight tear in his eye, he began telling her about the conversation he had with Frank earlier. It was probably a good time to get everything out in the open, so he informed Susan that somebody cut their phone wires. They weren't destroyed by an animal like they previously thought. Susan sat forward as she listened to what Charlie was saying. He continued talking about this afternoon's meeting with Frank. Charlie told Susan her father was already released from prison; and he feared Mark might have had something to do with all the mysterious events since her visit to town. He acknowledged how none of it made any sense at this point; but the circumstances made it appear that it was very possible her father was involved somehow.

Susan's first reaction was anger. She was angry because the father that claimed to want to meet his daughter may be no different than some of the criminals she has represented. Her next feeling was great sadness. How terribly sad to learn that her own flesh and blood might be the cause of all the bizarre events. Susan finally realized fear may be the most appropriate emotion for this situation. Here is a strange man coming to see her for reasons that may not be pure. No telling what this man, her father, has endured in prison all these years.

Nothing was making any sense. It was Susan's turn to wonder what to do next. Should she call Mike to cancel his visit? She didn't want to put him in danger too. Should she pack up and leave to avoid this unknown threat? No, she would never leave her grandpa knowing his life could be in danger also. Susan needed to clear her head to figure out what to do. It was never her personality to back down from a challenge. She was going to form a plan as to the best way to deal with this situation. Susan refused to run from the problem.

When she thought Mike might be in her life forever she knew she would eventually tell him about her father. When she decided to break off their relationship she was glad she hadn't mentioned anything. When she left Springfield Susan wasn't sure if she would ever see Mike again. She just wanted time to sort her feelings before making a major commitment to him. It didn't seem necessary to share her past while she was still undecided to stay with Mike or not. Now that Mike was coming to Grandpa's house, she would have to explain everything about her past so he could understand what dilemmas she is now facing.

Although it wasn't the way she envisioned telling him, it might be better to tell him on the phone…before he arrives. Susan thought it was a good idea to warn him of the situation right away, rather than later. With that, she started dialing the phone. She decided telling him over the phone now would provide him the option to change his mind about coming. Mike might feel there is too much drama going on. He might choose to back away from the problem and stay in the city. Susan thought this might be the perfect circumstance to find out how sincere he is on wanting to be with her. He'll either come to her in spite of the issues at hand; or he'll run. This phone call will make or break them in terms of a relationship.

To Susan's surprise, Mike told her he didn't care what or who her parents were. He told her he loved her in spite of anything her dad might have done. Mike told her he was leaving his office immediately to rent a car for the trip. He promised to get there as soon as possible, but didn't want to wake her grandpa if he arrived in the middle of the night. Susan told him where they kept the spare key so he could let himself in if they were sleeping when he got there. She told him she'd have a pillow and cover on the couch waiting for him. They blew a kiss through the phone and hung up.

Charlie was standing in the doorway with a smirk on his face. He admitted he heard most of the conversation. He was tickled to know Mike was coming. Charlie could see that Susan was also happy Mike would be here for her. He told Susan that from what he knew about Mike so far, he liked. He even reminded him a lot of himself when he was younger; so of course he must be a pretty good guy! They both giggled at that comment. Susan felt some of the tension from the day leave her body. They decided to get some sleep for now; and be ready for Mike to arrive. Grandpa was looking forward to getting acquainted with Mike; and thought it might be good to have an objective person help them sort through the recent disasters. After all, three heads were better than one!

Feeling relieved that Mike was on his way; Susan was able to fall asleep immediately. Her dreams were pleasant and she would be fully refreshed by the time he got there. Charlie didn't fair as well. Although he was tired from so much worrying, he couldn't sleep. About the time he found a comfortable position in his lumpy bed, he started to drift off. Suddenly he was startled by a thumping noise outside his bedroom. He leaped out of bed, grabbed his rifle, and tip-toed to his doorway. Charlie peeked into the living room, but saw nothing. He expected to see an intruder but there was nobody visible.

Quietly he walked into Susan's room. She was softly snoring and was sound asleep. At that point Charlie assumed he must have been hearing things. He had a lot on his mind; and the mind tends to play tricks on a person when they're overtired. He knew if he stayed up he'd be miserable; so he went back to bed. As he lay in his bed he listened for sounds, but everything seemed to be quiet. Charlie guessed he was probably alarmed by some animal rooting around the house. He rolled over and fell asleep.

5

The next morning Susan woke up, anxious to see if Mike came in during the night. She silently slipped her robe on and looked in the darkened living room. She saw Mike sprawled out on the couch, one leg on the floor. The blankets were tangled as if he had a wild night sleeping. Susan smiled to herself and admitted he was a welcomed sight to see. Barefoot, she walked into the kitchen and started fixing a pot of coffee. She knew Mike loved to wake up to the smell of freshly brewed coffee first thing in the morning. That was the least she could do for him since he rushed to be with her.

As she predicted, Mike woke up with a large grin on his face. He was delighted to wake up to see Susan sitting across the room from him. He was happy to smell the aroma from the pot of coffee as well. He reached for her to sit next to him. They snuggled for a long time, not wanting to let go of each other. Mike released Susan long enough for her to get their coffee. As soon as they situated themselves with their warm mugs of coffee, he asked Susan to tell him what was going. The flood gates opened. She told Mike the entire story. She began with her first night in town to finding out about her dad. Mike listened and didn't interrupt. When Susan finally took a breath between words, he asked if she would repeat the story more slowly. There was so much information to sort through that he couldn't keep up. Susan started from the beginning, explaining everything more slowly.

When he was sure Susan had told him everything he suggested they get a pen and pad of paper. Mike thought it was important to write everything down. Once it was in writing they could take each point and possibly figure out some answers. Susan was more than willing to try anything, so she got up to find a paper and pen.

At that moment she realized Grandpa still hadn't gotten up. It was unlike him to sleep so late. He was usually awake by sunrise. She thought she should check on Charlie before she looked for the pen and paper. Shocked, her grandpa was nowhere to be found.

Susan dashed out of Grandpa's room, ran back to the door, and called his name. Sometimes Charlie would get up to watch the sun rise. His theory was that a new sunrise could shine a new light on your problems, giving a new perspective to solving the issue. It may be a corny idea, but Charlie believed a new day provided hope to any problem. Susan didn't find him on the porch where he normally would sit in the early hours. Mike was watching her dart from room to room, but wasn't sure what the problem was. Finally Susan flew past Mike and yelled that her was missing

Mike got up to follow Susan to the door. Grandpa's car was still in the driveway. Mike's car was parked right behind Charlie's. Nothing had changed since last night from what they could see. Susan called his name but there was no response other than the birds squawking in the tree. They walked around the house where they found Charlie crumpled on the ground. With her heart in her throat Susan knelt down to feel for a pulse. She found a strong one. What could have happened, she wondered.

They managed to get Charlie back into the house. They gently laid him on the couch where Mike had been sleeping only minutes ago. Her grandpa looked like he was sleeping, but instead he was unconscious. Mike called Susan's attention to a spot of blood on the back of Charlie's head. When she wiped it, she felt a large lump in that same area. They decided the best course of action was to get him to the hospital the fastest way they could. Mike's rental car was blocking Charlie's car, so they had no choice but to risk getting the rental bloody from the injury. Susan didn't care at that point. She just wanted to get her grandpa help. Mike picked Charlie up carefully. He carried him to the car like a baby, laying him in the backseat. They rested Charlie's head on Susan's lap and sped away to the hospital.

While Susan handled the paperwork the Doctor's began checking on their patient. When she finished the insurance forms, Mike whispered some reassuring words to her. The nurse came out to tell them Charlie was awake now and on his way to get x-rays. She suggested Susan go to the cafeteria for a while until they brought her grandpa back to a room. The nurse was comforting, letting Susan know he was in good hands.

They found a table in the corner and nibbled on a donut. Susan was having a difficult time swallowing the pastry because her stomach was churning from the stress. Her nerves were shot. Thankful that Mike was with her, she relaxed for a minute. But having Mike there wasn't enough to keep her from releasing a flood of tears. She prayed her grandpa was going to be okay.

Mike nudged her gently, asking if she'd rather go back to the emergency waiting room since she wasn't going to be able to relax. He could see that Susan wasn't going to be able to eat or drink, so he thought she might feel better returning to the waiting room to be closer to her grandpa. He was right. She took him up on the idea immediately. She dropped her half-eaten donut in the trash and hurried back to the elevator. Mike could hardly keep up with her.

While they were waiting to hear from the nurse or doctor, Susan started thinking about the series of events the past few days. It seemed obvious someone was trying to cause her family harm.

Before she thought her father might be the cause of all the upheaval. Now she was wondering who else might do these things. In her job she angered a lot of people. She had prosecuted and won many cases. Any number of those folks could be seeking revenge. In the middle of her thoughts, the doctor came out to talk to her.

Doctor Felix worked on her grandpa. He stated Charlie suffered a mild concussion, which caused memory loss. Charlie does not recall what happened; nor does he remember why he was outside where he was found. In addition to the concussion, he had a contusion that required a few staples. They wanted to keep him overnight for observation; and Susan agreed. Doctor Felix told Susan she could see her grandpa for a few minutes, but then had to let him rest. Both Susan and Mike went into the room.

Susan knocked softly on the door. She peeked in to see if Grandpa was ready for visitors. Charlie was sitting up in bed, motioning for her to come in. Walking over to his bedside she wondered what it was about hospital beds that made people look so frail and helpless. Before she had a chance to ask him how he felt, Charlie grinned and told her he was fine other than a throbbing headache. Just then Mike poked his head in. He shyly asked if he could come in the room too. Charlie told him to come on in so they could meet. He told Mike he had a bone to pick with him.

He proceeded to tell Mike it wasn't necessary to knock his block off just so he could spend some time with his granddaughter alone. Mike had a flabbergasted look on his face, which sent Charlie into gales of laughter. The amusement caused his head to hurt, so he had to settle himself down with a few giggles instead. Once the pain subsided he told Mike he was just joking. Charlie admitted he had no clue what happened to his head.

The nurse knocked on the door to remind them it was time for Charlie to rest. Susan and Mike needed to leave for a while, but they could come back later in the evening. Kissing her grandpa goodbye she whispered in his ear that he didn't have to worry about her because Mike was there. He would protect her while Grandpa was gone out of commission. She also told him to concentrate on getting better so she could bring him home soon. They left the hospital as it began raining.

Running to the car they noticed a note on the windshield. Someone had written "*I know who you are. I know about your father.*" They looked at each other in disbelief. Mike attempted to make light of the note. He said nobody could know whose rental car this was, so maybe the note was put there accidentally. Susan was no dummy. She knew the note was specifically written to her.

There was nothing they could do about the note, so Mike suggested they at least get something to eat. He was starving after not eating since yesterday. He thought Susan should at least try to eat something before she made herself sick. She admitted she was also hungry, so they headed to the café her grandpa took her to. The waitress on duty happened to be Lois. Lois asked where Charlie was. She assumed Charlie was with Susan, but noticed he wasn't anywhere in the café. Susan briefly explained what had happened to her grandpa; and that he was still in the hospital. Lois was horrified! She asked if she could go visit Charlie when she got off work. Susan told Lois her grandpa would be pleased to have a visitor.

In a small town such as this, Susan realized most people were going to hear about Charlie's mishap sooner or later. There weren't too many secrets kept in little towns. The good thing about everyone knowing everybody's business is that they all cared about each other. They would be sincerely concerned about Charlie when they heard the news. Lois finished taking their orders and shuffled off to the kitchen.

As they waited for the food to arrive, Susan asked Mike if he thought they should take that ugly note to the sheriff's office. Mike thought a minute, then stated since they didn't know who wrote the note it might seem ridiculous to run to the sheriff with it. He reminded her it could be some kid writing nonsense just to be annoying, so he suggested she let it drop for now. However, he did think it was a good idea for them to stop at the sheriff's office to see if they had any news about the body Susan found and her car that's been missing. Susan agreed they could do that after they ate.

While they were eating Susan glanced out the window. She had to take a second look because she thought she saw someone across the street staring at them. There was nobody there when she looked the second time. She looked over at Mike to see if he noticed anything, but he was concentrating on his food. He didn't seem to be alarmed about anything. She finished her meal feeling like she was just acting paranoid over nothing.

Of course Susan had every right to feel paranoid. With all that has happened in the past few days it wasn't surprising the thought of a stranger was lurking around every corner. To make things worse, it caused her grandpa serious harm that could have cost his life. Thankfully he was going to be okay after a few days of rest. Still, Susan wondered how long his memory was going to be affected. It would be nice if his memory came back soon. If he could remember who hurt him, they might be able to figure out more pieces to this terrible puzzle.

In the meantime, Susan had to decide what to do next. Mike agreed they needed to visit the sheriff to get an update on her missing car. He didn't seem too enthusiastic about finding out who the prowler was though. It made Susan curious why Mike would be more concerned about a stolen car than who had hurt her grandpa. She was uncomfortable about Mike's priorities. Surely he didn't mean to place more importance on her car than her grandpa's life. She needed to shake these negative feelings away and quit letting paranoia take over.

After lunch Mike went to the restroom before they left the café. Lois brought the bill over to the table. Susan picked it up and noticed there was a note folded under the bill. She unfolded the note so she could read what it said. In large print, the note said, "IMPORTANT, PLEASE CALL ME AT 555-1234 TONIGHT."

After Susan read the note she looked up to ask Lois what the note meant. Too late, Lois was already walking back to the kitchen. Susan put the note in her pocket; and then paid the bill. By that time Mike came out of the restroom. Obviously Lois didn't want to talk in public, so she guessed she'd call her later tonight. She was curious to find out what the note was all about. She was also interested to know how private the note was meant to be. Susan wondered if Lois wanted the information to be kept from Mike. She decided to keep it to herself. After she speaks to Lois later she'll know whether or not to tell Mike what it was about.

More than likely Lois was just concerned about her grandpa. She probably wanted to know how he was doing; and didn't want to discuss it at her work. No point in making a big deal about the note unless she finds out it is something to worry about. Susan turned to Mike to ask if he was ready to go to the sheriff's office. Afterwards they would go back to the hospital to check on Charlie. Maybe she'd see Lois there as well. With any luck, maybe her grandpa recovered some of his memory by now. The doctor stated Charlie had "selective memory loss", which could be considered a good thing. It meant that her grandpa at least knew and recognized the people in his life...he just couldn't recall recent events. The doctor assured Susan that this type of amnesia was generally temporary.

When they pulled up in front of the sheriff's office they noticed several people hanging around the building. Some were shouting, some were cursing, and several were mumbling about not feeling safe in their own town. What the heck, Susan wondered. They literally had to push their way through the crowd to get in the door. The phones inside were ringing like mad. People were talking so loudly you could hardly understand what anyone was saying. It was total chaos in the once quiet sheriff's office. Susan looked around hoping to find a familiar face. The sheriff had been her grandpa's friend for years, so she was trying to find him. Frank was nowhere to be found. She asked one of the deputies where Frank was, but all she got was a snarly response. Nobody seemed to know where Frank had gone for the day.

From the bits and pieces they got out of the pandemonium, it sounded like the sheriff and new deputy had left this morning on a call. They never came back; nor did they call the office to explain why. Frank and his hand-picked deputy were two responsible men. It wasn't like them to just up and leave, not telling anyone of their whereabouts. For such a small town, they were fortunate to have plenty of officers on staff. They were never short-handed for help during their routine calls. The residents were still outside yelling about not feeling protected with no sheriff available. Susan heard one man say his wife was disabled and they were upset that the law hadn't done anything about the cut wires. The phone was their only means of contacting an ambulance. Without a phone his wife was at risk of not getting help if she needed it.

Another woman was crying about her phone line being cut. She was a widowed woman with three young children. Her phone was her lifeline to the outside world. She was frightened that a criminal was in their town cutting everyone's wires, making the entire town powerless to get help. She and the children felt vulnerable and afraid. Those were the types of comments they were hearing from the crowd. Susan realized her grandpa's house wasn't the only one affected. Somebody was vandalizing several homes, causing problems for everyone. She didn't know whether to feel better knowing they weren't singled out or to feel worse because the whole town is being victimized. Maybe that's why Frank wasn't available. He could be busy trying to find the culprit.

There was no reason to hang around the sheriff's office any longer. They weren't going to be able to find out anything with everyone in an uproar. Mike and Susan decided to head back to the hospital and check on Charlie. She looked forward to seeing his smiling face again!

They saw the doctor as soon as they walked into the hospital lobby. He assured Susan that Charlie was doing well, all things considered. He was resting comfortably and was expected to have a full recovery. The doctor told them Charlie was getting restless sitting all alone in his room. He needed visitors to perk him up.

After a little small talk, Charlie told Susan that the sheriff had stopped by to see him earlier. Frank was in a good mood when he came because he caught the guy who had cut everyone's telephone wires. Susan and Mike just looked at each other. How odd, they thought. Frank comes to the hospital to inform Charlie they caught the guy; but he failed to report to work or tell the other deputies. Even so, Susan was glad to hear Frank succeeded in catching the guy. The town's people will be glad to know too.

Susan asked what time Frank had visited Charlie. He told her it was sometime around noon because he remembered Frank saying he was going to the café for some lunch. Susan realized noon was around the time her and Mike was at the café. She was positive Frank wasn't there because she would have seen him. Mike spoke up next, asking Charlie if Frank's Deputy was also with him. Grandpa told him Frank mentioned his new deputy came to the hospital too, but was busy in the hallway flirting with all the nurses. Charlie didn't see the deputy at all, but believed Frank's story about him being out in the hall.

Suddenly it occurred to Susan that her grandpa's memory might be coming back. If he was able to remember events from the afternoon it could be a good sign of his full memory returning. She decided to quiz him a little to see exactly what he did or didn't remember since his incident the night he was hurt. Without wanting to put words in his mouth, she asked him bluntly what happened to his head. Charlie hesitated briefly; and then told Susan he remembered getting out of bed because he heard a noise. He went outside to look around, but he slipped on something which caused him to fall. That's all he remembered until he woke up at the hospital. Susan believed that's how he remembered it; but she had doubts that it was a simple accident like he just described. There was something sinister about the whole thing. In her heart she knew somebody purposely wanted him hurt. She had no idea who or why; but for now she had to accept that the injury was officially being called an accident.

What nagged her most about her grandpa's "accident" was knowing her biological father happened to be in town at the same time. She was unaware why he would want to cause Charlie harm; yet, the timing was rather bizarre. She couldn't help but wonder how her father fit into this unique scenario of events. Hopefully it was all a coincidence. Susan wanted to believe her father changed. She wanted her father to be the type of man she could be proud to call her dad. At the same time she wondered why she hadn't heard from Mark this whole time. He was in town long before she arrived, so he's had plenty of time to contact her.

Susan jumped from one issue to another. One minute she was thinking about getting her grandpa back on his feet. The next minute she was dwelling on her father's agenda. From that she thought about her car and the body she found. No wonder her head felt like it was ready to explode! There was just way too much going on at one time. Susan was having a difficult time sorting everything out. Then she remembered the note that Lois had given her earlier. She would have to remind herself to call Lois tonight after she gets home from the hospital.

Lost in her thoughts, she realized she had been staring off into space for several minutes. While she was daydreaming in her own little world, Charlie and Mike were just laughing it up. They hit it off very well. Her grandpa had Mike laughing at stories of Susan when she was a kid. Mike had Charlie laughing equally hard at his stories of being a cop in the big city.

Susan was happy to see they were enjoying each other's company. Charlie admitted he hadn't laughed that hard in a long time. Now his head was beginning to hurt, so he needed to put the stories on hold. Susan could see that he was tired, so they got ready to leave so Charlie could get some rest. He was grateful to have them visit, but he was also happy to see them go home so he could get some sleep. He promised the doctor he would follow his orders so he could go home the next day.

As they left the hospital Susan checked her cell phone for messages. She realized her battery was almost dead, which could be a major problem. Her battery charger was in her car; but she no longer had her car. Therefore, she no longer had a phone charger. Mike noticed her checking her phone. He asked if there was a problem, so she explained the battery was nearly dead and she had no charger for it. Mike suggested they stop at Wal-Mart to get a new one. While they were there she could pick up some new clothes too. Unfortunately, her suitcase was in the car when she started walking that first fateful night. Luckily she kept a few raggedy jeans and sweatshirts at her grandpa's, so she didn't have to run around naked. Even so, she did want some decent clothes to wear during her lengthy visit. They headed for Wal-Mart to get the items.

They drove past the sheriff's office on the way to Wal-Mart. The crowd had decreased, so things looked more normal again. Susan wondered if Frank and his deputy ever got back. She wasn't going to dwell on that thought right now. She was making a mental list of what items to buy, trying to figure out what personal items she might need. One thing for certain, she had to buy some soap and shampoo. Grandpa only had some manly toiletries; and she wanted more feminine ones. Inside the store a lady approached Susan. She asked if Susan was Charlie's granddaughter. She nodded her head that she is.

The lady proceeded to tell them how sorry she was to hear of Charlie's accident. The lady wanted to continue talking, but Susan told her they had to finish shopping and get back home. She thanked the lady for inquiring of her grandpa's well-being; and then went to the cash register. There she was approached again. It seemed everyone in town had already heard about Charlie's accident. They all meant well, asking how he was doing. Susan chuckled to herself about small town gossip, how everyone knows everybody's business. Mike, on the other hand, was insulted that too many people knew their business. He told Susan he didn't appreciate so many people knowing everybody's business. It made him uncomfortable. Susan told him to lighten up. That's the way it is in small towns.

6

On the way back home they had to drive past the sheriff's office again. This time Susan wanted to stop to talk to Frank. She guessed Frank would be back by now; and she wanted to know if there was any news regarding her car or the body she found. The crowd was gone now and things appeared to be back to normal.

When they went inside one of the deputies told them they'd find Frank at his desk. She knocked softly on his door, expecting Frank's cheerful self to answer. Instead she was greeted by a grumpy voice telling her to come in. Poking her head in the door she asked if she could have a word with him. Frank softened his voice when he realized it was Susan knocking on his door. He told her he was planning on stopping by Charlie's house on his way home tonight; but since she was here he'd go ahead and tell her his news. Susan was glad they decided to stop after all.

Frank wasn't thrilled to see a stranger with Susan. He gave Susan a look that let her know he wasn't thrilled telling his news in front of a total stranger. He wanted to talk to Susan, but he wasn't so sure about telling her friend what he had to say. Susan took the cue and introduced Mike to Frank. She identified him as her boyfriend, which didn't make Frank feel any better about it. He was still a stranger as far as Frank was concerned.

Susan could sense Frank's discomfort, so she thought it might help if she explained that Mike was also a police officer in Springfield. Generally officers had a certain kinship, like brothers. Maybe now Frank would talk more openly in front of Mike; and tell the news he wanted to share.

Frank told Susan he went to see her grandpa earlier. When he left the hospital he intended to have lunch at the café; but instead he received a phone call from some hunters who found a burned car in the woods. Frank drove straight out to the location to investigate. This explained why Charlie said Frank had visited him; and afterwards Frank was going to have lunch at the café. No wonder he didn't get to do that. This was also why he couldn't be found at the office when the wild crowds were beating down the doors.

The sheriff described the car as a Ford SUV, similar to Susan's vehicle. The car was so badly burned he couldn't make a positive identification that it was her car. He was almost certain it was though. For now they'd have to wait for the lab results to know for sure. They were comparing Vehicle Identification Numbers to learn if her car matched the numbers from her insurance company.

Frank then asked Susan to tell him about the night she first arrived. He requested she explain every little detail she could remember…from the time her car ran out of gas until she got to her grandpa's house. She wondered why he wanted her to repeat the details of that night; but was more than willing to cooperate. She told him every detail she could remember. When she talked about the horse that almost knocked her down, Frank mentioned his deputy found a wild horse running along the road that night. The last thing Frank brought up was the dead body Susan discovered. He then informed her that when they found her missing car, they also found a burned body.

He went on to say the body was burned beyond recognition.

Susan felt as if she were going to faint. It was bad enough that she had found a dead body in the woods. It seemed even more gruesome knowing there was also a dead body in her car. Frank explained it was more than likely the same body. The body Susan found was removed from the area she discovered him. The impression the dead body made in the mud matched the body found in Susan's car. It was likely one in the same. Susan didn't know what to say.

Frank told them a DNA test was being done. They hoped to learn from the DNA report who the dead person was. Susan was numb. She hoped to hear they found her missing car; but she never expected to hear a dead body was found in it. This only happens to people in the movies or people she prosecuted in court. She never expected anything like this to happen to her. Suddenly she realized Frank might be thinking she had something to do with this. She asked if she was a suspect. He almost laughed at her question, but realized she was serious. He didn't want her to worry because there was no reason to suspect Susan of any wrongdoing.

Besides, if Frank was going to believe Susan had something to do with her own car missing or the dead body, he might have to start believing she was really evil and caused her grandpa's accident. That was the farthest thing from his mind. It was strange that two such events happened; but no reason to believe Susan was connected in either situation. She was grateful to hear that. The last thing she needed was to end up on the other side of the courtroom. She was a prosecutor, not a defendant!

When they got back to the house Susan tidied up a little. She wanted to make sure everything was in proper order before they brought Grandpa home. To help keep her mind off her troubles, she decided to make a peach cobbler to celebrate Charlie's return. Her grandpa loved the smell of baked goods; and Susan wanted to make his homecoming as welcoming as possible.

Mike decided to join her in the kitchen so they could chat while she measured ingredients. Once the cobbler was in the oven, Mike warned Susan that she's probably going to be asked what her purpose was for visiting Charlie. She thought it was odd for anyone to question why she would visit her grandpa. What was so strange about a granddaughter wanting to visit her grandpa? Mike also told her she'd probably be questioned about family squabbles or fights over money. Susan knew that question would be totally ridiculous so she wasn't concerned. She wasn't thinking very clearly though or she'd wonder why Mike was planting these absurd ideas in her head.

If anything, she loved visiting her grandpa. There was no reason for anyone to question why she would come. The real question might be why she chose this particular time to come. Susan didn't want to share that information with Mike, since he was part of the reason she came when she did. She wanted to get away from Mike because she was thinking about breaking up with him. That's why she wanted to come to her grandpa's when she did; plus the fact that her grandpa wanted her to come this particular weekend. Charlie was her "rock". Whenever she felt troubled over something, it was Charlie that she turned to. This time was no different. So, if anyone questioned why she came when she did…she'd have to admit it was because of Mike.

This wasn't a good time to discuss their relationship though. She was glad he was with her to help her get through this rough time; but that didn't mean she wanted a long term relationship afterwards. They could talk about that later. For now she had to concentrate on the unknown dead body. She wondered why someone would steal her car and use it to bury a person. Why did they feel it was necessary to burn somebody beyond recognition? She wondered if she might even be accused of causing the chaos surrounding her. These were the questions foremost on her mind. Her relationship with Mike was secondary.

Before her cobbler was finished baking the doorbell rang. It was Frank standing at the doorstep. Susan invited him in, teasing him that he must have smelled the aroma of her peach cobbler. Frank wasn't smiling. He even declined a cup of coffee, so Susan knew he was only here for some serious business. Frank wanted to get right down to the facts. He began telling Susan and Mike they got the lab results back on the car and dead body.

First of all, Frank stated the car was identified as being Susan's vehicle. The Vehicle Identification Number matched her SUV, so there was enough proof. Secondly, he didn't have all the lab results for the dead body, except to verify the body was a man. At this time they still didn't have the results on his age, race, height, or any distinguishing features he may have had. Frank confirmed it often to several weeks to get detailed lab results in cases like that. They were all going to have to be patient.

There were no fingerprints found on the SUV. The vehicle was burned so badly that much of the metal melted, taking any fingerprints with it. Even with limited information, Frank was confident this case would remain a priority. They all wanted answers. He knew Susan's crazy story of stumbling in the dark, hearing horse hooves, and seeing a dead body was legitimate. He assured her once more that she was not being considered a suspect in the case. Susan was relieved to hear that; but it still made her queasy knowing her car was used in a crime. She had prosecuted many criminals in her career; but has never been so personally involved in a crime herself. It was difficult to shake the nauseous feeling in the pit of her stomach.

When the sheriff left, Mike decided to play detective. He found a pencil and paper to take notes with. He requested Susan repeat all the events that happened on her first night in town. She was exhausted and really didn't want to rehash it again; but agreed to repeat everything if it would help.

At least she didn't have to think about her car sitting in the middle of a field with a dead body burnt to a crisp. Mike would keep her mind occupied with details of the other things instead. Mike asked her when she learned about the cut phone lines. As she pieced that together, she realized Grandpa had kept that information from her for a while. Susan guessed it was another one of Grandpa's ploys to protect her from bad news. She continued her story, ending it with the morning they found her grandpa getting hurt.

7

Mike had an idea for them to do some investigating on their own. Since Charlie couldn't remember what happened or how he got hurt, maybe it would help if Mike and Susan did some searching. They might find some clues if they retraced Charlie's step, so they began by taking a walk out the back door. Even though everyone "assumed" Charlie just slipped and fell, maybe some little detail got overlooked. Maybe something or someone may have been lurking outside that night. Charlie could have been startled and fell; or worse...maybe someone caused him to fall.

Flashlights in hand, they began their search in the backyard. It hadn't rained in a long time, so the ground was pretty dry. Susan wondered if Charlie might have tripped over an object. Yet, she remembered he thought he had slipped on something wet. As they looked around they didn't find anything wet. There were a few rocks here and there; but Susan was sure her grandpa was familiar with every inch of his own yard. It would seem unlikely he would trip over something that was normally there. She guessed it was possible an unfamiliar object may have been in his way though.

Susan gasped! Mike turned around to see what was wrong. She pointed to the ground where Charlie was laying when they found him unconscious. Mike looked closely at the area she was pointing at. He didn't see anything unusual. Susan kneeled down to get a closer look. She lifted a piece of sticky cloth. Mike didn't see any significance in the object she was holding. He looked anyway.

Dangling between her fingers was a torn piece of fuzzy material. Mike asked if Susan knew what it was that she was holding. She replied it was the material her lost Pluto was made out of. Still perplexed, Mike asked what or who Pluto was. She explained that it was her favorite stuffed animal her father had given her shortly before he went to prison. It was a very special stuffed animal that she kept at her grandpa's house for years. Susan explained when she moved to the city she decided to leave Pluto behind, keeping a spot warm for her when she came back to visit.

Now she remembered the first night she arrived she had seen Pluto propped up on the stool. It was always the first thing she looked for when she'd visit Grandpa. Later she recalled looking over at the stool and Pluto was gone. She thought her grandpa had moved it when he was cleaning, so she didn't give it another thought. With everything that happened since she arrived, she had forgotten to ask Grandpa where Pluto was. After finding pieces of Pluto in the back yard she was really curious why her stuffed toy was outside. She knew there was no reason for Charlie to bring him outside. There was no logical explanation for anyone to take Pluto outside.

At a closer looked, she noticed the piece of material was stained with something sticky. It looked a lot like dried blood. With that, Mike and Susan came to the same conclusion…somehow her Pluto was involved with Charlie's concussion. How and why was the real question? Knowing the possibilities, Susan knew she would have to call Frank. She was sure a police report needed to be taken, even though she had no idea what the connection might be. Before she had a chance to call Frank, he was calling her. Frank told Susan he was nearby and could get back to her house quickly. They went inside to wait for the sheriff. Susan could feel her stomach getting queasy again. The idea of her and Mike investigating was turning into a real Sherlock Holmes caper. She wasn't so sure she liked playing the role of detective.

While Frank was collecting the pieces of material they found, he wondered if he should tell Susan what he's learned so far. He was tempted to tell her he received the DNA results of the dead body she found. Frank decided it wasn't a good time to tell her, so he chose to keep it under his hat for now. He remembered the sadness he felt as he read the DNA report. It verified the dead body was that of Mark Mitchell, Susan's biological father. Now he knew why Mark hadn't made any attempts to contact Charlie or Susan. The man had been dead for at least several days, maybe longer. This case file was getting larger and larger as the hours passed.

When the sheriff left Charlie's house, he decided to drive down the road a little farther. He had heard the Maddock place was sold recently; and new people moved in. Frank was hoping one of the new folks might be the mysterious girl Susan saw on the horse. The Maddock place had facilities for horses, even though the previous owners didn't have any. In a small town like this, any time new people moved in, everyone knew all about it right away. This time it seemed hush-hush. The regular gossip mongrels hadn't been spreading the word about a new family moving. Frank wondered if maybe this family stayed to themselves, not giving the gossipers a chance to talk about them.

Turning into the drive it didn't appear anyone was using the overgrown path. After bouncing up the road in his old truck he noticed someone was outside doing work on the house. Frank drove a little closer and got out. While walking up toward the porch he noticed somebody had replaced the boards and shored up the porch. Just as he was ready to knock on the door, a girl came around the corner. She looked to be in her late teens. When she saw big, burly Frank standing at her door she let out a scream. He apologized for startling her; and then introduced himself. He told the young lady he heard new folks had moved in, so he wanted to welcome them to his town. With that she smiled.

She told him her name was Paula White and she was sorry she couldn't stay to chat. Her horse had gotten out through a broken fence; and she had to chase him down. Before she left Frank mentioned a neighbor reported seeing a horse running loose through Grady's field a few miles away. Frank offered to drive Paula there to get her horse so she wouldn't have to walk so far. Paula was a little apprehensive about his offer; but decided to take him up on it. She didn't want to walk miles in an area she was unfamiliar with. Paula felt like she could trust Frank. After all, he was the sheriff so he must be pretty safe.

During the drive Frank asked Paula if she happened to be the young lady that found Susan walking in the woods when her car ran out of gas. Paula readily admitted that she was the same girl. He asked if she also saw the body that Susan had stumbled upon. She explained that she was riding her horse that night and found Susan huddled on the ground, quite shaken. Paula stated she jumped off her horse to see if she could help Susan; but otherwise didn't see anyone else that night. Paula explained how Susan screamed about a body; but Paula didn't see it herself. She went on to say she hurried up back to her house so she could get help for Susan. Her brother John was home, so she told him to call the police. He wasn't able to call though because the telephone lines were down.

Paula said her and her brother took his jeep to drive back where Susan was supposed to be waiting. When they got there Susan was nowhere to be found. She explained that the lights from the jeep gave them pretty good vision to the entire area; but neither of them saw any dead body. John even got out of the jeep searching with a flashlight. After several minutes of an unsuccessful search, they headed back to their own house. Paula said she hoped Susan was okay. Frank assured her Susan was just fine.

Frank asked Paula if she was absolutely sure they had driven to the area in the woods where she left Susan. She was positive it was the right place because she remembered a big oak tree, plus they found her horse's hoof prints in the dirt. He continued to ask minor questions; and Paula complied with everything he asked. She didn't seem like she was trying to hide anything. At one point Paula even volunteered additional information. She told the sheriff that they couldn't find Susan's missing car either. Her brother got a little frightened at the whole ordeal. He just wanted to get back home and be safe. Paula mentioned how they were new to the area; therefore, they didn't know who they were dealing with.

Frank knew he had probed as far as he should without making Paula nervous. He lightened up the conversation and talked about horses. That was a topic Paula seemed more comfortable talking about. He asked a few things about her brother, but kept it simple.

Frank suggested she was pretty young to be living in a big old house with just her brother. At that point, Paula stated they lived with their father as well. Paula told him her dad's name is Phil. Without trying too hard, Frank gathered a lot of information from Paula on their brief drive. He was pleased that he stopped by to meet the Whites.

Getting to Grady's house, the sheriff honked his horn. Out came Grady, walking as slow as a turtle. Frank got out of the car to meet Grady half way. He apologized for dropping in so late, knowing Grady went to bed with the sunset; and woke up with the sunrise. He was worried Grady might be a little cranky for interrupting his sleep routine. He hoped Grady would understand why he was coming there so late once he knew why. Paula needed to rescue her horse and get him out of Grady's field.

As Frank predicted, Grady was angry to have people come over this late. He snarled at having his routine interrupted. Muttering under his breath, Grady told Frank he could have just gone in there for the horse without bugging him about it. Frank just grinned. He knew Grady kept a loaded shotgun by his door; and Frank wasn't taking any chances on sneaking in Grady's yard!

When they reached the barn where her horse was, Paula remembered she forgot to bring a bridle with her. Now she wasn't sure she'd be able to ride the horse home. She had never ridden bareback before, so she hoped Grady had a rope or something she could run through the horse's halter. He started digging around in one of the other stalls looking for a rope. Instead he found an old bridle and saddle wedged in a corner. He told Paula they were old, but in good condition. Grady's grandkids used to ride his horse when they were little; and although the horse had died years ago, he kept the equipment.

Paula thanked him for letting her borrow the saddle. As she began mounting the horse she noticed in the corner of the stall was several gasoline cans. Turning to Grady and Frank, she warned them how dangerous it was to keep gas cans in a barn with all the straw. Grady huffed, stating the cans had been there for so long that all the fumes had probably evaporated by now. Frank didn't say anything, but he was thinking Paula was probably right. She said her good-byes and rode off.

As Frank was ready to leave, he decided to check the gas cans. He would feel terrible if there was ever a fire because he didn't take the time to check it out. He'd rather be safe than sorry. As he got closer to the cans he realized they looked brand new. There was no dust covering them, no cobwebs sticking to them, nor was there any rust from sitting out in all kinds of weather. Of course, Frank was a cop so it was easy for him to be suspicious of anything out of place or out of the ordinary. Grady said they were probably old cans; but that doesn't mean he really knew if they were old or new. Grady just assumed they were old. He never paid a lot of attention to things he didn't want to be bothered with. The cans weren't in his way, so he likely didn't even notice them being there. He was almost deaf too; so he wouldn't hear any noise if someone hid them there. That's just how Grady was. Frank asked if he could take the gasoline cans back to the office with him. He thought it might be wise to have the cans checked for finger-prints.

His suspicion grew as he thought about the whole evening. When he was at the White's house nobody invited him in. Paula said her father lived in the house too, but she didn't offer to introduce them. He wondered if they had something to hide. On the other hand, maybe Frank was just getting overtired and letting his mind wonder. One of the downfalls about being the sheriff is always looking for the worst in people. Frank wished he wouldn't do that, but it came with the territory. He decided there was no reason to believe Paula was anything except a nice kid.

8

As he approached the middle of town, Frank decided to stop at the café. He was getting pretty hungry; and didn't want to rattle pots and pans in his own kitchen because it would wake his wife. His wife loved him with all her heart, but she hated being woken in the middle of the night. Getting a bite to eat at the café was the smarter choice, he decided. When he got closer to the café he saw a truck coming directly at him. The truck had no lights, but was surely going to hit him head-on! Frank jerked the steering wheel to get out of the truck's way. Steering too far to the right, he found himself in the loose gravel on the shoulder. This caused Frank's truck to slide down the hill on the side of the road. His truck rolled over several times before coming to a stop in the ditch below.

He could feel his body aching from the way his body was being tossed around as the truck rolled. When the car finally came to rest he had to catch his breath. Frank took his time trying to move each limb to see if anything was broken. When the truck was rolling down the embankment, Frank thought the seatbelt was so tight it was breaking his bones. Luckily all his body parts seemed to be intact. When he attempted to remove his seatbelt, he found that it was jammed. No matter how hard he tried, he could not get the seat belt off. He decided if the seatbelt was the worst of it, he could consider himself lucky to be alive. He wanted to call for help, using his police radio; but realized his knees had hit the dashboard, breaking the radio. Naturally, Frank hoped somebody would come for help soon; but he was so far down the ravine he wasn't sure anybody would find him.

What seemed like hours of total silence were actually only minutes. Frank couldn't tell how long he had been trapped in the car. He knew he wasn't far from Grady's house, so somebody should have seen or heard something. Of course, Grady is almost totally deaf, so he wouldn't have heard anything. He wondered if he was too far from the White's house for them to hear the crashing noise. From inside the car it seemed deafening as he plummeted down the hill. Frank had no choice but to sit and wait for help. Maybe in the daylight he would be able to figure a way to loosen the seatbelt himself. He hoped he wouldn't have to wait that long though.

While Frank was lying in his car, Susan and Mike were a few miles away getting ready for bed. Before she fell asleep Susan recalled the note Lois handed her earlier. The note mentioned how important it was that she call her tonight, so she got out of bed to find her cell phone. The phone hadn't been on the charger very long, but there was probably enough battery to make one phone call. She waited until Mike was in the shower before dialing. Susan slipped out on the porch to make the call, partly dreading to hear what Lois had to say. Yet, she was also anxious to know what she had to say. When nobody answered, she put the phone back on the charger. She thought to herself that she would try calling Lois again tomorrow, after they picked Charlie up from the hospital.

The next morning was a beautiful sunshiny day. Susan was looking forward to having her grandpa back home. She knew he could re-cooperate a lot quicker in his own surroundings. Most people did. Mike and Susan skipped breakfast so they could get to the hospital right away. When they walked into the hospital room, Charlie was dressed and ready to go. The bandage on his head looked like a turban. Susan giggled when she first saw him with the gauze headpiece. Charlie told her he had been up for hours waiting for her to pick him up. He said he was anxious to get home because he missed Susan and he couldn't handle one more hospital meal. He wanted some home cooking again!

Susan asked Charlie if he wanted to stop at the café for breakfast. They had the best home cooking around, second to her own. Besides, she wanted the opportunity to talk to Lois if she was working this morning. She would let her know she tried to call but there was no answer.

Apparently Lois didn't work the early shift because a different waitress took their order. Charlie asked where Lois was; and the waitress told him that she was new so she didn't even know who Lois was. Susan guessed she would call Lois at home later. Charlie was thinking the same thing because he was looking forward to seeing his friend after being away so long. They would both have to wait.

When the three of them arrived at Charlie's house, the deputies were spread out checking the grounds for clues. Frank had promised he'd send the deputies over, but Susan hoped it would be later, after she had the chance to inform her grandpa what's been going on the past few days. She wanted to be able to tell Charlie how they found parts of Pluto and the blood on the material before the sheriff showed up. It was too late. Charlie's welcoming home party turned into an investigation of the premises. Not what Charlie expected, but was pleased to see the deputies working on the case.

As he looked around the yard, absorbing this latest tidbit of news, he suddenly had a flashback of the night he was hurt. He remembered hearing a noise that caused him to look outside. The next thing he knew he felt something hit the back of his head. He realized now that he didn't slip and fall. He was hit on the head, causing him to fall. Without saying a word, Susan and her grandpa knew what each other was thinking. They both wondered if this incident had anything to do with her father being back in town.

In their search, the deputies found a few more pieces of Pluto's material scattered throughout the yard. They placed the evidence in a plastic bag, sealed it, and put it in a box to be send to the lab. In addition to finding Pluto's material, one deputy found an old horseshoe hidden behind the bushes and a key. Both items had blood on them. The shoe was taken as evidence along with Pluto's remains. The lab could see if the blood matched each object. Hopefully they would know if the blood on the horseshoe and/or the material from Pluto matched Charlie's blood from his head injury. If the blood matched, it would seem the horseshoe was used as the weapon that hit Charlie's head. If it was the weapon, Charlie was very lucky to have survived with just a concussion.

Coming home to find deputies crawling around his yard searching for weapons seemed unreal. Charlie felt overwhelmed at the scene. He told Mike and Susan he was going inside. He needed to take his pain medicine and lie down for a while. Charlie said maybe he'd be more prepared to talk after a good nap. This was not at all what he expected to come home to. He started thinking that maybe he should have stayed at the hospital an extra night.

While Charlie was napping, Susan tried calling Lois. After all, if Lois wasn't at work, maybe she'd be home to answer her phone. On the very first ring Lois answered. Susan identified herself and Lois seemed pleased to hear from her. Lois asked how Charlie was doing; and she wanted to know if she could come over later to visit. She was making some chicken noodle soup (one of Charlie's favorites), so she wanted to bring it over for him. Susan told her how nice that would be. Charlie would be pleased to have visitors. Susan thought she noticed a spark in Lois's eyes when she looked at Charlie the day she met her at the café. It seemed like Grandpa had a cute little twinkle as well. When he introduced Lois to Susan it was obvious they were more than friends. She thought it was sweet; and looked forward to getting to know Lois better. Susan was glad to know her grandpa had somebody to spend his lonely nights with.

Getting impatient with Lois for avoiding why she wrote the note, Susan finally brought it up in the conversation. Lois just laughed. She said she guessed she was just being overly dramatic the night she wrote the note. It really didn't mean anything. Lois just wanted to make sure Charlie was okay, so she thought if she wrote the word "Important" on the note that Susan would make sure to call. Susan thought that explanation was very strange. She would have liked to quiz Lois further about the matter, but it was clear that Lois had nothing more to say about the mysterious note.

Mike told Susan she really looked tired. He suggested she take a nap while her grandpa was lying down. He told her it was better to be well rested so she could take care of her grandpa when he was up. Without an argument, Susan took advantage of the opportunity. She decided a catnap would feel pretty good, so off to her bedroom she went. Mike decided to take a walk in the woods while the two of them slept. He could do a little exploring on his own; and get some fresh air at the same time. It was a beautiful day to be outside to enjoy nature in its finest.

About thirty minutes into his walk he came across a gravel road. With his police instincts he thought the gravel appeared to be somewhat disheveled. In fact, he noticed what looked like swerving tire tracks along the edge of the road. Mike felt sorry for anyone who might have veered off the road in this location because it sure was a steep drop. He thought it might be wise to follow the path of disturbed gravel to see where it might lead. What he could see was how tire tracks ended on the road, but continued down the ditch. As he peered over the edge he could see a car turned upside down. He recognized the car from earlier.

Mike was sure that was the same car the sheriff had. From where he was standing he couldn't see anyone in the car. Yet, he didn't want to go for help until he was certain nobody was inside. He ran down the ditch towards the car. As he got closer he thought he saw some movement inside the vehicle. Moving quickly, Mike lost his balance running down the steep hill. He stumbled over twigs and rocks, but regained his balance and finally managed to get to the car. He got down on his knees to peer inside the turned over car. He found the sheriff dangling sideways, unable to get out of his seatbelt. Mike then reached through the broken glass to check Frank's pulse. Feeling a strong pulse, Mike proceeded to cut the seatbelt, releasing Frank from the peculiar position he'd been in.

When he touched his arm, Frank opened his eyes. This startled Mike at first, but he was relieved to see Frank was still alive. Mike asked if he thought anything was broken, but Frank said he didn't think so. He was stiff from lying there for so many hours; but was otherwise okay from what he could tell. With Mike's help, Frank attempted to squeeze out of the window. After a few tries it was obvious he wouldn't be able to. Leaving the choice up to Frank, Mike offered to either go get help or continue trying to pull him out. The sheriff elected to try getting out again because he didn't want to be stuck in the car any longer. Holding Frank's shoulders it soon became apparent that the roof was too smashed in for him to have enough space to get out. Mike had no choice but to leave Frank behind while he ran to get help.

It took him about twenty minutes to run back to Charlie's. Tearing inside, he woke Susan up and asked where her cell phone was. While she got the phone off the charger, Mike was telling her about finding the sheriff in a ditch. He told her to call the sheriff's department to report the accident; and to send EMT's as quickly as possible. In the meantime, while they waited for help, Mike was going to take some water and a blanket to Frank. He knew it was important to keep Frank quiet and comfortable until help arrived.

Making it back to the sheriff, Mike slid down the hill into the ditch once again. In the distance he could hear the sirens approaching. Getting back on his knees, he called out to Frank to take a drink of water. Taking the bottle from Mike, he almost drank it all. He offered Frank the blanket, but he declined. They could both hear the sirens now. Help was near. Mike told Frank he was going to run back up the hill to make sure the EMTs would know where to stop. He didn't want to take a chance that the driver would pass them by.

Shortly after the EMTs arrived, the deputies drove up. They were the same officers that had just been at Charlie's house that morning. However, right now it seemed like ages ago that these same men had been looking for crime evidence. Now they were here to save a life. Mike motioned them to follow him down the hill where Frank was waiting. Being the tough guy that he was, Frank tried to make light of the situation. He teased the EMTs and deputies about taking so long; that a man could starve out here before being found! The EMTs ignored Frank's attempt to be funny and kept working on getting the car door open. They finally decided to use the Jaws of Life, because the door was too demolished to pry open by hand.

Finally, they were able to open the door and extract Frank from the wreckage. Gently they put him on a gurney to take him to the hospital for observation. Still being the officer, Frank started quizzing his deputies about their search at Charlie's place. He demanded to know if they had found anything; but the deputies told him he'd have to wait until after he was checked out by the doctors before they would discuss the case. Irritated, he quit asking about the case. They were going to make sure Frank was okay before they discussed work stuff with him. He trained these deputies; and they were only doing what they were trained to do. He couldn't be mad at them for following procedure.

When Mike got back to Charlie's, Susan was waiting for him at the front door. She wanted to know everything that happened; and if Frank was going to be okay. Mike explained what he could, making sure she knew Frank was fine. The sheriff was one of her grandpa's best friends. She didn't want anything to happen to him. She certainly didn't want her grandpa to feel guilty for Frank's accident. It wasn't Charlie's fault that Frank happened to be on duty that day.

About that time Charlie walked in and asked what the heck was going on. He said several police cars passed him on his way home. Charlie stated they were driving like crazy men, speeding on the dirt road. That made him think something serious was going down, so he rushed home to make sure Susan was okay. Charlie could see for himself that Susan was fine, so he turned to Mike to see if he had any answers. Mike told him what happened to Frank, so he was ready to jump back in his truck to go to the hospital. Instead, Susan gently took his keys from him and offered to drive Charlie to the hospital herself. She knew he'd want to see Frank, but she didn't want him driving while he was so upset. Without hesitation they got in the truck and headed for the hospital.

Mike declined to go with them. He said he wanted to snoop around a little more while they were gone. Since the deputies had to leave so abruptly earlier they may have missed something during their search. He wanted to take this opportunity to do some investigating on his own, with nobody else to bother him.

Susan was glad Mike didn't come with them. She felt she needed time to herself to sort things in her mind. She needed to put everything in perspective somehow, without him nagging her about details. Besides, she rarely had the chance to be alone with her grandpa. During stressful times like this, she needed alone time with him more than ever. She offered to stay in the waiting room while Charlie went to visit Frank. Susan told him to take his time. She needed the quiet time away from Mike anyway. She was only sorry it was under these circumstances.

Frank lay in the hospital bed looking like he had picked a fight with an eighteen wheeler and lost. He was covered with bruises and cuts, some of which had to be stitched. Charlie sat down on the bed next to his good friend. He teased Frank about being jealous. Charlie told him it wasn't necessary to get banged up just because Charlie had a head injury. He reminded him they didn't need to compete on who could suffer the worse damage. Frank laughed, holding his side to ease the pain. Eventually Frank told Charlie he believed he was run off the road deliberately. Charlie nodded in agreement. Both men knew somebody was out there to cause problems; they just didn't know who or why.

Sitting up in bed to get more comfortable, Frank called the nurse to get a pain pill. Before the nurse returned with the medication, Frank told Charlie he had one more thing to ask before he got too groggy to hear the answer. Frank asked what Charlie knew about Susan's boyfriend Mike. He told him he really didn't know too much. From what Susan had told him, she had been seeing Mike for a few months. They met at the court house where she works. Frank then asked if Charlie if he knew what Mike's last name was. After thinking a moment, he realized he had never heard Susan mention Mike's last name. He couldn't answer that question.

The questions were making Charlie feel uncomfortable. Obviously Frank had good reason to inquire or he wouldn't have brought it up. He wondered what Frank wasn't telling him. Frank had taken his pain pill by now, so he was getting sleepy. He just mumbled that it's just the nature of a cop to question everything. There was nothing more to his inquisitions than curiosity. Charlie knew his friend too well, so he wasn't buying that story…but it was clearly not the time to pursue the line of questioning. Frank need to rest.

When Charlie got home he went straight to bed. He was tired, but wasn't able to fall asleep right away. It was as if a movie continued to play over and over in his mind. He couldn't stop thinking about all the events of the past few days. He even chuckled to himself thinking he's never had this much excitement in his 70 years as he's had in the last seven days. Convincing himself he had to go to sleep, he rolled over thinking about more pleasant things. Once he started thinking about his dearly beloved wife, he was able to find himself in dream land.

Once Charlie was sound asleep, Susan thanked Mike for saving her grandpa's best friend. Mike shyly accepted the compliment, but told Susan anyone would have done the same thing if they had found the overturned car. He didn't feel like much of a hero; but he was glad the situation gave Susan something positive to think about. After everything she's been through recently, she needed to feel good about something!

Mike was also glad she was in a good mood right now. What he had to say next might make her unhappy. He had to tell Susan he needed to get back to his office soon or they'd be sending a search party for him. Mike didn't want his sergeant to think he abandoned his duties, so he needed to get back to work soon. Mike hoped Susan would understand. She wouldn't want him to lose his job. If he could go back to work for a day he could then request a formal leave of absence. Then he could come back to Charlie's and help them deal with the ongoing investigation.

Susan listened as Mike apologized for having to leave. She said nothing. Mike reminded her he'd come back as soon as possible. With tears streaming down her cheeks, she assured him she did understand. She would miss him. Her only request was that Mike would come back as soon as possible. He agreed he would. Together they packed his few belongings and put it in the rental car. Now he could be ready to leave first thing in the morning.

Susan was standing at the passenger side of the car while Mike was loading his trunk. Out of the corner of her eye, she thought she saw something glittery on the floorboards. On closer look she noticed there was a metal object sticking out from under the passenger side seat. As she focused on the object she realized it was a metal clasp from the back of Mike's cell phone. How odd she thought. Mike had told her in the rush of leaving his apartment he forgot to take his cell phone. During his visit he had been borrowing hers to call work.

Susan pointed to the phone on the floor and asked Mike why his cell phone would be inside his rental car if he had left it at home. He calmly explained he must have grabbed it at home without realizing it, and then it fell on the floor. If that were the case the battery would be dead by now...yet, Susan could see the light blinking on the phone. A blinking light indicated there was a message waiting. If the battery was dead the light couldn't blink. Mike was obviously concealing the truth about his cell phone; but for what reason?

Susan asked Mike why he didn't bring the phone inside and recharge it on her new charger. At least then he'd have a working phone on his trip back home. He told her he'd stop somewhere and purchase a charger. That way he could plug it into the cigarette lighter to recharge on his trip home. Mike told her he wouldn't want to risk the chance of forgetting his phone again, so he should just keep it with him in the car. Susan was too tired to argue. Mike could do whatever he thought best regarding the charger.

When she went to bed, Susan couldn't stop thinking about Mike's phone. She wasn't sure exactly what was bugging her about it; but she couldn't shake the feeling there was something untruthful about Mike's explanation of the phone being in the car after he said he left it at home. Susan decided she was being silly. Mike had no reason to be deceitful...especially over a cell phone. Maybe he really did forget that he brought it with him. Her last thoughts before falling asleep were not about the cell phone. Instead, she kept wondering who was out to harm Frank. First there was her grandpa's accident; and now Frank's. Obviously some person is out there with an evil mission..... But who?

Mike and Susan both woke to the wonderful aroma of bacon cooking. Charlie was busy in the kitchen, making bacon, eggs, and toast. He wanted to start the day with a big breakfast, while at the same time be able to treat his granddaughter to a nice surprise. On the table was a jar of homemade jelly. It was from the last batch Susan's Grandma had made before she passed away. Susan enjoyed every morsel. With each bite there was a great memory attached, thinking about her grandma. Mike, on the other hand, gobbled his food so quickly his tongue didn't have a chance to taste the food. He seemed anxious to leave, planning on gulping a cup of coffee first. Instead he was faced with a feast he felt obligated to enjoy. Of course, he didn't want to be rude to Charlie, so he joined them in the big breakfast gala.

To add a nice touch, Mike insisted on cleaning up afterwards. He really hoped they would decline his offer so he could get on the road. To his surprise, Susan took him up on the offer. She enjoyed being pampered. While Mike cleaned the kitchen she took a shower. At least she could feel pretty and fresh for Mike before he left. Throwing the towel around her, she reminded Mike that her grandpa was just in the other room. With a grin on his face he proceeded to remove the towel anyway. Mike whispered in her ear that Charlie wasn't home. He went into town, so they had the whole house to themselves. Needless to say, Mike didn't leave as promptly as he thought he would.

9

When Mike left, she decided to call her boss, Matt, to check on the status of some of her pending cases. Her boss told her everything was fine; and she should stay with her grandpa as long as necessary. Matt told Susan he had already divided her caseload and given them to her associates. He promised her there would be plenty of cases for her to dig into when she returned.

When Susan hung up, she thought to herself how lucky she was. She was blessed with a loving family, a wonderful boyfriend, and a good job. What more could she possibly want or need? Mike had only been gone a few minutes, but she already missed him. She was glad she accepted Mike's decision to come here. Things were working out very well, except for the doubts she had regarding some of his vague explanations of things…such as his cell phone.

As she was changing sheets on the beds, Charlie walked in with the sheriff right behind him. Susan wondered what the two of them were up to. As old friends, the two of them often got into mischief. The way they were laughing right now made her think they were up to no good again. She joined them in the living room. Suddenly their smiles turned into frowns. Susan looked down at herself wondering if maybe she had a stain or something on her clothing. What could have possibly happened from when they walked through the door until now? Taking charge, she told them both to sit down and start talking. Like two little boys, they did as they were told. Susan reminded them both that she was an adult; therefore, deserved to be treated like one. She wanted to know what they were trying to keep from her.

Susan sat across from Frank and Charlie. She wanted to face them so she could see their eyes as they talked. In her opinion, eyes never lied. Whatever they had to say would be reflected in their eyes as well.

Frank began telling Susan what she already knew. She already knew the lab identified the burned car as being registered to her. That was no secret. What she didn't know was what Frank had to tell her next. Not only was the car hers, but the burned remains of the body inside was her biological father, Mark. Susan started to speak but the sheriff stopped her. Frank held up his hand, letting her know he wasn't finished speaking. He told her she could ask questions when he was done telling the rest. Frank also told her that the material from Pluto did have traces of blood on it.

Susan asked whose blood it was, although she suspected it was her grandpa's. Frank told her it matched Charlie's blood type. Thinking Frank was finished talking she bowed her head in deep thought. Breaking her concentration he told her there was more to discuss. Frank asked her how well she really knew Mike. She was rather shocked by the question, but wanted to know where this line of questioning was going. Susan told him she knew his name was Mike Hayes; and he was a police officer in Springfield, IL. Looking for an expression on Frank's face, she found none. He was treating this conversation very business-like.

She went on to say they met at the court house where he was observing a case she was prosecuting. Frank asked what she knew about his family. With that she remembered Mike telling her his father was a security guard for Brinks armored cars. She added that Mike's father was killed in the line of duty, guarding a bank. Saying it aloud, Susan realized how similar their lives were. Mike's father was killed while on duty as a guard; and her own father was in prison for killing a guard. She had never made that connection until now, as she verbalized this to Frank. Apparently she blocked these similarities from her mind before; not wanting to admit there might be a connection between the two families.

Charlie's face crumbled into lines of sadness. Susan was gradually becoming aware that her boyfriend might be involved with something criminal. Frank wouldn't be questioning her about Mike's background if he didn't think he was seriously implicated. Charlie knew the last name of the guard his son-in-law had shot. Even if the name hadn't been etched in his brain during the trial, he would never forget it. Earlier Frank told Charlie that he contacted the Springfield police department to inquire about an officer they had named Mike. They only had one Mike on the force. His last name was Smith.

At this point Susan felt the two men were still keeping some facts from her. She told them to stop treating her like a child. Whatever they had to say, she could handle it. Charlie explained that he thought Mike was the son of the guard that Susan's Dad shot. To Susan's credit, she didn't fall apart. She sat there feeling numb instead. She was doing everything to hide her feelings. She wanted to act like she was calm and cool. She wanted to act the role of a controlled lawyer, like when she prosecutes criminal in a court of law. This was too close to home though. Inside she could feel the mounting pressure. She was afraid she'd break down any moment. Mostly she was crushed to learn her boyfriend might not be as honest and upstanding as she once believed.

She wondered if Mike knew who she was before they got involved. Could he have known she was the daughter of the man who shot his father? Before Mike came to Charlie's she broke down to tell Mike all the sordid details about her father. Although she hated telling Mike over the telephone, she felt obligated to warn him before he arrived to Charlie's house.

At the time she didn't know if he'd be appalled and wouldn't want to see her anymore. Instead, he told her he didn't care about her past or anything her father might have done in his lifetime. She believed him. Now she wondered if he already knew all about her dad before she told him. Why would Mike betray her like that? What could his motive possibly be?

This made her think about the strange story he came up with about his cell phone. His story didn't seem plausible at the time, but she was too tired to argue about it. Yet, she was a logical person and knew it made no sense to say he forgot his phone when it was lying on the floor of his rental car. She began reflecting on all their conversations to see if anything else he said didn't make sense.

Now Susan was getting angry. She was anxious to confront Mike about all of this; however, she wanted to do it in person. She'd have to wait until he comes back to Grandpa's house in a few days. She definitely wanted to see his eyes when she confronts him about his background.

The sheriff was about to say something else, but Charlie caught his eye and shook his head. Frank immediately understood Charlie's signal, so he didn't say any more. Charlie felt as if Susan had enough information to process without adding more. Charlie would have liked to shield her from the news about Mike; but Susan was too smart for that. She would have figured out they were holding information back. He knew it was best to be open and honest with her instead. He could tell Susan was having a very difficult time coping with everything she just learned. Charlie also knew his granddaughter was strong and would work through it in time.

Susan needed some fresh air. She told Charlie and Frank she was going to take a walk to clear her head. She wanted to sort out all the information she just heard. Charlie told her if she needed him he would be back shortly. He was going into town to pick up some items they needed. He assured Susan he would return as quickly as possible. Charlie suspected Susan might need a strong shoulder to lean on after her walk.

Driving into town, Frank asked Charlie why he didn't want to tell Susan that Mike had asked for three weeks leave of absence from his work. He explained his granddaughter had enough to handle, without adding more problems right now. Even though she was a sharp attorney and could cope with a lot; Charlie was sure Susan had limits on dealing with personal issues. Frank could tell her the rest later.

Frank asked Charlie if he thought it was strange that Mike's request for leave of absence happened to be at the same time Mark was being released from prison. Charlie told him he didn't know what to think. It could be a fluke; but what were the odds that Mike would happen to take off work the same time Mark was getting released from prison? The timing was too coincidental not to be suspicious. Yet, neither understood the connection at this point. Why would Mike want to be here in town when Mark arrived? That was the real question; and neither had the answer. Knowing Mark was the dead bank guard's son was disturbing. Red flags went up in both their minds.

Since they were talking about Mark, Charlie thought it was a good time to mention his feelings about that long ago robbery. He asked Frank if he thought Mark was alone in planning the robbery or if he might have had partners. Frank said he had wondered the same thing before, but didn't know. He didn't think Mark could have been the lone bandit. It was a well thought out heist, so maybe there were more people involved. One thing for sure, they never recovered the money that was stolen that fateful day. The police caught Mark shortly after the robbery and killing. He didn't have a penny on him; and swore he had nothing to do with it. Yet, he was convicted and spent many years behind bars.

After he dropped Frank off at home, Charlie was driving past the café. He thought about Lois, wondering if she was working. He really wanted to see her, but he promised Susan he'd come home right after he dropped Frank off. He decided his granddaughter would be okay if he was gone a little while longer. His excuse for stopping at the café was to thank Lois for the soup she brought him when he was first injured. Maybe he'd have a cup of coffee while he was there as well. If he was lucky, maybe Lois could take her break and have a cup of coffee with him. Charlie knew Susan wouldn't mind.

While Charlie was busy flirting with Lois, Susan was still on her walk. She was in no hurry to get home just yet. It was a beautiful day; and the fresh air felt wonderful. She wasn't paying any attention to which direction she was walking. Susan was familiar with the woods and fields around the area, so she wasn't concerned about getting lost or anything. She was surprised when she came upon the Maddock place. That's when she realized how far she had walked. Seeing a girl out by the old barn, Susan walked toward her. The closer she got, she realized it was the same girl that had been on the horse the first night she arrived.

Paula saw Susan walking toward her. She called out to Susan, asking her where she had run off to the other night. Paula and her brother were concerned when they went back to get Susan and she wasn't there. She explained how scared she was after finding a dead body, so her instinct was to run as far away as she could. She apologized for not waiting for

Paula; but no apology was necessary. Paula said she would have probably done the same thing if she had been in Susan's shoes. At least she could see that Susan was okay, in spite of that awful night.

They chatted a while longer, getting acquainted. Paula told Susan she normally would invite her in the house, but her father was having a bad day. He'd be upset if she brought anyone in when he's in one of these moods. She explained that her father was confined to a wheelchair after an accident a long time ago. She added that most of the time her dad just sits in the house feeling sorry for himself. Paula and her brother rarely had anyone over because it generally upset their dad. With that, Susan noticed the time. She told Paula it was getting late; and she needed to get back home. Susan didn't want her grandpa to start worrying about her being gone too long. They waved goodbye to each other; and went their separate ways.

It so happened that Charlie and Susan got home at the same time. They both laughed when they met in the driveway, realizing they didn't need to worry about each other after all. Susan told her grandpa how she ran into Paula at the Maddock Place. Charlie told her it would be nice if she could make friends in the area; but to be careful because nobody seemed to know much about the White family. Hardly anyone has had the opportunity to meet them since they mostly stayed to themselves.

Tomorrow he was going to ask Frank if he knew where the White's moved from. He was just curious, but thought it might be a good thing to know. If anyone knows the town folk's business, it would be Frank. Maybe Susan got to meet Paula's family while she was there. He asked Susan if she met the others; but she told him Paula couldn't invite her inside. She went on to tell Charlie how Mr. White had been in an accident, so he was in a wheelchair. Otherwise, that's all she really knew. Paula didn't talk too much about her brother at all.

Now that she's had time to think about Frank's comments regarding Mike, she wondered if it was a good time to discuss it with her grandpa. Susan fixed them each a cup of hot cocoa and sat together on the couch. Charlie knew his granddaughter too well. He knew she was up to something. As an attorney Susan knew exactly how to fish information out of somebody. He was prepared to start answering questions any moment. Sure enough, Susan asked him to tell her everything he knew regarding Mike. She wanted to know why Frank was asking such probing questions about her boyfriend. She wanted to know if Frank suspected Mike of any wrongdoing. Charlie knew there was no point in stalling. He may as well tell her what he knows and what Frank suspects. Frank was going to tell her anyway; so he might as well be the one to lay it all out on the table.

Charlie asked Susan if she was aware that Mike had previously asked his employer for three weeks leave of absence. He added that Mike hasn't been at work for the past three weeks, even though he's only been in town since last weekend. Charlie explained that Frank was unable to account for Mike's whereabouts during the first three weeks Mike had taken off work. At least he hadn't figured it out just yet. Susan sat a moment, thinking about it. It had been about a month ago when she first told Mike she needed her space. She was very upfront, telling him she wanted a separation from him. At the time, Mike was livid. He kept pestering her to rethink her decision. He didn't want to break up; but he was the one who encouraged her to visit her grandpa for a while to think things through. Mike told her she was probably under a lot of stress at work. In fact, he agreed she needed to get away for a while. He just didn't agree about breaking up. Mike told her they could discuss their relationship when she returned from her visit. Even though he wanted to go with Susan to Charlie's house, he'd stay behind if that's what she preferred. He even told her to take all the time she needed to think things through. Mike promised not to pressure her, but was really hoping she'd change her mind and invite him to go with her. In the end, Susan opted to go to Charlie's by herself; in spite of what Mike wanted.

When Charlie first asked Susan to come visit this particular weekend, she almost declined. As much as she loved visiting her grandpa, the weekend he asked her to come was a busy time for her at work. She hated asking her boss at the last minute to let her take time off; but, at the same time, Susan was anxious to get away from the big city so she could sort out her personal issues regarding Mike. Also, it was out of character for Charlie to "request" a visit; so she felt uneasy declining the offer. It was obvious to Susan that her grandpa had something important to discuss with her in person or he wouldn't have asked her to come on a moment's notice.

She didn't think he wanted to discuss her personal life; but even if he did, she wasn't quite ready to have that conversation with him. If the opportunity arises, she would tell her grandpa about her rocky relationship with Mike. Charlie would never pry, so she didn't have to worry about him pressuring her to discuss it.

Instead of having the opportunity to discuss her love life, the visit turned into a nightmare of other events. Next thing he knew Mike was coming to visit and be supportive. Mike was no longer the priority at that point. Unfortunately, now it looked like he might have had a totally different motive for being here. His motive didn't necessarily have anything to do with his relationship with Susan.

From what Frank told her, Susan realized Mike might have been on vacation or leave of absence for several weeks before he came to her grandpa's. Frank implied that Mike may have been in town all along. All their phone conversations had been on their cell phones, so she never had reason to doubt he was calling from the city. She assumed he called her when he had a break at work or when he got home from work. Little did she know at the time he was actually calling from his cell phone. Now Susan realized he could have been making those phone calls from anywhere, including Charlie's back yard. Just because Mike said he was at work in Springfield didn't mean he was being truthful. At this point they were only guessing where Mike was when he called. Of course, Susan was smart enough to know his whereabouts didn't make him guilty. Yet, she was too intelligent to ignore the fact that he has been lying all these weeks. It was peculiar that he would let her believe he's been working all this time if he hasn't been.

Susan began wondering what was wrong with her. How could she miss the obvious signs that Mike wasn't the man she thought he was? Her grandpa was right. There are far too many coincidences to exclude Mike from being involved in the recent events. She had to ask Charlie if there were any other secrets about Mike that she didn't know. He told her there was one final concern. Charlie proceeded to tell her that when her father killed a guard years ago, that guard had an infant son named Mike. The child would be the same age her boyfriend is. He added that Frank was doing a background check on Mike, hoping to learn his true identity. Charlie promised to keep Susan informed of any new information they learn. He would not keep secrets from her, even if it's painful to hear.

Knowing Frank was investigating Mike, she decided to hold off on confronting him just yet. She would let Frank do his background check first, find out what other evidence he might obtain, and then confront him. Otherwise, if she confronted him with the information she knew thus far, Mike would be backed into a corner. He would attempt covering his wrongdoing with some lie, hoping his girlfriend would believe him. Under normal circumstances he might be able to pull that off. Knowing what she knows now, Susan will have a tough time believing anything he says. She decided to wait until Frank does his background check to see if it implicates Mike in any criminal activity. Until then, she needed to let Mike believe Susan doesn't know anything. Let him get caught in his own lies. Her lawyer skills prepared her to be able to see through most lies and deceptions. She just never thought she'd have to use these skills against her own boyfriend.

They wanted to end the evening on a lighter note before going to bed. Susan began teasing her grandpa about his "girlfriend" Lois. All red-faced and stuttering he couldn't get the words out quickly enough to deny having a girlfriend. Susan could see right through that mask. She began laughing uncontrollably. Grandpa knew he wore his feelings on this sleeve, but didn't think he was that obvious. Then Charlie admitted he *might* have a little crush on Lois; but that didn't mean he still didn't love his dearly departed wife! Susan assured him it was okay to have a special lady friend in his life. He deserved not to be lonely; and it meant a lot to her knowing he was being taken care of when she wasn't around.

Feeling a little awkward about talking to his granddaughter about his love life, he wanted the conversation to end soon. Susan was bullheaded though. She continued teasing him and blowing kisses at him, calling out Lois's name. Charlie finally caved in and giggled too. Actually, Charlie felt relief that it was out in the open. Now he didn't have to sneak around to visit Lois. He was glad his granddaughter was able to accept the situation. Charlie hated keeping secrets anyway. Maybe now he could invite Lois over for dinner some evening so his two favorite women could get acquainted. No more pretending Lois was just a casual friend. Susan thought it was a great idea. She was looking forward for the three of them to share a meal together.

Later the two of them had their nightly cocoa, but neither felt like going to bed just yet. Susan suggested they go outside and sit in the swing for a while. It was a gorgeous night to gaze at the stars. Charlie remembered how he and Susan used to sit on the swing in the evening after Nora went to bed. Those were simple times, but some of the best memories developed from those nights on the porch. Susan confessed to her grandpa that he was her hero. She talked about how he had always been there for her when she was younger. She recalled the time she was excited about going out with one particular boy. She was excited that he finally asked her out; but later found out he only asked because he was dared to take out the girl with the killer father. She was so hurt when she found out. Charlie nodded he remembered that night. But, her grandpa told her she didn't need a boy like that. She deserved much better; and there would be plenty of others that would call on her. Susan knew her grandpa was usually right. He always gave good advice.

In a lighter mood, Charlie asked if she remembered the time her grandma came out with her broom because she thought some one was trying to break in the house. While standing there with the broom, looking vicious, Charlie and Susan burst out laughing. They asked her what the heck she planned on doing with it. Nora would find herself laughing at the two of them afterwards. They continued reminiscing about old times for a while. Finally Charlie admitted he was getting sleeping. Before they turned in for the night, he told Susan how much he enjoyed her company tonight. They could go to bed with happy thoughts on their mind. He ended the evening by assuring her that bad things have a way of working themselves out. He wanted Susan to go to bed with pleasant thoughts instead of worries.

10

Susan woke up first the next morning. She decided it was her turn to make breakfast. After looking through the fridge she decided to make French toast and sausage. She heard Grandpa stirring, so she hurried to get the table set. He walked in the kitchen appreciating the wonderful smells of a hearty breakfast. One of the many things he missed since his wife passed away was the daily aromas from her cooking that filled the house. No matter what the agenda was for the day, he and Nora always had breakfast together. They used that special time to chat about their plans for the day. With her gone he's had many lonely mornings at the table. He hated not having anybody to talk to over breakfast.

Susan reminded Charlie that they agreed to have Lois over for dinner. She was hoping he would like her to come tonight because she already had a menu planned. Charlie said he'd go to the café and asked Lois right away, before she made other plans. Susan said she'd get the groceries while he was at the café. She was sure Lois would accept the invitation. It was going to be fun.

Before he left, Charlie wanted to check the phone to see if the wires had been fixed. He was pleased to know the service was back in order; and they could use their phone again. He was still perplexed wondering if the phone wires getting cut had anything to do with all the other strange events that have happened. Nobody seemed to know at this point.

On the way into town Susan realized she hadn't called her insurance company about her car. She really needed to take care of them so she could get another vehicle. For now she was sharing her grandpa's truck; but it was inconvenient to both of them. Charlie didn't mind sharing it with his granddaughter, but it would be nice if they each had their own car to get around in. Transportation was necessary to have whether they were in the country or the city. She would have to remember to call her insurance agent as soon as she gets back to her grandpa's house.

Dropping Charlie off at the café, Susan drove on to the sheriff's office. She asked if Frank was in, but was told he had not been in at all today. The deputy informed Susan that Frank called in earlier and said he would be in the office later this afternoon. Disappointed, she went back to the truck and headed to the grocery store. She would have to wait to talk to Frank.

When she got home, she put groceries away before calling her insurance company. The agent told her she would need a copy of the police report to verify her car was totaled after being stolen. They couldn't reimburse her for damages without the report. Susan had plenty of time before she had to cook dinner, so she drove back to the sheriff's office. She asked the deputy if he could fax the police report to her insurance agent. She gave the deputy the necessary fax number so he could take care of it right away.

By the time she accomplished that task, it was time to pick her grandpa up from the café. As she got closer she thought she saw the same rental car that Mike had been driving when he was in town. Turning around she headed after the vehicle to get a closer look; but the car disappeared from her sight. Susan drove up and down a few of the side streets, but still had no luck finding that car. She pulled back out on the main drag and headed for the café. The entire drive she kept a sharp look out for the car. She was curious to know who was driving that same car.

There were no other customers in the café when she picked Charlie up. Lois motioned her over to the table so the three of them could sit. Charlie told Susan that Lois agreed to have dinner with them tonight; but she wasn't able to get off work until 4:00 p.m. Together they decided they'd have dinner around six. That would be enough time for Lois to rest her feet a while before eating.

Charlie asked if Susan had gotten her business at the sheriff's office taken care of. She explained how she had a deputy fax the police report to her insurance company. Naturally, she hoped they would be able to settle the claim soon so she could buy a new car. Charlie told her not to get her hopes up. These things can sometimes take forever to resolve. Susan admitted he was probably right. Maybe she would get lucky and not have to wait too long.

The lunch crowd started coming in all at once. Lois's shift was about to get busy. Charlie and Susan got up to leave so Lois could get back to work. Before they walked out the door, Charlie winked at Lois, reminding her he'd see her at six. She winked back, telling them she couldn't wait. Susan thought it was cute watching her grandpa flirt with Lois. Tonight's dinner ought to be interesting, she thought.

On their drive home, Susan thought she saw that same car again. It appeared to be the identical rental car that Mike had. With Grandpa in the car she didn't want to go chasing after it again. Instead she tried to memorize the license plate so she could have one of her legal buddies check it out. Susan didn't want to be too obvious checking with the car rental place. She didn't want to raise anybody's suspicion on what she was up to. She made a mental note to call her private investigator friend in Springfield to see what he could find out. Maybe it was nothing. When Mike turned in the car, somebody else apparently rented it.

After lunch, Charlie admitted his head was hurting a little. The doctor told him it was common to have headaches after a concussion; and he advised Charlie to rest when that happened. He told Susan he was going to take a nap because he wanted to be well-rested when Lois got there. Susan thought a nap was a good idea; and she would use the quiet time to plan their evening with Lois. She began by getting out the candles and special table cloth. She might even use the good china tonight if she could find where her grandpa keeps all the good stuff.

She didn't want to wake Charlie to ask where he kept the candles, so she just started checking various places throughout the house.

As she was looking in her grandmother's antique cabinet she came across some old pictures. Knowing she had a little time before she needed to start dinner, she leisurely started thumbing through the pile of photos.

Susan wondered how often Grandpa got these photos out to look at. It appeared they were shoved under a mess of papers, so he probably hasn't looked at them in a very long time. She decided to leave the photos out so they could look at them together. Charlie could give her the background of the people in the pictures. Together they could take a journey down Memory Lane.

Putting those pictures aside for the moment, she glanced back to a drawer in the cabinet. She noticed an official looking envelope hanging out the opening of the drawer. Unable to resist, she took it out. To her surprised, the envelope was addressed to her! The postage date was over ten years ago. The return address was the prison where her father was. Her hands were shaking as she held the envelope tight. She didn't know whether to read what was inside or just put it back where she found it. It was obvious nobody had ever opened the envelope. Still, she wondered why neither of her grandparents had ever told her she had this mail.

Susan wasn't so sure she could handle any more surprises right now. She decided to concentrate on fixing dinner instead. She took the unopened envelope to her room, tucking it under her pillow. Maybe she would read it later. For now it was time to start cooking dinner. If she waited much longer to cook, they'd all be starving. She washed her hands and plunged into a cooking frenzy. Susan was going to make this a meal her grandpa and Lois would never forget!

The fragrances of a wonderful home-cooked meal woke Charlie. As he rolled over in his bed he was pleased to realize his headache had subsided. He was feeling well enough to be able to enjoy the delicious dinner Susan was making. The bonus was that he would also be able to enjoy Lois's company. Charlie decided he must be one of the luckiest men in town. With that he walked into the kitchen to see if he could help the chef.

Susan was finished cooking. The table was set beautifully, soft music was playing on the radio, and the lighting was perfect. There was nothing left for Charlie to do, except admire the atmosphere his granddaughter created for the evening. He had just enough time to wash up before Lois arrived. She rang the doorbell, but before Susan could get to the door Charlie was already there. He escorted Lois to the living room. Not wanting to come empty-handed, she brought them some homemade cookies.

Any time Susan was with her grandpa alone, he talked endlessly about Lois. He practically told Susan all of Lois's life history in the short time she's been there. There was no question in Susan's mind how interested her grandpa was in Lois. She couldn't remember him talking about anyone as much as he talked about her. She couldn't help but notice the way Charlie and Lois interacted together. They were clearly a couple in love. It was beautiful how they looked into each other's eyes; like two puppies ogling each other. It was another unexpected turn of events during her visit. At least it was a pleasant surprise, unlike the other things that have happened since she arrived. Susan was happy for them both.

Charlie and Lois were pleased when Susan rejected their offer to help in the kitchen. They enjoyed being pampered. Lois wasn't used to this kind of attention. During her brief visit, Charlie often mentioned Lois's past. As a waitress for many years, she was used to being the one to serve others. It was a rare occasion for her to be the one served. Susan also knew Lois had a difficult adult life…Apparently she was widowed at a young age. She had two small children when her husband died, forcing her to be a single parent with minimal income. Her husband had no insurance, leaving her penniless when he died. In a small town there were few employment opportunities. Lois felt fortunate when she was able to get the waitress position. Even though it wasn't an easy job, it provided enough income to put food on the table and clothes on their backs. Now her children were grown and living in Springfield. Lois didn't get to see them often, but they did call her several times a week.

Susan delighted in being able to play the waitress role for a change. It made her happy to know Lois was enjoying being the guest instead of the hostess. Charlie and Lois toasted each other with their glass of iced-tea. They raised their glasses to Susan in appreciation for the excellent dinner before them. Afterwards Susan made the happy couple go into the living room while she tidied up the kitchen. She could do dishes later, but wanted to clear the table at least. She wanted to use this time to get better acquainted with her grandpa's girlfriend instead of fussing in the kitchen.

They all enjoyed each other's company throughout the evening.

Lois didn't seem at all like a stranger. They talked as if they had known each other for ages. It was a comfortable and fun evening for all of them. They purposely avoided any discussion of the serious problems the town has recently faced. Nothing was going to ruin their night.

Just as Lois was preparing to go home, there was a knock on the door. It was Frank and his deputies. They all looked at each other knowing this couldn't be good news. Susan invited them inside and offered them some of Lois's cookies and coffee. Frank said he would love a hot cup of coffee, but he needed to skip the cookies because of his diabetes. After a little friendly conversation Charlie couldn't stand the suspense any longer. He told Frank he knew he didn't come here just for coffee. Charlie told him to blurt out whatever was on his mind. No point in keeping everyone in suspense.

Lois asked if she should leave, but Frank told her it would be important for her to listen to what he had to say. He began by asking Lois a question. Frank asked if she had ever met Susan's boyfriend before. Lois responded by saying she did meet Mike once when he and Susan stopped at the café one day. She introduced him as her boyfriend. Prior to that, Lois had never met him. Charlie asked Frank why he would ask Lois such a question. What could Mike possibly have to do with Lois?

The question sparked everyone's interest. Susan was reminded of the day Lois slipped her a note saying it was important that she call her. That was the same day she introduced her to Mike. Maybe this was a good time to bring that up. She turned to Lois, telling her she remembered the day she introduced her to Mike. Susan added that it was also the day she gave her that odd note telling her to call her. Lois looked at Frank, and then turned to Charlie. Finally she looked at Susan. The silence could be sliced with a knife at that point. Frank broke the silence. He asked Susan what note she was talking about. She excused herself a moment so she could retrieve the note from her jacket pocket. Sitting back down, she handed the note to Frank. Frank asked Lois to explain what the note meant.

With her head down, Lois explained how she overhead Mike on his cell phone when he went to the restroom. She described how the entry to the restroom was near the cash register where she was standing, so she was able to hear bits and pieces of his conversation. Lois stated she didn't intentionally try to hear what he was saying. She wasn't eavesdropping. She just happened to be standing close enough to hear some of what he was saying in his phone. She explained that most of the time Mike was whispering in the phone; but every once in a while he raised his voice. This caught her attention. When he spoke loudly enough, his voice echoed and she could hear him. What she was hearing unnerved her. She felt she needed to warn Susan about what she heard, so she wrote the note. Lois hoped Susan would call her when Mike wasn't nearby so she could tell her what she overheard.

Susan quickly reminded Lois that when she did call Lois back Mike was already in his car heading back to Springfield. Susan even mentioned that Mike was gone when they finally did talk. Yet, Lois didn't reveal anything about overhearing Mike having a conversation that worried her. Lois apologized to Charlie for doing any of this behind his back. Before Charlie could respond, Lois continued telling them the rest of the story. Lois wasn't alone the night Susan called her. Her neighbor Lydia was at her house, so she wasn't able to talk freely. Lois didn't want to discuss this information or her concerns with Susan in front of anyone else. That's why she pretended to have a normal conversation with Susan. She couldn't discuss what she really wanted to say. For Lydia's benefit, she spoke to Susan about everyday things instead.

Lois assumed she would have another opportunity to talk to Susan privately; so she would wait until then to tell her about what she heard. In fact, Lois thought about bringing it up tonight; then changed her mind because she didn't want to ruin their evening.

Everyone was quiet, waiting to see what Frank had to say about all of this.

Frank took a deep breath. He acknowledged that he heard everything Lois just said. Now he wanted her to repeat the entire story so he could take notes. Frank particularly wanted her to provide him as many details as possible about Mike's conversation. He told Lois to think hard about the bits and pieces she did hear. He said even if it didn't make any sense, it was important that she try to recall as many of the words she could. Frank told her it helps to remember details when you relax your whole body first. Take a deep breath and blow it out slowly. Then begin to challenge your memory bank.

Lois did as she was told. She took several deep breaths, and then blew it out slowly. She shook her arms to get the tension out, followed by resting them by her side. Lois felt relaxed enough to try to piece together the words she heard Mike say in his cell phone. She specifically heard him mention he found one key in the stuffed dog. He did not find a second key. The person at the other end of the phone must have gotten angry at what Mike was saying, because she could hear shouting through the phone. Mike also talked about tearing up the dog, but that didn't make sense to Lois. She couldn't imagine what it meant for him to tear up a dog.

Next thing she remembered was Mike talking about safe deposit boxes. He asked the person on the other end of the line to make sure he had his information correct. Basically, what she gathered from the conversation is that Mike was looking for something and couldn't find it.

Charlie had been watching Susan the whole time Lois spoke. He tried to pick up on what she was feeling right now. He knew she became an expert on covering up her feelings. As a lawyer she had to remain objective at all times. What Charlie was seeing though was the tell-tale signs of stress. She sat stiffly with her hands folded tightly in her lap. Susan's back was too straight, showing signs of tension. Charlie reached over to take her hand. He wanted to offer any comfort he could.

Instead of accepting her grandpa's comfort, Susan got up to pace the floor. She turned toward the sheriff asking him to give it to her straight. Frank looked at her with a puzzled face. He wasn't trying to hold anything back. He assured Susan he was trying to obtain information because he had nothing new to tell them right now. Frank told all three of them that he had no reason to hide information. If anything, he would rather keep them well informed of everything going on. He felt it was important they know so they could remain alert.

Lois got up to leave, apologizing for her part in spoiling their night. Susan assured Lois that their evening was not damaged.

She was glad to know the truth about the note; and they wouldn't let this news interfere with the rest of their plans. Frank and his deputies let themselves out; and Susan asked Lois to stay. She wanted to make sure Lois understood nobody was mad at her for what she told Frank tonight. To brighten up the rest of the evening, Susan brought out the pictures she had found earlier. She was determined to resurrect their dinner party from the grave it had just gotten blown into. Maybe some old photos would bring a smile back to their faces.

At first Charlie and Lois were still tense. As they shuffled through the photos Susan was relieved to see they were more relaxed again. After a marathon of picture-looking, Susan excused herself. She reminded her grandpa that she didn't get a two hour nap like he did, so she was tired. In reality she was still wide awake. She just wanted to give Charlie and Lois some time alone. Before he let Susan sneak off to bed, he reminded her they didn't have their customary hot cocoa yet. He said without cocoa they would all have bad dreams. Lois got up saying she would fix it. Susan had worked hard enough fixing the fabulous meal, so she wanted to do her fair share.

While Susan waited for her cocoa, she told her grandpa she was concerned about what she had learned about Mike. She's never been able to put her finger on it, but for some time now there was something about him she was uncomfortable with. As she talked she could see Lois in the kitchen. She realized how well Lois seemed to know her way around her grandpa's kitchen. That thought got her mind off of Mike.

Lois brought the cocoa in on a tray. She sat the tray down, handing each of them their cup. As they sat quietly sipping the warm drink, she suggested that Charlie and Lois take theirs outside so they could sit in the swing. Looking at Susan he knew that was his cue to give her some time alone. Taking Lois outside was a perfect way to give his granddaughter the space she needed.

When Frank got home, he found his wife Judy fast asleep. He didn't want to disturb her but found himself drawn to her bedside. Gently he reached down and kissed her forehead. Judy stirred a little, but didn't wake up. Frank was aware of how many lonely nights his wife endured because of his job. He might need to consider retiring soon so they could enjoy more time together. As soon as this case is closed he was going to submit his papers to retire. It was time. The job was getting to him.

As he got ready for bed he remembered taking Paula White's fingerprints. The day he stopped at her house he performed a casual wipe-down of her door. He used the excuse that he had gotten grease or dirt on the knob; and he wanted to clean up his mess. She didn't question what he was doing. He remembered putting the fingerprint test in his car when he left. The problem was the test kit was probably destroyed during the car crash. Even if he found the test kit, any prints he might have gotten are probably unreadable. He would go back to the crash site in the morning and see if he could find the envelope the test was in. If the envelope wasn't anywhere near the crash site, Frank would check inside the car.

The next morning he was still thinking about the White family. He really would like to meet the rest of them. When he attempted making inquiries about Paula's father or brother he didn't get anywhere. It was as if this family didn't exist prior to moving to this town. Frank knew it would be important to discover where they came from and who they really were. How he missed the old days when his little town was quiet and peaceful.

When he got to his office he asked his deputy, Butch, if he received a fax or message from the Springfield police. Butch told him there were no messages; nor were there any faxes. Frank told Butch about Lois overhearing a strange phone conversation that Mike made. He gave him the details as Lois described; and Butch just scratched his head trying to make some sense out of what he was hearing. Frank asked Butch to give him his opinion on what's been going on recently. He wanted somebody else's opinion. His deputy was young, fresh out of the training academy. Maybe he would have some insight how to handle this case. Unfortunately, Butch said he was well-trained for small town law enforcement; but wasn't prepared to handle a case as complicated as this one.

Since he didn't have any messages, Frank decided it was a good day to just go home. He had a splitting headache anyway, so it would do him more good to rest than to rack his brain on this case. Even driving was a chore today, so he made a wise decision in going home and spending some time with Judy for a change. She'd be surprised to see his ugly mug show up at home this early.

Susan spent the morning cleaning. This gave her a chance to stay busy and not dwell on everything she's learned recently. It was nagging her about Mike. She was convinced he was guilty of something; but she didn't know exactly what part he played in this puzzle. It bothered her thinking the man she almost wanted to spend her life with could possibly be a criminal.

Right now she would concentrate on keeping her family safe. She would deal with Mike after she collected a few more facts about his role in this mess. She turned her thoughts to something more positive. Susan was pleased to know her grandpa had a girlfriend. It almost sounded silly to say, but it was certainly fun. Since Lois was an integral part in this drama, Susan felt obligated to help protect her too. She suddenly had an idea. Why not ask Lois to move in with us? If they were all under the same roof, they could keep a better eye on each other. It made sense to Susan. Now she hoped Charlie and Lois would agree.

Susan joined the couple on the porch. Before Charlie or Lois had a chance to speak, Susan blurted out her idea that Lois should move in with them. Lois blushed and looked over at Charlie. It was almost as if she was trying to signal his permission before she answered. At that point Charlie chimed in. He announced that it wasn't a question. He insisted Lois stay with them. Lois quietly agreed. Susan giggled to herself thinking they didn't take very long to answer. She wondered what they had in mind for sleeping arrangements; but she didn't have to wonder long. Charlie put his arm around Lois and escorted her to his bedroom.

When Susan woke up the next morning she smelled coffee brewing. Lois was already gone. Charlie explained Lois had to go home to get her uniform because she was scheduled to work today. Susan and Charlie continued to drink their coffee when the phone startled them. They had forgotten the phone lines were fixed, so they were surprised when the phone actually rang. Susan could hear her grandpa giving yes and no answers to whoever the caller was. When he hung up he told Susan the call was from Frank's deputy, Butch. He requested that Charlie and Susan come to the sheriff's office as soon as they could. Charlie added that the deputy thought they might have some new information to share with them. Naturally, Charlie told Butch they would be there within the hour.

Frank was waiting at his desk when they arrived. After a few minutes of small talk, Frank showed them a piece of paper. It was a document from Public Records. The document listed an arrest record for a person named Michael Smith. Some were minor offenses; but many were serious drug trafficking arrests. Susan was shocked. The last thing she expected was Mike being involved with drugs.

Charlie asked Frank how it was possible to get hired as a police officer if the person had a criminal record. Frank assured him he was checking into that. He didn't have all the results back yet, but he agreed with Charlie that police departments did not hire former criminals. There was something suspicious about Mike's background. Either Mike lied on his application or someone else had used Mike's social security number. Chances are, they agreed, Mike lied on his application form.

Susan couldn't remember if she told Frank or her grandpa about the lie she caught Mike in. When he first arrived to town he told Susan he was in such a rush to get to Charlie's house he accidentally left his cell phone at home. Yet, later Susan discovered he actually had his cell phone in the rental car the entire time. In fact, Lois had witnessed Mike talking on his cell phone. She didn't know if this was important information or not; but she wanted to make sure she told Frank anything and everything she knew.

Frank agreed that any piece of information might be useful. He took notes as Susan described the evening she discovered Mike's cell phone on the floor of the rental. She also told him her stuffed animal Pluto was at Charlie's house the night she arrived. It was only later that she discovered her favorite toy missing. The sequence of events was beginning to fall into place. No matter which way you looked at it, Mike appeared to be guilty.

Just then, out of nowhere, it occurred to Susan that the night she arrived and stumbled across a dead person it was probably her own father. She wondered how she didn't figure that out before. Frank and Charlie probably already knew this, but kept it from her. With that final thought, Susan collapsed on the floor. One of the deputies ran to get a wet paper towel and began massaging the back of her neck. He didn't know if it would be helpful or not, but he saw somebody do that on TV when the person fainted.

Within seconds her color returned. Susan sat up slowly, realizing that she must have fainted. She had never done that before so she was unprepared to feel so shaky and nauseated. Charlie crouched down next to her, telling her not to move until she was sure she could get up without passing out again. Wiping her face with the wet paper towel made her feel somewhat better. As she recuperated from the nauseous feeling in the pit of her gut, Susan was able to stand. She felt like a fool, but everyone in the room assured her it was okay. Obviously all this negative energy was taking a toll on her. Susan admitted her body and mind were falling apart recently.

She explained to Charlie that she felt as if her brain exploded. Her brain capacity to absorb all the horrible news was full. Her body shut down temporarily, allowing her brain to absorb the latest bits of news about Mike. Before she could process any more information, she passed out. Now Susan was ready to start over. She pulled herself together and sat in a chair. She let all the men pamper her a few more minutes, and then told them she was fine. Susan refused to allow herself to fall apart again. She insisted she would be fine to continue their conversation about Mike. It was important for her to know the truth; no matter how queasy it made her feel. Susan composed herself, waiting for Frank to continue.

With hesitation, Frank told Charlie and Susan that he had fingerprints taken from Paula. He did it without Paula's knowledge so she wouldn't be suspicious of what he was doing. The problem was, Frank added, that he didn't know if the prints survived the car crash. The lab was still checking to see if Paula's prints were readable enough to use. He wanted to do a thorough background check on her; and the prints would be very helpful. Frank admitted he wasn't confident that Paula was actually guilty of anything. Instead, he had a gut feeling that the White family in general had something to hide.

In the meantime, while he was waiting for those results, Frank had called the Springfield Police Department. He talked to one of the

Sergeants there who was willing to talk about his officers. Frank discovered Mike was indeed a police officer there about a year ago. Mike was fired for lying on his application about having a criminal background. Apparently, from what Frank learned, Mike had a felony charge that disqualified him from being a police officer. He was fired from the force about six months ago. Once again, indicating Mike was a liar about a lot of things.

This piece of information shocked Susan; but she was able to handle the news without fainting. She had to force herself to stay strong even though she felt like a rag doll at this point. She felt a little woozy, but was determined not to crumble. Susan took a sip of water to help keep her mind clear. By this time Susan thought she couldn't learn any more about Mike that she hasn't already heard. Unfortunately, Susan was very wrong.

She thought back to the day she met Mike. It was a spring day, flowers blooming, birds chirping, and a beautiful warm breeze blowing. Susan remembered the details of the day very well. She had successfully prosecuted a well-known criminal that day; and reporters were waiting on the court house steps to take pictures and get her statements. It was a proud day and she was more than happy to answer all the reporter's questions.

As the reporters scattered to get back to their offices, she noticed one gentleman standing nearby. Susan remembered what a handsome man he was. As he began approaching her, she assumed he was just another reporter out to get a story. Ready to answer more questions, she was pleasantly surprised to find out he just wanted to congratulate her for winning her case. He introduced himself to Susan, making sure she noticed the badge clipped to his shirt. They spoke briefly, their eyes locked on each other. He suggested they go somewhere to get a cup of coffee and get away from the court house crowds; and she accepted.

It was an unexpected date; and they hit it off immediately. They began seeing each other on a regular basis after that; and fell in love. Now, a few years later, she was questioning the entire relationship. Susan reflected on that first meeting. She wondered if Mike had been at the court house specifically to meet her. In her mind she questioned if it had really been a chance meeting; or was it something more sinister? Was it possible that he purposely wanted to meet her and be involved in her life, pretending it was an accidental meeting? Yes, she still had a lot to learn about this man she used to call her boyfriend.

Frank could tell Susan was looking a little pale again, so he wanted to make sure she was alright before proceeding with the rest of the news. Assured she was ready to hear the rest, Frank started talking again. He walked around the room while thumbing through his notes. He took a breath and began telling the group the rest of what he knew.

Frank told the group he was able to confirm that Mike was the son of the guard that was killed by Susan's father. In his research he also learned that Mike had a younger step-sister and step-brother. Mike's step-sister's name is Paula. Her whereabouts where not known at the time he received the report. Everyone immediately suspected the new woman in town was likely the same Paula that is related to Mike. Frank added that the report did not disclose Mike's step-brother's name. He was aware that Paula White had a brother named John; but the report couldn't confirm or deny this information.

The only explanation for John's name not being on the report is if John had lived in a different state when his father and sister moved into the house or if John had a different last name from his sister. It was unclear why only Paula's name would be included on the report.

Susan began thinking of all the times she thought she saw Mike driving around town since he supposedly left. Now she knew he didn't really have a job to go back to, so maybe he was still in town. She wondered if revenge was the reason Mike would be involved in this horrid mystery. Of course, she was jumping ahead of herself with these thoughts. At this point nobody knew for sure if it was Paula White that is related to Mike. Right now they are just speculating. As a lawyer she was sensitive to knowing facts before making accusations.

Frank brought the conversation back to what he's learned in the last 24 hours. He added his information to what Lois mentioned regarding the phone call she overheard. Now he needed to piece together the importance of the key Mike found inside Pluto. More importantly, Frank wanted to know where the second key is that Mike mentioned. He had checked with the local banks first to see if there might be a Lock Box connected to either of the keys. They agreed the key they had as evidence did belong to a Lock Box. If there is a second key, it might mean there is a second Lock Box. Frank wanted to know who would have originally hidden the one key in Susan's stuffed animal. There was still a lot of investigating to be done.

Charlie had been very quiet when Frank disclosed the new information. He was silent because his own thoughts were dodging in several directions. After listening to Frank describe the latest evidence, it occurred to Charlie that Mike is probably the person who hit him on the head that awful night. He would have had the opportunity to sneak up behind him and knock him out. At the time Charlie was pleased to finally get to meet Susan's boyfriend...but now he wondered if this man really came to their house to search for a key. Worse yet, did he come to kill Susan's father in a fit of revenge for his own father's death?

They were all sitting around Frank's desk, lost in their own thoughts of the situation. As Frank slid his chair away from his desk he informed everyone he was going to pay a visit to the White family. He hoped to be able to see all of them. He wanted to meet Paula's father and brother.

Charlie and Susan took their cue. The informational session was over. As they got up to leave, Susan asked Frank if there was any possibility that Mike was not involved. Looking at her, Frank told her it didn't look very good for Mike. She couldn't deny how the guilt seemed to point to Mike, so Frank's opinion of him was probably correct. Susan wondered how she could have misjudged him so much. She realized her heart must have clouded her logic when she fell for him. Looking back, there were often times when Mike would dodge questions. At the time Susan thought it was the nature of a police officer to be evasive sometimes. Now she realized he must have been hiding the truth about many things. She obviously missed several signals to indicate he was less than an honest man.

11

As Charlie and Susan drove home, her cell phone rang. She glanced at the caller ID and saw it was Mike. There was no way she could talk to him right now. She didn't want to hear anymore lies. The things she learned about Mike tonight were too fresh in her mind. It would be too difficult to have a conversation with him until she had time to sort all the information out. Besides, it would be like talking to a stranger. She didn't know him at all. All these years she knew him as Mike Hayes. Now she finds out he is really could be Mike Smith. She didn't know this man at all. It would be a mistake to answer his call at this point.

When they got home Charlie noticed the photos were still on the coffee table. Thumbing through them, he noticed that there are several pictures of people he didn't recognize at all. One picture had four people posing. One person was his daughter, one was his son-in-law, but he didn't recognize the other two men in the photo. As he looked through more pictures he found the same two men in several of the snapshots. When Frank had been there they didn't go through all the pictures, so many were overlooked. Charlie decided it might be helpful if he took the photos to Frank to see if he knew who the two men were. He tucked those pictures in his pocket to take to the sheriff's office after lunch.

As they were eating lunch, Susan told her grandpa that they needed to discuss something. With all the other things going on, she almost forgot to ask Charlie who was responsible for Mark's funeral arrangements. She knew Mark's parents were deceased, so she wondered if that left the responsibility to her. Charlie thought a moment and admitted he hadn't given it any thought before. He acknowledged the task of making funeral arrangements would indeed be theirs since they were the closest kin. He quickly added that he didn't mind taking care of it; and he promised to keep it simple.

Susan asked if Charlie thought anyone from town would even come. He admitted it wasn't too likely for anyone else to show up; but felt it would be nice to at least hold a private service so they could have closure. She agreed that would be the decent thing to do, so they proceeded making the arrangements.

While Susan and Charlie made funeral arrangements, Frank was on his way to the White's house. Once again he found himself bouncing along the bumpy road. He noticed a jeep parked in front of their house, hoping that was a good sign that somebody was home. He parked his car behind the jeep, blocking anyone from leaving. As he was ready to knock on the front door, it opened. A man held the door open while Frank introduced himself. The man held out his hand, introducing himself also. He was John White, the brother of Paula. As they walked into the living room, Frank saw an older gentleman in a wheelchair. He assumed this was Paula's father from what he had learned so far. John introduced Frank to his father, Phil White. Phil told Frank to sit down and make himself comfortable.

Frank started by apologizing for coming unannounced. Phil shook his head with indifference. He told Frank not to worry about it. If he didn't want visitors they wouldn't answer the door. Simple as that. Frank explained he was in the middle of an investigation, trying to gather as much information as he could. He was asking all the neighbors what, if anything, they saw the night Susan came to town. In fact, he wondered if Phil or his family noticed anything going on recently that is out of the ordinary. Frank continued his questioning by asking if Phil had heard about the dead body that was found in a burned car. Phil's response to most of the questions was that they hadn't lived there long enough to know what was or wasn't ordinary in this town. He hadn't noticed anything strange. If his kids noticed anything peculiar they would have mentioned it. He tried to convince Frank he didn't like gossiping. Phil was a loner and wanted to keep it that way.

Trying to keep the conversation friendly, Frank asked where they moved from. The answer was vague. Phil stated they were from a little town in Illinois that if you blinked you missed it. Before he could ask anything else, John stood up and told Frank they'd let him know if they heard anything that might be considered unusual. He walked toward the door, giving Frank the indication the visit was over. With that, Frank thanked them for their hospitality and he got in his truck. He decided it was a very unsatisfactory visit for sure. He didn't feel like he learned anything. The lack of hospitality only made Frank more curious; and determined to come back another time. In the meantime, his walkie-talkie buzzed, interrupting his thoughts.

His deputy Butch was calling to find out when Frank would be back in the office. There were a couple men in the office waiting to see him. He told them he'd be there in just a few moments because he wasn't far away. Frank wondered who the two men were. He hoped it wasn't the cranky old brothers that lived on the outskirts of town. They were always complaining about one thing or another. He wasn't in the mood to listen to their nonsense.

To his surprise, the two men waiting for him were FBI agents. They introduced themselves as Agent Roy Adams and Agent Ken Jones. Agent Adams told Frank they were there to find out why Frank has been making inquiries about Mike Smith. They were aware that Frank had been snooping around trying to get background information on Mr. Smith; and they needed to know why. Frank sat down, absolutely speechless. What next? Now he had the FBI coming to his little town to question him. He was definitely going to retire when this case was solved!

Frank pulled himself together. He told the agents he hoped he didn't mind if he called the FBI Headquarters to verify they were who they said they were. Agent Jones acknowledged they respected Frank for checking on their identification. Frank made the appropriate phone call and found out both agents were legitimate.

Once he knew the Agents were serious about questioning him, Frank told them the whole story about the crime he was investigating; and how Mike was implicated. He started from the day Susan arrived through his visit with the White family. Agent Adams thanked him for telling them about the investigation. He added that the FBI was familiar with the investigation too. Frank was surprised with that knowledge. He had no idea this crime had become a federal investigation. Interesting, he thought.

Agent Jones spoke up at that point. He told Frank that the information he was about to disclose could go no further than Frank's ears. They had to be certain Frank could keep this to himself. He was willing to do that, but was curious to know what the big secret was. Jones continued. He explained that Mike Smith was working for them as an undercover agent. They are currently in the middle of busting a huge drug ring; so they had to fabricate Mike's whole background record.

Frank was forming several questions to ask. He started by asking exactly what part of Mike's record was accurate and what part was made up. Adams explained that it was true about Mike's father being the guard that was killed in the robbery long ago. It was also true that his real name is Michael Hayes, not Mike Smith. Susan apparently knew him by the correct name after all. He was anxious to tell Susan, but realized he just promised the agents to keep all of this information to himself.

Adams told Frank he'd be seeing them around town for the next few days. They were going to be poking around a little, looking for additional information for their case. He suggested Frank just ignore them while they're hanging around. They didn't want anyone getting suspicious about them being there…especially if they're seen with the sheriff. Frank agreed he would pretend they didn't exist. He would go on about his daily business as if they weren't around.

Adams and Jones got ready to leave, but Frank had one more comment. He admitted this case was out of control and way over his head. He told the agents he was grateful for their involvement; and he hoped they could get to the bottom of the case soon. Frank admitted he didn't like keeping secrets from his friends. It made him uncomfortable, but knew it was necessary for now. With that he thanked the agents and went back to his desk.

Frank dwelled on the situation the rest of the afternoon. He knew it would be most difficult to keep this secret from his best friend Charlie. They discussed everything; and Charlie would know if he was keeping something from him. The only way to remedy this problem was to avoid Charlie as much as he could. If he didn't see or talk to Charlie, he wouldn't slip and say something he shouldn't. Of course, Charlie might begin wondering why Frank was ignoring him after a while. He would make Charlie believe he was working on a different case at the same time, making him too busy to have their daily chats. Frank couldn't think of any other way to deal with the secrecy issue.

Susan was trying to stay busy so she wouldn't have time to dwell on Mike. While she was vacuuming in the hallway, something metal got hung up in the vacuum brush. The metal object clanged noisily until she finally turned the vacuum off. Susan tipped the vacuum upside down to see what had gotten sucked up. At a glance she could see a shiny piece of metal glimmering from the sun. As she reached inside the bristles, she felt the smooth edge of a flat metal object. It didn't feel like a coin, but it was clearly something that needed to be taken out. She had to find a screwdriver to loosen the cover around the brushes. When the cover opened, a key fell to the floor. Susan started to pick the key up; but remembered Frank talking about a key to a lock box. This could be the missing key everyone was talking about. She immediately called Frank to tell him what she found. He would probably come get the key and have it checked for fingerprints. When she called Frank he wasn't available.

Luckily she was able to talk to Frank's deputy, Butch. He told her not to touch anything; and he would be there within thirty minutes. By the time she washed her hands and made a cup of tea, Butch was already at the door. Susan was thankful he got there so fast. Butch scooped the key up with a tiny hook-like instrument; and then dropped it into a plastic evidence bag. Afterward he asked Susan if it was okay for him to measure the distance from the back door to where the key was found. Butch was hoping he'd also find some footprints in the carpet or other telltale signs of footsteps that didn't belong to Charlie or Susan. Susan was anxious to let the deputy do anything that could help this investigation. She told him he was free to check whatever he needed to.

Butch collected as much evidence as he could and started toward the door. Before he left he asked Susan how she was feeling. He remembered how she fainted after hearing so much bad news, so he wanted to make sure finding this key didn't send her over the edge. Susan assured him she was fine. She didn't anticipate that happening again. Butch then inquired how she was doing after learning her boyfriend was a criminal. Susan was somewhat shocked at that question. She felt it was none of his business how she was feeling about Mike. Yet, she felt obligated to come up with some kind of response because he did seem sincere. Susan told him she was more than disappointed to find out what she's learned; but she was quite able to deal with it. She still thought it was rude of Butch to even bring it up. He hardly knew her to be asking such personal questions. Susan guessed he might be a good deputy, but he certainly had the personality of a slug.

As soon as Butch left she began cleaning the mess from the vacuum cleaner disaster. Charlie came home shortly after she got the mess cleaned up. Lois was with him and was carrying a suitcase. Today Lois was officially moving in with Charlie and Susan. The room was ready for her to unpack her things.

While Charlie and Lois were busy putting her things away, Susan's cell phone rang. It was Mike again. Her first reaction was panic. She almost dropped the phone when she saw his name on caller ID. Susan decided to answer the call this time. With a calm voice she said, "Hello." Practically yelling, Mike asked why she hasn't answered any of his messages. He told Susan how worried he's been not hearing from her. After he got that off his chest, he finally asked how she was doing. Without answering his first question, he jumped into his next question. He wanted to know how the investigation was going. She paused to see if he was going to ask anything else before she answered.

When Mike didn't say anything else, Susan told him she was doing fine. She added there wasn't anything new on the case. She waited for him to respond to her answers, but all she could hear was heavy breathing. She could also hear noises in the background; but couldn't distinguish what the noise was. Susan listened very carefully to hear how he was reacting to what she just said; but there was no audible response. She thought she heard him sigh. Was it a sigh of relief or a sigh of boredom? She couldn't tell. She was curious to know what he was thinking, but knew there was no point in asking him. Susan will never believe anything he tells her anymore.

She felt obligated to ask how he was doing. Mike told her he's been really busy at work. He said they were swamped with a lot of cases, so he wouldn't be able to get away for a while. Mike told Susan he would try to finish up as quickly as possible, but couldn't promise her when he could return. She assured him there was no need to hurry back. She explained how she and her grandpa were busy with a lot of family obligations recently, so she didn't have a lot of free time to deal with him. Mike got a little defensive with her last comment, asking her what she meant. Before she could answer him, she heard somebody else trying to talk to him. Susan concentrated on the other person's voice, hoping to see if she could recognize who that person was. The last thing she heard Mike say was that something had come up and he was going to have to hang up. They said their goodbyes; and hung up the phone abruptly.

Susan told Charlie and Lois about the strange phone conversation she just had with Mike. Charlie suggested the next time he calls just to let it go to voice mail. He told her maybe it wasn't a good idea trying to have any conversation with him right now. He asked that she wait at least until they learn more of Mike's involvement in the recent crimes. Susan mentioned she considered having her phone number changed. At least then she wouldn't have to know Mike was trying to contact her. Charlie agreed that might be a good idea, so Susan dialed the telephone company to change her phone number.

Once that was taken care of, she decided she better call her boss to let him know her new number. Susan thought she also needed to call Frank. She wanted to make sure he had a way to contact her.

After she called her boss, she immediately called Frank. He jotted down her new number, asking why she had the number changed. She told him about the conversation she had with Mike; and how she made up her mind she didn't want him to be able to reach her. Susan wanted nothing more to do with a man who could be guilty of harming her grandpa or her. Nor did she want to communicate with a man who possibly murdered another man.

Frank told her he understood. He didn't blame her for being upset. He wished he could tell Susan she didn't have to be afraid of Mike; but for now he had to honor his promise to the Federal Agents not to say anything. He wasn't so sure it was a good idea for Susan to lose contact with Mike totally. Frank kind of liked the idea of having an open line between Mike and Susan so he could continue to learn things that he tells her. If Susan won't allow Mike to contact her, he didn't have any way to keep checking on Mike's activities. Yet, if Mike isn't truthful, he guessed he really wasn't learning the truth of what was going on anyway. He'll be glad when the time comes so he can tell Susan it was okay to talk to Mike again. She'll be happy to find out he isn't the bad guy after all.

Frank sat in his office daydreaming of the day they could close this case, tell Susan her boyfriend is a good guy, and get their town back to normal. While he was sitting there thinking of all these good thoughts, his police mindset kicked in. He realized he might be jumping to conclusions about Mike being guilt free. The more Frank thought about it, the more he began thinking about possible motives for Mike to want to join forces with the FBI. He was concerned about the fact that Mike's father was shot in the robbery. It actually made more sense that his motive to work with the FBI was to get closer to the FBI records. As a partner to the agents, Mike would have access to all the records regarding the bank robbery where his father got killed.

Frank wondered if Mike's ultimate goal was to get revenge on the person who killed his father. He would have inside knowledge about the case if he were on the investigative team; and then he could check on Mike that way. Unfortunately, Frank wasn't on the team; so the best he could do was stay in contact with the team members and learn things about Mike from them. This position would give him access to all the information involving the shooting and robbery. With Frank's years of law enforcement experience, it was easy for him to think like a criminal. From this standpoint, Frank believed Mike looked more like a suspect than a trustworthy investigator. He hated thinking this way, but his gut instinct told him he was right. In spite of what the FBI agents said, Frank was sure Mike was not to be trusted.

The deputy knocked on Frank's door, disrupting Frank's train of thought. Butch told the sheriff he had something to show him. With that, he showed Frank the evidence bag that had the key in it. Frank asked if that bag held what he thought it did. The answer was yes. In addition, Butch was proud to tell him there was a partial print on the key; and he already sent it to the lab. Frank told the deputy he was doing an excellent job assisting him with this case. They were both anxious to learn whose prints were on the key.

After talking to Frank earlier, Susan remembered she needed to call her insurance company. She wanted to make sure they had her new number so they could contact her as soon they processed her accident claim. Once that was taken care of, Susan wanted to check on Lois to make sure she was settled in her new room.

She peeked in the open door to find everything was already put away. Lois was finished unpacking; and had all her things put away. Susan walked down the hall towards the kitchen when she heard voices talking. She thought she heard her name mentioned, so she didn't want to barge into the kitchen making them feel uncomfortable. Instead, she casually walked in pretending to still be talking to the insurance company. Susan never did find out what they were talking about, but figured if it was important they would tell her later.

Charlie was getting ready to take Lois to work, so he asked Susan if she'd like to ride along. She told him that would be a great idea because she wanted to find a place where she could rent a car. Charlie fussed a little, telling Susan he didn't mind sharing his truck. He hated seeing her waste her money on some rental. She assured him the insurance company was going to pay for the rental until she found a car to purchase. He didn't argue with her because he understood that she wanted her own car. Charlie really didn't mind sharing his, but he knew Susan wanted the freedom to come and go when she liked instead of depending on him.

After they dropped Lois off at the café, Charlie drove Susan to Quincy Rental Agency. Susan picked out a Jeep Wrangler. Since she had to do some paperwork before driving away with the Jeep, she told her grandpa to go on home. She'll be right behind him shortly. Charlie told her he was going to do some errands, so there was no hurry for her to get home.

After what seemed like forever, Susan completed all the paperwork. She was looking forward to driving the Jeep. It seemed like a fun vehicle, albeit not practical to purchase. As she walked out to the parking lot she noticed the rental car that Mike had used when he was in town. The only reason Susan knew for sure it was the same vehicle is because it had a large ugly scratch on the passenger door. Two cars couldn't have that same design on their door, so it had to be the one Mike rented.

Playing investigator, she went back inside the rental office to inquire about the car. She explained her boyfriend had rented it previously; and then she made up a story how he left his wristwatch on the front seat. Susan told the clerk she'd take it back to him if they found it. The clerk explained the company's privacy policy, which meant he was not at liberty to discuss another customer's business with her. He did suggest, however, that Susan tell her boyfriend to call them and they could discuss any lost item with him.

Susan tried her next ploy. She attempted flirting with the clerk. She hoped he'd be more willing to talk if she flirted. To her dismay, he didn't budge. This clerk was honest. He wasn't going to break any rules about divulging information, so she might as well give up on learning anything new here.

Susan decided if she couldn't get information from the clerk, maybe an official sheriff could. She stopped at Frank's office to tell him about the rental car she saw on the parking lot at Quincy's. Frank didn't seem overly impressed just because she saw Mike's rental car there. Susan wouldn't let up though. She insisted either Frank or one of his deputies go there and check it out. She pleaded that maybe, just maybe, Mike could have left a piece of evidence behind.

Frank realized Susan was groping for more clues at this point; but maybe she was right. He promised her he would go to Quincy's tomorrow and see what he could learn. He would prefer to have a search warrant on hand; but knew he didn't have sufficient grounds to get file for one. The most Frank could do was question the people that worked there; and see what he could learn. Frank also reminded Susan that she was not allowed to bring him anymore ideas or problems because she already met and passed up her quota. With Frank's comment, Susan blushed. She knew he was teasing her. Even she had to admit that maybe she was grasping at straws. Susan was so determined to get to the bottom of this mystery that she was willing to turn the whole town upside down if need be.

12

With that, Frank considered sending his Deputy, Butch, out to check the rental car. Maybe Butch could casually snoop around unofficially and discover a piece of evidence accidentally. In the meantime, he was really busy and needed to get back to work. Susan could tell Frank was acting a little strange. No matter how busy he was, he always took out time to talk to her or her family. Concerned with his abruptness, she asked him if he was okay. Frank told her he was sorry to be so rushed, but had several deadlines to meet. Susan excused herself, but left with a gnawing feeling that Frank was holding something back. Frank sagged in his chair with relief when she left. He wanted so bad to discuss what he learned about Mike through the Federal Agents; but he knew he couldn't. This was a difficult situation at best, Frank thought.

Shortly after Susan left, Frank decided to make a return trip to Phil's house. Something was nagging him about the visit, but he couldn't put his finger on it. The last time he was at Phil's house he noticed the house was fairly clean, even though it was cluttered with a variety of items. If his memory served him correctly, Frank thought he saw two black boxes next to Phil's chair. It wasn't uncommon for people to keep their personal papers in locked boxes, so he didn't give it any thought at the time. But today when Butch brought him the key Susan found hidden at her house, it triggered Frank's thoughts to the missing locked boxes from the bank heist long ago. Frank didn't have grounds to request a search warrant; so he decided he would just casually look around next time he visited Phil.

Arriving back home before Grandpa and Lois, she wanted to relax a few minutes before fixing dinner. Sitting on the couch she remembered the letter she found from her father. She still hadn't read it yet. Now was as good a time as any to get it out. With trembling hands, Susan carefully opened the envelope. Susan took a deep breath before unfolding the letter, unsure of what she would learn. Very slowly, she began reading. The letter said,

"*To My Sweet Little Girl:*

I will always wonder when you received this letter and if you have chosen to read it. With all my heart I hope you can believe me when I tell you I love you more than life itself. I wish I could be with you to tell you this instead of relying on words in a letter. Either way, I hope you grow up knowing how happy I was to know my baby girl was born and became the love of my life. I wanted to hold you in my arms, kiss your cheeks, and be able to tell you how much I loved you. No matter what has happened, I will go to my grave being proud to call you My Sweet Girl.

I realize how much shame and embarrassment I brought to you and your mother. I am truly sorry for that. It was never my intention to bring harm to either of you. All I wanted was for my family to be well and taken care of. I wanted to be the one to provide that for you; but I made a terrible mistake that cost all of us the family you so deserved.

I am also sorry for the pain I'm sure you had to endure growing up. Having a father in prison for murder probably caused you a lot of pain and the brunt of many cruel jokes. You didn't deserve that; nor did your mother. I would give anything if I could only go back in time and undo all the wrong I have done.

I've heard the other men in prison saying things like that; and I don't know if they mean it or not. But, I mean every word of it. The pain I have caused you and your mother was so wrong. There is nothing on this earth I wouldn't do to change what happened.

I just needed you to know that I will always be sorry for causing our family to be torn apart. I will always regret missing the chance to watch my Sweet Girl grow up. I miss being with your mother. I do cherish the memories I have of you when we were together briefly. You were the most beautiful baby and little girl. You were only three years old when I went to trial, then directly to prison. I am so thankful that I got to spend those special three years with you. After I was taken to prison I knew I may never see you again. I was always afraid you would hate me and never want to see me. That's why it is so important to me to write this letter. If nothing else, I want you to know how much I loved you then and love you now.

No matter what you've been told before or what you believed before, I hope when you read this letter you will realize that you and your mother have always meant everything to me.

I made a terrible mistake in judgment when I took part in robbing a bank. I was only the driver and didn't know things were going to go wrong. I'm not making excuses for my part; but I wanted you to know I was desperate at the time because I didn't have a job. Very foolishly, I agreed to drive the getaway car, hoping to get enough money to hold us over until I found another job. Wrong is wrong. My pride took over my logic that day. I was wrong and will pay for that mistake for a long time. The part that hurts me the most is that you and your mother have to pay for my ignorance as well. I never wanted that to happen.

I hope you still have the little stuffed animal I left for you. Some day it could be important for you and your mother; and I wanted you to have it to remember me as well.

The only thing that keeps me going is hoping that someday you might forgive me and let me meet you. I look forward to that day. I know I can't make up for all the time lost; but if you will give me another chance I'd like to prove what a good father I can be. I love you with all my heart. Your Dad"

When she finished reading the letter, she could almost touch the emotions Mark was trying to express in his words. Almost every line mentioned something about the love he had for his daughter. In between the lines he showed remorse for his part in the robbery that caused him to be in prison. Mark repeated over and over how sorry he was that his dreadful mistake had costs him to be taken from his family. In the letter Mark never denied his guilt or involvement in the robbery or shooting the guard. Yet, at the same time, he never explained what his participation was, other than being the driver of the car.

When she put the letter down she had huge tears streaming down her cheeks. Susan cried uncontrollably as she placed the letter back in the envelope. For the first time in her life, Susan finally had proof that her daddy did love her. She always wondered, even though her grandpa told her she was her daddy's pride and joy. Susan wanted to believe her grandpa when he would tell her how Mark loved her. But was afraid Grandpa only said those things to make her feel good.

This special letter was the confirmation she needed that her father was a loving man. Even though he allowed himself to get involved in a robbery, there was a side to him that was good. It was hard for Susan to imagine what it must have been like for her mother. How awful it must have been for her mother to know her husband was a robber and murderer. Susan realized her grandparents must have had a difficult time as well. Their only daughter was forced to raise a child alone, with no income. How very sad for her grandparents to witness their daughter struggle through that rough time. Susan knew her grandparents sacrificed a lot to help them. She would always be grateful to them for everything they did.

Although she wasn't proud of what her father did, Susan was consoled knowing he wasn't heartless. There was a part of this stranger that loved his family. It meant a lot to Susan learning this side of her father. She was thankful she found the letter. At least now she knew a little about her father. He was no longer just a stranger that shared her DNA. After reading the letter, she was better prepared to finalize the funeral arrangements. It was no longer just an obligation. This was something she wanted to do.

While Charlie was waiting for Lois to get off work he decided to drop in on Frank. He often stopped by Frank's office, so it wasn't out of the ordinary for him just to pop in unexpected. When he walked into the office he was greeted with a cool welcome. Charlie pulled up a chair like he always did. He settled into his favorite chair, waiting for Frank to tell him one of his jokes. Instead, Frank apologized for not being able to have one of their friendly chats. He explained he was swamped with paperwork that had to get done before the end of the day. Before Charlie had time to respond, Frank stood up and walked him to the door.

In all the years Charlie has known Frank, he has never been that abrupt. He couldn't help but feel hurt with his curt response. He really wanted to say something, but Frank's facial expression made it clear the conversation was over. Charlie grabbed his jacket and walked out the door. He wondered if he had said or done something wrong to make

Frank upset. He was very troubled being treated like this. Charlie couldn't think of any explanation for Frank's behavior.

When he picked Lois up from work he told her about the brief visit with Frank. Lois was as perplexed as Charlie. Neither could come up with a plausible reason for him to act this way. Both agreed Frank has been working hard lately, so maybe he was just tired. Nothing else made any sense.

Changing the subject, Lois started telling Charlie about the fancy-dressed strangers that came to the café. She told him she had never seen these guys before; and she thought it was odd that they just sat around like they were sizing the place up. The guys didn't even order any food. They sat there for a few hours just drinking coffee. Lois continued talking about the two strangers. She stated they seemed pre-occupied staring at everyone coming in or out of the café. Neither said anything to anyone, even when some of the town's folk try to strike up a conversation with them. Lois described them as being unapproachable with their fancy suits and uptight attitude. Charlie couldn't envision who they might be or what they were doing in town.

When they got home Susan showed Charlie and Lois the letter she found from her father. She excitedly told them how happy she was reading it. Knowing she didn't need any more negativity, Charlie was pleased to know the letter made Susan so happy. Susan went further to say she was ready to make funeral arrangements for her father. Charlie was a little surprised, but pleased to hear his granddaughter wanted to do this. He asked her what she had in mind for arrangements.

Susan told him she'd like to have a private service. She assumed not too many of the town's people would be interested in attending; and this would be a good way for her to say her personal goodbye. She had never done anything like this before so she relied on her grandpa to guide her through the process since he was only too familiar with having to make funeral arrangements. Of course her grandpa was more than happy to help her. His first suggestion was to use the funeral home where his wife and own daughter had their services. Susan immediately agreed and asked how she should go about contacting them.

Charlie went to his bedroom to get the papers from the funeral home. The yellowed papers had all the information they needed to begin. He wrote the phone number down for Susan so she could call them in the morning. They decided to continue the planning from the kitchen. As they sat at the table, Susan asked Charlie if he knew approximately how much the funeral would cost. He admitted he had no idea because he and his wife had a pre-arranged funeral that was paid for long ago. By now the prices have surely gone up. They would learn everything they needed to know tomorrow. With an afterthought, Susan asked her grandpa if he thought it was okay to have her dad's body cremated. Charlie told her the decision was hers; and he would go along with whatever she chose.

She asked Charlie if he would mind telling her more about her father. She especially wanted to learn more about Mark *before* the robbery. Susan suspected the man that married her mother was a good person or her grandparents wouldn't have allowed their daughter to marry him. This is the Mark she wanted to learn about.

Susan wanted to know as much as possible about her father before she buried him. It was important for her to feel like she knew him a little before sending him to his final resting place. Since this was going to be her first and only time with her father, she wanted to make sure it was meaningful. Susan was grateful to have found the letter when she did. Now she could have the closure she's waited for all these years.

Charlie wanted to help Susan get better acquainted with Mark's memory. He understood her need to feel she had a connection with her father before the funeral. He suggested they look over some old pictures. That would help spark his memory of the event connected with the photo. The first album was Susan's parent's wedding pictures. She was surprised that no one had ever shown her these before. Of course, it never occurred to her to ask anyone if there were wedding photos to look at.

As they thumbed through the photos she saw a very happy young couple posing for the photographer. Mark was a dashing young man with a broad smile and wide shoulders. Her mother was a beautiful woman with deep dimples, long reddish hair, and eyes that glistened. Her last memories of her mother were when she let Susan brush her hair. They would giggle together; and her mother's dimples would deepen the more she laughed. The wedding photo was just a younger version of the mother she remembered.

One thing for sure, her parents were a handsome couple. They appeared very happy in every photo. Charlie said they were thrilled when their daughter announced her engagement to Mark. They thought he was a fine man. He had good manners and a decent job. What more could parents want for their daughter?

Unfortunately, shortly after the wedding Mark lost his job. The company modernized, replacing many of the workers with robotics. With no job, Mark was forced to collect unemployment benefits. With a heavy mortgage and baby on the way, Mark became desperate for more money. Susan's mother wasn't able to work at the time because she was having a difficult pregnancy. The financial burden fell on Mark's shoulders.

Before long, Mark ran into one of his old school chums. He convinced Mark that he was working on a deal that could help get him out of debt quickly. Being young and naïve, Mark accepted his friend's deal. Unfortunately, what he didn't know was that the so-called deal was also illegal. The arrangement wasn't a real job after all. It was a "get rich quick" scheme that included robbing a bank in another town. At first Mark declined to participate. He was determined to find employment to keep their head's above water. He wanted to take care of his bills the right way, not through illegal methods.

Mark had too much pride to turn to Charlie and Nora for help. He was strong-minded; convinced he could handle the debts on his own. When he learned their house was going to be repossessed he felt desperate. That's when Mark called his so-called chum. He agreed to do whatever it took to save his house; but he made it clear that he would only do this one time. He just needed enough money to get house payments caught up so they wouldn't end up homeless. Mark would take any legitimate job after they got their bills caught up. He didn't want his wife to know how desperate they were. She had enough to worry about with the difficult pregnancy.

Nobody knew what Mark was planning. He convinced Susan's mother he would just be out of town for a few days to do a business deal.

He didn't want her to know what the real plan was or she would have tried to talk him out of it. Mark explained to his wife that he was going with his friend on Thursday and would be back by Sunday. On Friday morning Susan's mother and Grandparents were having breakfast when the police knocked on their door. To everyone's shock, the officers informed them that Mark was involved in a robbery where a guard was shot and killed. Mark had been arrested and needed an attorney. Silence filled the room. None of them could believe what they were hearing.

Charlie explained to Susan how the next few weeks were a blur. Shortly after Mark's arrest, Susan's mother went into early labor. Little Susan was born the same day Mark was put in a jail cell to wait for a trial date. He asked if he could go to the hospital to be with his wife and newborn baby girl; but was denied. He wanted more than anything to see his tiny daughter; but he could not be released from jail unless bond was paid. Mark knew there was no money to pay for bond; so he was going to have to sit in jail until the trial date was set.

Of course he would always regret not getting to at least see his new baby. Mark knew he may never get to hold if he was convicted. He was also aware that his wife might never forgive him for what he had done. Mark knew he deserved her anger. It broke his heart knowing the birth of his daughter should have been the happiest day of their lives. Instead, it was the beginning of the worst time in all their lives.

Due to a few technicalities, the trial was postponed and delayed many times. Mark's friend had the funds to pay for his bond to release him until they had a court date. By this time his house had been repossessed, so Mark had no choice but to stay in a hotel while he awaited trial. He begged his wife to stay with him during the court delay. As much as she was appalled at what Mark had done, she still loved her husband. She chose to stand by his side as they fought the legal battles. She would never be happy at the choice he made to commit a crime in order to save their house. She understood his motive, but wished he would have come to her instead. Maybe together they could have found a way to get through their financial difficulties. Now they would never know.

Mark's friend eventually ran out of funds to help them. Mark depended on his friend's help because he wasn't able to find employment. With a pending court date, nobody wanted to hire him. Due to just giving birth Susan wasn't able to work either, so they had to depend on her parents to support them during this ordeal. Both Mark and Sarah were ashamed about their predicament. They hated putting Charlie and Nora in the middle of the situation, but there was nothing else they could do.

While they were living with her parents, Sarah developed a form of Parkinson's disease. The combination of Parkinson's disease and taking care of a baby, her health progressively failed. She also began having problems with her equilibrium. Sarah could only walk a few steps at a time and would lose her balance. She would fall several times a day, becoming bruised from head to toe. Her condition continued to worsen. In addition to bruises, she sustained a concussion, broken bones, and depression.

This new information helped Susan realize how much her mother had suffered. She also understood that her memories as a little girl had been somewhat distorted. Sarah was embarrassed and angry that her disease was so disabling. She felt she couldn't take care of her own daughter, putting the entire burden on Charlie and Nora. She didn't want Susan to remember her as a bruised and fragile person; so she went out of her way to cover up the obvious bruises. Susan was saddened to learn how much her mother had suffered.

Susan was only three years old when Mark received a certified letter announcing the court date. It was time to face the dreaded trial. Mark's freedom was about to come to an end. Susan's parents had three years together rebuilding their relationship and making a home for their child. Charlie and Nora didn't like that their daughter's life was so difficult; but they respected her for trying so hard to keep their family together. It all came to an end by the time the trial was over. Mark was convicted and sent to prison.

As Susan listened to her grandpa relate this story, she had a whole new appreciation for everything her parents had gone through. The most beautiful part is they survived a great hardship together. She was able to acknowledge to herself how proud she was to have been born to two people so determined and strong. Susan realized her parents must have loved each other dearly. Together they were determined to provide a home for their daughter and make the best out of a bad situation. It made her very proud to learn this about her parents.

Without her letter or Charlie's recollection of events, she may have never known how wonderful her parents were. She would have never known the good side of her father either. Susan was very thankful she found that special letter from her father. It provided the opportunity to learn all these wonderful things about her parents that she would have otherwise never known. Susan felt this was the first incident during this visit that turned out so positive and meaningful.

While they continued looking through the photos, Frank was back in his office reviewing lab results. Paula's fingerprint results were on his desk, but he hadn't opened the envelope yet. Next to that packet was a second lab result, marked "Key". Which envelope should be opened first, he wondered. Frank didn't know if he was hoping Paula was related to Mike or not. He wasn't sure which would be the better scenario. And the key…what will he learn when he finds out who touched the key? Frank sat back in his chair and opened Paula's fingerprint envelope first. Before he had a chance to read the results, the phone rang. It was Mike. He wanted to know if Frank had spoken to Susan recently. He explained that he had been trying to call her, but kept getting a recording that it was out of service.

Before he told him anything about Susan, Frank used the opportunity to tell Mike he knew about the aliases he had been using. Mike was taken aback by Frank's comment. He was surprised that a small town sheriff would have taken the time to dig up that kind of information on him. Mike wasn't sure why the sheriff was checking into his background; but he knew now he better watch his step around Frank. Mike guessed something triggered the sheriff to start delving into his records and background. He had no idea what or why he was checking on him.

While Mike was trying to figure out why the sheriff was so interested in him; Frank broke the silence. He told Mike that he didn't want to get in the middle of his and Susan's problems. He did tell him that Susan changed her phone number; and if she wanted Mike to have her new number she'd have to give it to him herself. Frank wasn't going to meddle in their relationship so there was no point in Mike bugging him about it.

Mike composed himself, telling Frank he appreciated his candor. He didn't expect the sheriff to get involved in his relationship with Susan; and he respected that Frank didn't want to. After buttering him up as much as possible, Mike told him that he was aware of the visitors he's had recently. He was talking about the Federal Agents, letting Frank know he was aware of their presence in town. Frank didn't deny or admit anything about the agents. He was sticking to his promise not to discuss anything about them visiting the other day. Frank remained close-mouthed.

Mike realized he wasn't going to get any information from Frank, so he was going to hang up. Before he was able to do that, Frank asked Mike about the day he arrived at Charlie's. More specifically, Frank asked if he happened to move Pluto, the stuffed animal. Mike decided to cooperate with Frank's questions so there'd be no suspicion placed on him. Mike told Frank the night he arrived he was exhausted. He simply let himself in with the key Susan left under the mat for him. Within minutes he fell asleep on the couch. Mike added that he didn't touch anything other than the pillow and blanket. Frank then asked if Mike heard Charlie get up during the night. He also wanted to know if Mike noticed anything strange or unusual that night.

Mike insisted he didn't see or hear anything. He was too tired that night; and he went straight to sleep on the couch. Everything seemed quite normal as far as he could remember. Frank told him that was all the questions he had for now. Mike didn't want to linger on the phone any longer. He was anxious to drive back to Charlie's so he could confront Susan and find out what's going on. He wanted to hear Susan's reason for changing her phone number. Mike needed to know why she was avoiding him.

After their conversation, Frank leaned back in his chair thinking about Mike. He was going to have a lot of explaining to do when he comes to town. Once again he picked up the envelope with lab results in it. Frank pulled out a sheet of paper that was on top of the actual results.

He was specifically looking for one particular thing in the letter. As he glanced through the paragraphs he found what he was looking for. It was confirmed. Paula and Mike were related. This also means Paula's brother is Mike's half brother. Knowing this, Frank is now positive Mike is involved.

While Frank was sorting through all the lab results, Susan was back at home enjoying the evening reminiscing with her grandpa. She suggested Lois and Charlie sit in the swing while she fixed their nightly hot cocoa. It sounded good to them, so off they went to get cozy on the porch. Sitting together they discussed how Frank had acted earlier. Although Charlie wasn't upset anymore, he was truly concerned at his friend's odd behavior. He thought about it for some time and came to the conclusion that Frank must be worried about something very serious. Charlie knew his pal inside and out. He was certain Frank was avoiding him to protect him from something.

Just then Susan came outside with the cocoa. As she handed the cups out, she could tell Charlie and Lois were having a serious conversation. They were talking so intently they didn't even notice Susan had come out. Susan caught their attention and asked what they were talking about. Lois stated they were concerned about Frank. She explained that Frank had been short with Charlie today, which was out of character for him. Susan replied that she thought the same thing. She had also visited Frank earlier and he cut their visit short as well. They felt for sure Frank was hiding something. Charlie decided he was going to confront his friend tomorrow. Satisfied with that plan, they all agreed to go to bed.

Waking up to the sounds of tree frogs and whippoorwills, Susan woke up happy. She had slept well; and was ready to face the new day. She found a note on the kitchen table. Her grandpa wrote that Lois had to be at work early today, so he didn't want Susan alarmed when nobody was there. She took the opportunity to putter around the kitchen and leisurely reread the letter from her father. Susan found the letter to be a great comfort to her. The sweet words from her father were very soothing.

It seemed ironic that on one hand she was reading the letter her father wrote; and at the same time planning his funeral. It was a task she didn't look forward to; but was pleased to have the opportunity to do something honorable for her father. He may not have been perfect, but he was still her dad…a man who loves his family. That's all she had ever wanted.

It was time to put her melancholy feelings aside and get down to the business of making the funeral arrangements. Susan called the local funeral home to find out what time would be best for her to come in. The funeral director asked a few questions; and when Susan told him who the funeral was for, she noted the director's voice change from friendly to cold. Susan choked on a few tears as she continued the conversation with the director.

It was clear he was not pleased to use his facility for a known killer; and yet, he didn't refuse Susan. She was hurt hearing the distain in his voice; but tried to understand that this man didn't know the real man her father was. Going to a different funeral home wasn't the answer. She proceeded to make the appointment and agreed to come later this afternoon.

When she hung up the phone, she wondered if she would get the same negative attitude from the florists. Before she lost her nerve, she immediately called the nearest florists to order the flowers. The saleswoman there was very friendly and didn't change her demeanor when Susan told her who the flowers were for. That was a relief. At least one stranger was sympathetic to the situation.

Nibbling on her toast she noticed the empty stool in the corner. It looked so empty without Pluto sitting there. She walked over to move the stool when she noticed something hanging off the bottom of the seat. Turning the stool over she found an envelope clued to the bottom. Apparently the glue was dry rotting, causing the envelope to fall away from its secure hiding place. Pulling it off the rest of the way, she reached inside the packet. There she found a small water-stained piece of paper. It appeared to be a document from a bank, but it was too worn to make sure. The ink had bled so badly she couldn't make out the written words.

It was obvious the document held some importance. Otherwise why would someone go to such lengths to hide it under a stool? Susan couldn't help but wonder if this had anything to do with the keys everyone talked about. She went to the kitchen to get a plastic sandwich bag, similar to the evidence bags the sheriff's office used. Susan wanted to take this to Frank, with the hope he could identify what the document was; and possibly use it for his investigation.

13

Grabbing her keys to the jeep, she heard a car pull up in front of the house. Thinking it was her grandpa she hurried to the door to show him what she found. Instead of her grandpa, it was Mike. Susan saw that he was driving a different rental car than last time. Not expecting to see him, she wasn't sure how to react. One thing for sure, she didn't want to show him the bank document she had in her hands. She quickly stuffed it into her pocket before walking out to Mike's car. Susan wasn't sure what she was going to say to Mike. She was totally unprepared to talk to him just yet. Mike put his fingers over his lips, letting her know she didn't need to say anything. He wanted to do the talking right now.

Mike asked her to at least give him a chance to explain things. He was aware that Susan knew about some of his background. He wasn't sure exactly how much she knew; but he was certain she knew enough to not trust him. Mike wanted to get back in her good graces, so he had to be careful how much to tell her without looking bad. Susan agreed to hear him out. Although she was torn about wasting her time listening to what he had to say; Susan decided it was the least she could do. She remembered how her mother had given her father a second chance. Her mother listened to Mark when he needed someone on his side. Wrong or right, she would let Mark explain himself before making any more judgments.

Mike began telling her he called Frank last night when he wasn't able to get a hold of Susan on her cell phone. He explained that he was worried when he couldn't reach her; and hoped that Frank would get a message to her for him. Mike continued, telling Susan he knew she learned about some of his supposed criminal records and aliases. She looked surprised when he admitted it. He then explained the reason he had to make up a new identity and forge some records. Mike told her he was working with the FBI as an undercover agent. He had to have the phony background so nobody would know who he really was. Susan didn't know whether to believe him or not. Some of his story sounded pretty iffy, she thought.

Still trying to convince Susan he was working with the FBI, he told her the reason he had to keep it a secret from Susan was so his cover wouldn't be blown. Plus, if anyone was aware that he was really an agent, they might take it out on Susan. He couldn't risk putting Susan or her family in danger; so it was necessary to keep his true identity from her to keep her safe from harm. It seemed like a far-fetched story to her. She was a lawyer and knew better than to believe this tale.

Mike could see that she didn't believe him. He suggested Susan talk to Frank tomorrow because he knew about the undercover sting Mike was working on. Frank could explain the whole cover-up; and maybe she'd believe him then. With that, she was more confused than ever. Now she wondered if maybe Mike was telling the truth. If Frank knew about this undercover business, it would explain why he's been acting so odd lately. If Frank was aware that Mike was an undercover agent, he wouldn't be able to tell Charlie or her. That could explain why Frank has been acting so distant to us lately. Yet, Susan was smart enough to remain very cautious. Without all the facts she couldn't determine if Mike was being truthful or not. She would talk to Frank tomorrow. She was confident he would tell her the truth.

At that point Mike asked Susan if they could go inside to talk instead of standing by the car. For a brief second she considered inviting him; but her instinct told her not to. Instead, she told Mike she wasn't in the mood for visitors right now. In fact, Susan remembered she still had to go to the funeral home to make all the arrangements. When she told Mike she had an appointment to make the arrangements, he offered to go with her so she didn't have to do it alone. Susan told him she preferred doing this by herself and didn't need any help. That's when she suggested he register at one of the hotels; and she would call him later. Mike put on his hurt look, but knew better than to argue with her. She told him the name of the nearest hotel, saying she would call him if she needed to contact him. Before he could say anything else, Susan had already gone back into the house. Susan wasn't interested in anything else Mike had to say. She wanted to talk to Frank before contacting Mike.

Charlie and Lois arrived home shortly after Mike left. Susan saw them drive past Mike as she peered out the window. Charlie recognized Mike in the rental car they passed. He ran into the house to make sure Susan was okay. Susan assured him she was fine. She explained how Mike had stopped by to tell his side of the story regarding his made-up identity. In her opinion, he seemed overly anxious to get his side told...too anxious, indeed.

Charlie usually didn't jump to conclusions or make quick judgments; but he told Susan he had a bad feeling about Mike. It wasn't so much what Mike said...rather, it was what he didn't say. He had nothing concrete to go on though. Charlie agreed with Susan that it would be best to talk to Frank about what Mike said. None of them were convinced that Mike was truly innocent. His story about working for the FBI didn't have a ring of truth to it.

Susan was anxious to call Frank right away, but she explained to Charlie that she was going to the funeral home to make the arrangements. Charlie offered to go with her, but this was something she wanted to do on her own, privately. He understood and told her to do what she needed to do. They would call Frank when she came back home. When Susan left he called Frank to let him know what Susan was doing; and that she needed to talk to him when she returned. Frank told Charlie to let him know when Susan got home and he would come over. It was better if they spoke in person rather than on the telephone; so he would be available as soon as Susan returned.

Meanwhile, at the funeral home, Susan was escorted to a private room with a large table and volumes of photo albums. While she was waiting for the funeral director, she began thumbing through the albums. That's when reality hit. Each album was filled with pictures of caskets, flowers, head stones, and everything connected to a funeral. Seeing all the pictures made her realize this was no dream. Susan began crying as the reality set in. She was here to plan her father's funeral; and it was more emotional than she anticipated.

When the director stepped into the room he could see his client was distraught. It was common for people to be emotional when planning a funeral; but he guessed his surprise was that someone would cry over burying a killer. Maybe he needed to rethink his position in helping her make these arrangements; and be more empathetic. He introduced himself as John Fitzgerald, while taking a seat next to Susan. She lifted her head to look into his eyes. There she discovered a warm pair of eyes looking at her. She felt more relaxed seeing the man as a warm human being, rather than the cold statue she visualized him to be.

John's immediate reaction to Susan was a feeling he had never experienced before with a client. From living in a small town, John had heard about Charlie's granddaughter…the hotshot lawyer in the big city. He expected to meet an uppity, somewhat cold-hearted woman that was stuck burying a man out of responsibility because she was the sole survivor. Instead, he was meeting a soft-spoken, lovely woman; that apparently was here to make plans to bury a loved one. It seemed they were equally surprised at each other.

John went through the brochures, explaining the various choices for a funeral arrangement. Susan stated she wasn't interested in a casket or any glitz. She wanted to keep it simple and private. John asked her if she had considered cremation instead of a burial; and she nodded that she had. In fact, she preferred a cremation. He asked a few more questions regarding whether she wanted a religious service or totally private, etc. At the end of the business discussion, Susan had chosen to have a very private funeral. She only wanted her grandpa, his friend Lois, and herself attending. They were not religious, so she didn't want to hire a preacher that didn't know her dad. That would be too much like hiring a stranger to attend; and she didn't want that.

In the end, Susan picked out the urn she wanted to keep the ashes in. John told her he would make the arrangements to have the body delivered from the coroner's office; and then he would call Susan to let her know what day they could have their private service. With that, Susan shook John's hand; and thanked him for being so understanding.

IMPENDING JUSTICE

John took the opportunity to apologize for being so rude on the telephone. He admitted that he was wrong in "assuming" anything. Susan smiled and left the funeral home feeling good about what she accomplished.

When she arrived home she found Frank already there. Leave it to her grandpa. He probably called Frank while she was gone so he could be there when she got home. Susan couldn't help but smile to herself. She felt so lucky to have Charlie as her grandpa.

Frank wanted to come to the house so they could talk in person. He agreed to come over right away. During the drive to Charlie's, Frank couldn't help wondering why Mike would disclose his undercover status to Susan. If he was really an agent, he would be more professional than to do something like that. Mike would know better than to expose his secret to anyone. Something was definitely not right about this.

While they waited for Frank to arrive, Susan remembered the envelope she found under Pluto's stool. She pulled it out of her pocket to show Charlie. He didn't recognize the document inside. He had no idea what bank it came from. The ink on the document was so smeared and blurry nobody could make out the words. They left it out on the table so they'd remember to show Frank when he got there. What they didn't know is Frank was bringing some documents to show them as well.

The first thing they did when Frank got there was to trade documents. Susan showed Frank the bank document she found; and Frank showed them the evidence proving Mike was related to the White family. There was so much information before them they didn't know which one to discuss first.

Frank admitted he didn't know the relevance of his news. The only thing he knew for certain was that Mike was related to the Whites. What connection that may or may not have on the case was still questionable. The bank document, on the other hand, was more obvious to Frank. He immediately recognized it to be a bank statement from the old bank that has now been replaced with a newer bank. The old bank happened to be the same one where the armored car was parked when the robbery and shooting had occurred. Years after the robbery they remodeled the old bank. At the same time, they modernized and started using newer forms compatible to computers. The document Susan found was an older version of the bank's forms. That meant the document was dated some time before or during the robbery timeframe.

Frank was a customer of the old bank when he was younger. He still had copies of some of his old bank statements, so he was very familiar with how they looked. Although they didn't need a forensic lab to identify what the document was; they did need help in figuring out how to read the detailed information on the document. With all the smeared ink, it was difficult to read the account number or name that was typed on it. Frank put the bank document in his evidence bag to take to the lab tomorrow. If they could find out the name and/or account number on the form, maybe they could figure out the connection to who was involved in placing it under a stool in Charlie's house. There could also be finger prints.

Susan read the papers Frank brought over. Now that she knew Mike was related to Paula, she wondered why he never mentioned it. It was one thing not to discuss his undercover business; but why would he keep an entire family a secret? Plus, she thought, isn't it a strange coincidence that her boyfriend happened to be related to neighbors of her grandpa's? Mike obviously didn't want Susan to know about his relationship with the Whites. She just couldn't figure out the relevance of keeping that information a secret.

Susan asked Frank if he was going to question Paula and her family. He explained that he had already done that. Frank told them he handled his visit with the Whites very informally. He didn't go there as an investigation during that visit. Frank admitted he wasn't satisfied with their answers at the time. He hired an investigator to do a thorough background check on the whole family. There was no doubt in his mind that something was fishy at the White's; so he hired an outsider to check out the situation. Frank thought he'd get the report back within the week. He didn't mention anything about the black box he noticed at Phil's the day he visited. Frank hoped the investigator would find it; and put it in his official report. Then he would have grounds to get a search warrant to take the box from the house.

Charlie and Susan were glad to hear that Frank was pursuing every detail. They felt somewhat uneasy knowing their new neighbors could be trouble. Charlie wondered if the White's had anything to do with the death of his son-in-law. Apparently Mike was killed around the time the Whites moved into town. Mark hadn't been out of prison very long before he was killed. It was bad enough having all these doubts about Mike's involvement with the recent crimes; but it was worse knowing it may not have acted alone. Mike's entire family could also be involved. This knowledge made everyone uneasy.

When Frank got ready to leave he reminded them to lock their doors and windows. He stressed the importance of protecting their safety from unknown intruders. Lois let out a giggle. Everyone turned to look at her, wondering what she was snickering at. She blushed a little, telling them this town has never had so much excitement. Lois explained that she moved to this small town to get away from big city crime. Yet, here they've witnessed more criminal activity in one week than she ever heard of in the city. Her innocent comment did lighten up the mood a little. Her observation was certainly true. None of them had ever experienced this kind of excitement before. With that, Susan began locking the doors and windows. It was time for bed.

After she was in bed her cell phone rang. Susan looked at the Caller ID and opted not to answer the call. It was Mike; and she was in no mood to talk to him right now…or maybe ever. As she put the phone back on the charger she realized she never gave Mike her new number. Susan wondered how he was able to get it. She made a mental note to ask Frank what she needed to do to stop Mike from calling her. The more she thought about it, the angrier she became. How dare he obtain her number and have the nerve to call after knowing he was the very reason she had the number changed!

When the phone rang the next morning she was ready to blast Mike for calling. Instead, it was Frank on the phone. With excitement in his voice he told her he needed to come to the house right away. Susan told her she'd wake her grandpa and have the coffee ready. When they hung up she had an inkling he had some good news to share. His voice sounded cheerful in his excited state. At least she was hoping to hear something good for a change.

Frank arrived before Charlie had time to get dressed. He had a handful of papers and was pulling something out of his tote bag. He spread the papers across the table for everyone to see. Included in the mound of documents were a few photos. The pictures caught Charlie's eye immediately. One picture was identical to the photo he found the other day. He was curious what the picture had to do with Frank's visit. Charlie wondered what his old friend was up to.

Frank told Charlie and Susan to take a closer look. He told them to take their time. Charlie concentrated really hard, trying to find what he was supposed to see. Susan also examined the photos very carefully. After a few seconds, both looked up from the pictures. They couldn't find anything in the photos other than various people posing for the camera.

Neither recognized any of the people in the pictures. Frustrated with the unsolved puzzle, Charlie asked Frank to point out what it was they were supposed to find in the photos. With a grin, he pointed towards the background of the picture. The people in the picture weren't important. What Frank found in the background was more interesting. With a second look, Charlie and Susan saw what Frank was so excited about. In the background, behind the people posing for the photo was a kitchen table. On top of the table there were two boxes. The boxes were clearly Lock Boxes from a bank. The bank logo was printed on the boxes, identifying them to be the Illinois State Bank and Trust Property. They wondered how anyone could have taken the boxes out of the bank.

The marking on the boxes that identified the boxes as property of the Illinois State Bank was identical to the marking on the bank document that was hidden under Pluto's stool. In addition to this remarkable discovery, the photo also showed Phil holding a set of keys. It appeared he was holding the keys like a trophy for the picture. The keys appeared to match the key found in Charlie's house, the day Susan vacuumed. Frank stated the lab would be able to magnify the photos, allowing them to read every detail on the boxes, including the account numbers written on the sides. With that information, Frank hoped they would be able to match the account numbers to the owners of the lock boxes. He felt they were finally getting somewhere in this investigation.

Lois had been in her bedroom getting ready for work, so she wasn't aware Frank was there. When she came into the living room, she could tell the three of them were having a serious discussion, so she didn't want to disturb them. Charlie saw her standing at the door and told her to join them. He couldn't wait to tell her what Frank found in the photos. In celebration, they gathered in the kitchen to have breakfast together. Charlie thought it was like old times. They ate and laughed; all feeling pretty happy with the recent discovery.

The telephone rang; and it was John from the funeral home. He told Susan that her father's body was going to be released later that day. He told Susan there was no hurry to hold the service; she could call him when she felt ready. The service itself would only about ten minutes, but the cremation would take several hours. He explained that if they had the service during the morning, Susan could pick up the ashes the following day. Susan thanked him for calling, telling him she wanted to talk to her grandpa before they decided what time to do the service. John told her he would look forward to her call.

When they were finished eating, Frank said he needed to get back to his office. He offered to take Lois to work on his way. After Frank and Lois left, Charlie asked Susan if she'd like to go on an old fashioned picnic. Just the two of them. He was still worried about Susan. Charlie could tell she wasn't sleeping well and often looked stressed. He thought a relaxing day together was just the medicine she needed. Susan loved the idea, but asked her grandpa if he would mind if they had the brief service for her dad first. It didn't seem like the greatest of ideas, but Charlie was willing to do whatever made his granddaughter happy. They could go on their picnic afterwards.

Susan quickly called John to ask if they could come to the funeral home within the hour. John told her it was no problem. Her dad's body was there and the cremation could be done later in the afternoon. She told him just her and her grandpa would be there for the service; and she would pick up the ashes the next day. For a moment Susan questioned if it was appropriate to have a service at the funeral home one minute, then turn around and go on a picnic...but she knew her father would have approved. He loved Charlie as much as she did; so he would be happy to know they were celebrating his life rather than mourning his death. She was convinced this was the right thing to do.

After the ten minute service, Susan asked John if she could see her dad one time before he was cremated. John explained that because his body was badly burned, he was beyond recognition. He convinced Susan that she wouldn't want to remember her father that way. Even though she was disappointed, Susan knew John was right. She wanted to remember the vibrant man she remembered her father to look like...if not in memory, at least in the photos she had of him.

When they got home, Susan packed fishing poles, blankets, and a basket of fruit. Now that the service was over, she was determined that she and her grandpa were going to have a stress-free day that they both deserved. She could relax knowing she did the right thing for her father; and would always cherish the wonderful letter he had left her.

They loaded the Jeep and headed for the lake. Susan chose the spot where her and her grandparents used to go on Sunday afternoons. Charlie reminded Susan how her grandma refused to bait a hook or take the fish off the line. Grandma Nora loved going fishing with her two favorite people, but hated getting her hands dirty. Susan remembered the time she had accidentally dropped the worms in grandma's hair. She never saw her grandma run so fast in all her life! Those were fun times, as she recalled.

The day slipped by quickly. Before they knew it, the sun was setting and it was time for Charlie to pick Lois up from work. As they were backing out of the wooded parking lot Susan noticed they weren't alone by the lake. There was a truck parked at the other end of the lot. Something about that vehicle seemed familiar to her, but she couldn't figure out what it was. Susan didn't give it a lot of thought. Nothing was going to ruin her wonderful day with her grandpa. It was probably nothing anyway.

After Susan unloaded her Jeep, Grandpa drove it to pick Lois up at the café. She hoped Grandpa and Lois didn't mind eating sandwiches tonight because she sure didn't feel like making a big dinner. She was totally relaxed, yet energized. Susan decided to take a walk before Charlie and

Lois got home. She found herself heading toward the White house. Susan didn't intentionally plan on walking in the direction of their house. She guessed she just didn't pay any attention which way she was going; and ended up facing the White's property. Susan mumbled to herself she should have been more alert to where she was going. Seeing the White's house made her start thinking about Mike again. She didn't want to ruin a perfectly good day by dwelling on anything negative. But, as she looked at the house before her, Susan couldn't help but start thinking about what Frank had told her earlier.

He told Susan that Mike was definitely related to the White family. For Mike to have a step-sister and step-brother, his mother must have remarried after Mike's father was killed. As she was piecing that information together, she walked around a large fallen tree on the White's property. When she looked up she observed the truck she saw at the lake earlier. Susan thought it was strange to find the very same truck at the lake and now in the White's driveway.

From a distance she heard raised voices coming from inside the house. Susan's first instinct was to find out if somebody needed help. As she moved toward the house she heard a familiar voice. She recognized whose voice she heard yelling. It was Mike's. Susan was pretty confident it was an angry voice rather than someone calling for help. Knowing it was Mike's voice, she became curious. She edged closer toward the house so she could make out what was being said. Suddenly she heard someone call out her name. Turning around she saw Paula coming toward her. The yelling inside the house ceased. It was so quiet you could hear a pin drop.

Susan walked closer to where Paula was standing. She really wanted to disappear, but it was too late for that. She also didn't want Mike to know she was out here. Paula asked Susan what she was doing. Susan explained how she had taken a walk and thought she'd come visit. As she got closer and realized somebody was arguing she didn't want to intrude. She was getting ready to turn around and go back home. Susan hoped this explanation was plausible. She wasn't about to mention the truck in the driveway.

As she got ready to leave, Paula offered to walk with her part of the way. Susan couldn't help wondering if Paula was just making sure Susan went home and didn't linger around. Paula walked most of the way with her. They had a pleasant conversation during their walk; but Susan was relieved to see Paula go back home. Susan wasn't interested in having any kind of deep discussion with her, for fear of saying something that might make Paula suspicious.

As she got closer to Charlie's house Susan could hear the phone ringing. She practically ran through the door to answer it before the caller hung up. Susan was expecting her boss to call, so she didn't want to miss it. As she hurried inside, she tripped over a piece of carpet causing her to lose her balance. She would have fallen flat on her face if someone hadn't caught her. Startled to find somebody was in the house, she began kicking and screaming at the intruder. He held her down long enough for her to see that it was Frank's deputy, Butch.

Still shaken, Susan asked Butch how he had gotten inside the house. He responded calmly, telling her he simply turned the doorknob to find it was unlocked. He let himself in thinking Charlie was home since his car was parked outside. When he realized nobody was home he was getting ready to walk out the door. That's when Susan came running in and almost mowed him down. Butch figured he happened to be in the right place at the right time to catch her before she fell.

Susan was grateful he prevented her from falling; but still felt uncomfortable knowing Butch was in her house uninvited. His explanation for being there might have made more sense if Susan trusted him. She couldn't put her finger on it, but there was something about Butch she didn't like. She was glad he was leaving. Susan didn't want to entertain him while she waited for her grandpa to get home.

Right after Butch left, Frank showed up. When Butch passed Frank on the road, he turned around to follow him. Susan was glad to see her friend, but noticed how tired he looked. In the short time she's been in town, it was obvious how Frank has aged overnight. She realized how this investigation was weighing heavily on her dear friend. Susan hoped this case would be solved soon so they could all get back to their normal lives. She would never complain about being bored again!

Frank's news verified nothing was going back to normal in the near future. He didn't want to repeat the news, so he preferred to wait until Charlie got home to tell them together. Susan told Frank her grandpa would be home shortly. Charlie was picking Lois up from work and planned on coming right back home. Susan suggested they have a cup of coffee and relax while they waited for Charlie. By the time she had the coffee brewed Charlie and Lois were walking through the door.

Frank announced he had the results of the fingerprints taken from the keys that were found. One key had Mike's prints. The second key had Phil White's and Paula's fingerprints. Everyone in the room looked at each other without saying a word. Frank explained the key did belong to a lock box from the same bank they discussed previously. He learned that Mr. White rented a lock box from that facility several years ago. Phil had one key, but apparently shared it with Paula. That's why both their prints were on one key. The other key only had Mike's prints.

Both keys fit the same box. Therefore, the White family and Mike had access to the same lock box. It was still unclear what was inside the box. Frank hoped he could learn the answers to this puzzle soon. He knew they were getting close to solving this case; and he was more than anxious to wrap it up so he can retire. His wife would be pleased to have her husband back too. With that goal in mind, he was ready to continue on with the investigation.

Frank didn't tell them everything though. He kept out the part where he obtained a search warrant and took custody of the black box he found at the White's residence. Frank was keeping the box in his truck for the time being; and planned on opening it with the keys they had for evidence. For now he was keeping this information under his hat. The fewer people that new of this finding, the better.

Everyone had watched and listened as Frank disclosed all the information he had. No one made a sound. Frank asked if anyone had any questions about what he just told them. Waiting to see if anyone spoke up, Lois stood up from her chair. All eyes turned to her, wondering what she was about to say. With tears streaming down her face, Lois told the group she had a confession to make. There wasn't a person in the room that could imagine what she could possibly have to confess about. Everyone focused on Lois, waiting for her to speak.

Frank requested she remain silent until he talked to her privately. He took Lois aside and asked if she was about to confess to a crime. If so, he wanted to make it clear she needed to have legal representation first. Lois assured him she hadn't committed a crime. What she wanted to confess was strictly of a personal nature. It was a secret that she had been holding back for too long; and she wanted to get it off her chest. Frank was relieved to know Lois wasn't a criminal. He asked Lois if it was something related to the crimes, because he would want to tape record whatever she had to say in case it was relevant. Lois agreed to have her confession taped, just in case it could be used in the investigation.

Frank had Butch get the tape recorder ready so they could proceed. While they were waiting for him to set up the recorder, Lois sat back down next to Charlie. She held his hand tightly; reassuring him what she had to say did not affect her feelings for him. Lois asked everyone to allow her to tell everything before they asked questions. Everyone agreed to abide by those wishes.

Lois cleared her throat and began to talk. At first she rambled, speaking too fast to be understood. Frank softly asked her to slow down, relax, and then continue. Lois repeated her first few sentences more calmly. She stated that she was previously married. Of course, everyone already knew that; so they wondered why she felt the need to mention it now. To their surprise, her next statement was to announce who her former husband was. With her head down, she said many years ago she was married to Phil White. Lois knew everyone in the room probably had their mouths wide open in shock; but she didn't want to look up to see their reaction. While she still had the nerve, she wanted to finish telling her tale.

Lois admitted she told her neighbors and friends that her husband had died. She was too embarrassed at the time to admit her husband walked out on her, leaving her and the children penniless. Lois was devastated when Phil left her. She felt betrayed, stranded, and alone. She had small children and no income. Rather than divulge her husband was a louse, she made up a fairy-tale about him. She let everyone believe her husband had died unexpectedly. It was easier for Lois to let people feel sorry for her for being widowed so young than to have people gossip about her for not being able to keep a husband. She wasn't very proud of herself for living with that lie; but she thought nobody would ever find out.

Charlie stood up and put his arms around her. He wanted Lois to know he didn't care about her past. He loved her for the woman she was today; not for the woman she pretended to be years ago. Charlie's show of affection gave Lois the strength to continue. She stated how she started a new life, assuming she would never see or hear from Phil again. His memory became a blur. She had all but forgotten him totally. Then one day her past came back to haunt her. She received a phone call from Phil, asking her a favor. Lois was very surprised to hear his voice. Surprised and disappointed.

Frank interrupted a moment, asking Lois when she received that phone call. He was curious if Phil called her before or after he moved into town. She thought it was about three months ago when she first heard from him. At the time she didn't ask him where he was living. Lois went on to relate how strange the phone conversation was. Phil called her to ask a favor; and informed her that he was going by the name of "White" now. Still dumbfounded that he was on the other end of the phone, she just listened. He told her he needed to find a key he had left behind those many years ago. Phil was hoping Lois could help him find it. She thought he might have described the key, but she didn't remember too much about the details of their conversation.

By the time they hung up the phone, Lois was in a daze. At the time she couldn't remember if he told her he'd call back or if she was supposed to call him. It was all kind of hazy. Lois tried to recall if he told her where the key was or if she was just supposed to look for it. When he walked out on her she gathered all his belongings and put them in a chest. She stored the chest in the attic; and hasn't been up there since. Lois was so angry at Phil at the time she just shoved everything of his in that chest. She didn't take time to go through his items. She was too upset to care what things he left behind. She recalled grabbing everything she could find and stuffed it in the trunk. To this day she had no idea what might be in that chest.

About a week after the initial phone call, Phil called her back. He was just as rude as the first conversation that had. He wanted to know if she found the key yet. Lois admitted she hadn't even looked for it. She informed him that when he decided to abandon his family responsibilities that she had put all his belongs in a trunk in the attic. Phil got a little huffy. She could tell he was angry at her for not doing as he had asked. With effort, he controlled his voice, trying to talk nicer. Lois was very suspicious of his whole demeanor by this point. She couldn't fathom why a stupid key could be so important. When they hung up she made up her mind to check the attic after all. Maybe it was time for her to exam what he left behind.

By this time everyone in the room was on the edge of their seat. They were all curious to know what Lois discovered in the trunk. Lois apologized for disappointing everyone. She could tell by the looks on their faces they expected to learn something meaningful. Instead, she explained that the trunk held nothing but clothing and a few photos. She checked all the pockets of the shirts and pants, but found nothing. Lois added there were a few coins, a scrap piece of paper with a faded phone number, and a paper clip under the clothes. Unfortunately, there was no key to be found.

Since she did find old photos, she took them out of the chest and placed them in her apron pocket that she always wore to work. Her intention was to look at the pictures when she went back downstairs. As she reached the bottom step, she was distracted by the phone ringing. When she answered the phone she forgot about the photos in her pockets.

Lois was exhausted but didn't want to break the momentum of telling her story. She admitted that she felt overwhelmed tonight when Frank talked about the key. When he said Phil's fingerprints were on the key, she realized it had to be the same key Phil wanted her to find. Lois was putting the pieces together in her mind, realizing Phil might be considered a suspect in this puzzling investigation. She wanted Frank to know about her former relationship with Phil; and she wanted him to learn it from her. Keeping it a secret any longer would just be an unnecessary burden. Lois wasn't looking for revenge against Phil for leaving her...but she sure wasn't going to let him implicate her in any crime he may or may not have committed. Lois had no choice but to confess everything she knew about Phil.

Charlie spoke up next. He told Lois he found photos in his hall closet the other day when they had stopped at her house to pick up more clothes. He didn't know whose pictures they were, but knew they weren't familiar. Charlie stated Lois hung her apron in his closet when she got home from work.

He concluded they were probably the same photos she found in the trunk, but forgot she put them in her apron pocket. Charlie said he put the pictures in his dresser, so he got up to get them. In the meantime, Frank asked Lois if she was aware of Phil ever being involved in illegal activity when they were married. At first Lois was shocked at the question. She soon realized it was a legitimate question and he had every right to ask. Lois stated she was unaware of him doing anything bad other than him walking out on her and the children. To her knowledge, Phil wasn't involved in anything illegal.

While they were talking amongst themselves, Butch was busy putting a new tape in the recorder. He had been taping the entire time Lois spoke, so the first tape was full. Charlie came back in the room with the photos. He handed them to Lois first, so she could see if they were the same ones she had stuffed in her apron pocket. She admitted they probably were the same pictures, but couldn't be positive. She glanced at the photos when she first found them in the chest; but her plan was to really look at them when she got back downstairs. She never got to do that, so she wasn't positive they were the same ones. Until tonight, Lois had forgotten all about them.

They fanned the pictures out on the table. Charlie immediately picked one up. It looked exactly like the photo Susan had questioned him about the night they were reminiscing over pictures. Holding it out for Susan to look at, she agreed it did look just like some of the pictures they had. Susan walked over to the drawer where she kept the pictures. After shuffling through the stack, she withdrew one. It was almost identical to the photo Lois had in her pile. The difference between the pictures was that one had Susan's father in it; and the other one didn't. Apparently Mark was the photographer of the photo he wasn't in.

After a thorough examination of the pictures Charlie picked the two "almost" identical ones to give to Frank. There were four people in each photo. One person was Phil (Lois's husband), one person was Mark (Susan's father), and the other two were unidentified. Nobody in the room recognized the other two gentlemen in the picture.

Frank asked if he could take the photos back to his office. He wanted time to study them carefully, hoping to find out who the other two men were. In the back of his mind, he was thinking this foursome might have been responsible for the armored car heist years ago. These old photos gave Frank the confidence that they were on to something. He wasn't sure exactly how the pictures would help, but his police instinct told him the pictures would be helpful in the current investigation.

Feeling good about the progress they were making, he didn't want anything to burst his bubble. Frank was ready to leave, but one thing still bothered him. Susan reminded Frank that Butch had already been at Charlie's earlier, before Frank had a chance to get there. It gnawed at him that his deputy showed up tonight without anyone asking him to. Very bluntly, Frank asked Butch how he ended up coming to Charlie's tonight. Seeming a little uncomfortable, Butch stuttered he happened to be in the neighborhood and thought it would be a good idea to check on things. Butch added he noticed Charlie's car had not moved all day, so he was concerned. So many things have happened recently that he wanted to stay on top of any problems. Frank was too tired to question his deputy any further, even though he wasn't sure he quite believed his excuse for showing up unexpectedly.

Walking them to the door, Susan stopped Frank from leaving just yet. She waited until Butch got in his car to leave, and then asked Frank if he had heard any more about Mike. Maybe he was being paranoid, but somehow Frank wasn't convinced that Susan really wanted to ask him that particular question. He wasn't sure what it was she wanted to ask, but he doubted if it had anything to do with Mike. At any rate, Frank decided to play along with the question. He told her he hasn't heard anything new.

Looking out the door, Susan saw that Butch finally drove away. She took that opportunity to asked Frank how long he's known Butch. Now he was sure she used the question about Mike as a cover up. Obviously Susan waited until Butch was out of earshot for her to ask him the real question. His first reaction to her question about the deputy was to ask Susan if Butch had done something to offend her. She explained how the deputy made her very uncomfortable. She couldn't put her finger on it, but there was something about Butch that made her uneasy. Frank told her the deputy had been on the force approximately four years. He admitted he wasn't the one who hired him; and quite frankly he knew very little about Butch.

It was late when Frank left Charlie's house. He was extremely tired and should go straight home. Instead, he decided it wouldn't hurt to make one last stop before heading home. He felt anxious to go to his office to check his mail and faxes. The federal agents told Frank they'd fax him their files on Mark, Susan's father. He was anxious to read them; and knew he wouldn't be able to sleep well if he didn't read them. As desperate as he was for some badly needed sleep, Frank didn't think it would hurt to take a few extra minutes to swing by his office. Afterward he would go right home and snuggle with his wife Judy.

As soon as he got to the office he checked his desk. He searched high and low, but did not find any mail or the faxes he was waiting for. Frank wondered if the secretary put them on her desk since he wasn't in the office today. As he got up to look, he found the documents still on the fax machine. With the files in his hand he decided it was worth coming to the office.

14

Most of what he read in the documents was the same information he already had. As he read further he did discover something new. The lab report identified some of the blood that was found at the scene did not match any of their suspects. Frank yawned, realizing he couldn't stay awake much longer. The words were all running together, so he needed to read this when he was more alert. Tucking the documents in his desk, he decided to go home.

Frank was walking out to his car when another vehicle whipped around the corner toward him. This set Frank off. He was way too tired to deal with some young punk playing around. Whoever it was probably didn't know he was messing with the sheriff. Frank didn't recognize the car, but thought he knew who the driver was. He approached the car, bending his head down toward the open driver's side window. The last thing Frank saw was the barrel of a gun pointed straight at him. Then there was an explosion. Before Frank's body hit the ground, the car sped off.

At about the same time, Lois's boss, Jimmy, was out walking his dog near the parking lot of the sheriff's office. Suddenly Jimmy heard the loud exploding noise, followed by the screeching of tires. His dog was barking and pulling at his leash. Jimmy thought the dog was going to run away, he could barely hold him down. The dog pulled him towards the parking lot, so he decided to follow. It was in the same direction the noise had come from just seconds ago. Just feet away Jimmy could see a crumpled body lying on the ground. At first he thought it might be a large wounded animal. As he looked closer, he could see it was a person lying in a pool of blood.

Yanking the leash, Jimmy and his dog ran as fast as they could. He didn't have his cell phone with him, so he had to get home as quickly as possible to call for help. When he called 911, he identified himself as James Duffy; and told the operator about a man being badly hurt. He told the person he didn't get close enough to see who the injured person was or what was wrong with him. The operator requested that he remain nearby so the police could talk to him when they arrived.

Within minutes, Jimmy could hear the sirens approaching. He went back outside to see if he could help. Jimmy wondered what happened out there. He had only been a few feet away from the victim, yet he didn't see what happened. He did remember hearing tires screech, as if somebody was in a hurry to get away. Jimmy guessed the police were going to question him about what he may or may not have seen. He would cooperate with them; even though he wasn't sure he had much information to offer.

When the ambulance arrived, Jimmy walked over to the scene of the accident. He watched the medics work on the unresponsive man. They found a weak pulse, so they continued using CPR. The man was placed on a gurney and rolled into the ambulance. Jimmy watched how the medics worked non-stop trying to keep the man alive. While he was admiring their efforts to save a life, a deputy pulled up where Jimmy was standing. He asked what, if anything, Jimmy had witnessed. He told him what he knew; and then he asked the officer if the guy was going to make it. The deputy stated it didn't look good. He added that Frank was a fighter, so they could only pray he would survive.

The officer noticed the expression on Jimmy's face. He turned white as a ghost as he learned who the victim was. Jimmy was shocked to find out the wounded person was the town's sheriff. The deputy apologized for blurting out that information. He assumed Jimmy recognized Frank was the victim. The officer took his arm to offer him support after learning such tragic news. Jimmy pulled himself together and thanked the officer for staying with him when he thought he was going to faint.

Jimmy asked who was going to contact Frank's wife. The deputy told him he would probably be the officer to break the news to Judy. Jimmy asked if he could go instead. He explained that Frank and Judy were good friends; and he didn't want Judy hearing about this from someone else. He felt that she would need a friend there than an associate. The officer agreed with him. It was his experience that spouses preferred hearing this kind of news from a friend instead of a uniformed person. The deputy insisted that he drive; but Jimmy convinced him to let him follow in his own car. He said it was official business and someone from the sheriff's office had to be there as well. Jimmy complied; and they each drove to Frank's house to give Judy the heartbreaking news.

Jimmy drove to Frank's house as quickly as he could without being reckless. As he drove along the dark road he was too numb to think. Jimmy couldn't believe what just happened. He just knew he had to get to Judy as fast as possible. All he could think about was seeing Frank's limp body lying in a puddle of blood. Even when he turned Frank over to check his pulse, he didn't recognize who he was. Frank was shot directly in the face at close range. There was not much of his face left to identify. Jimmy wondered if it was possible to survive such a catastrophe. He had to focus on getting to Judy before she heard it from someone else.

When Jimmy arrived at Frank's house he noticed the living room light was still on. He hoped that meant Judy was awake. He dreaded having to wake her from a sound sleep and giving her such dreadful news. Jimmy knocked gently on the door, taking a deep breath. Judy peeked through the window to see who was at her door so late. Once she realized it was Jimmy she immediately opened the door and invited him inside. Jimmy stepped in the entryway trying to decide how he was going to break the news. Before he could say anything Judy reached for Jimmy's arm and asks what was wrong. He blurted out that there had been an accident. Judy felt a chill go down her spine. She knew he meant Frank was in an accident, but she was afraid to ask how badly he was hurt. Jimmy went on to explain that he wanted to be the one to inform her of the accident so he could drive her to the hospital. Without another word Judy ran to her bedroom to throw some clothes on.

As they were driving to the hospital Judy wanted to know exactly what happened. Jimmy explained he really didn't have the answers yet. He told her he was walking his dog when he heard the screeching tires of a car nearby. He witnessed a car speeding off and noticed a man's body crumbled on the road. He didn't mention a shooting because there was no point in upsetting Judy anymore than she already was. Jimmy stated he immediately ran to help the man and then had to find a phone to call an ambulance. Jimmy didn't want to scare Judy so he didn't tell her how badly Frank was injured. As they got closer to the hospital, both were praying Frank's injuries were repairable.

What seemed like a lifetime of driving were actually only a few minutes. When they arrived at the emergency room, they were escorted to a private waiting room. Both Jimmy and Judy were aware that a private waiting room was not a good sign. They knew families were only taken to private waiting rooms when the news was serious or fatal.

Because the patient was also the town's sheriff, the doctors put an emergency rush order to get all test and lab results back immediately. Not only did they want to speed up the results to save Frank's life; the doctors knew there would be a high profile investigation involved. For investigation purposes, they would need all the medical findings immediately. The sooner they knew the extent of Frank's injuries, the sooner they could find who or what caused them.

The doctor sat next to Judy while he explained the details of Frank's injuries. He spoke softly but clearly as he informed Judy that Frank was shot in the face at close range. The doctor also told her that his chances of survival were very slim. He added that Frank lost a tremendous amount of blood and the bullet shattered Frank's brain into fragments. The doctor let Judy absorb what he was telling her. He wanted to give her time to sort out the overwhelming information; and then answer any questions she might have.

Judy didn't hesitate long before asking the doctor to help her understand how Frank's brain could be shattered. She really didn't want to know the medical jargon. She just needed a better understanding of how a bullet could literally shatter brain tissue. Judy was concentrating on the medical aspect to avoid the reality of her husband's injury. It was easier to discuss the physiology of the brain rather than discuss it on a personal level. Judy kept thinking, "Only bones shattered, not brains!"

The doctor had enough experience dealing with families to know that Judy really didn't want to hear the details of what a shattered brain was. Instead, she was searching for answers of what to expect in the future. Judy wanted the doctor to be honest with her; yet, she wasn't sure she was prepared to hear what he might tell her. Judy's real inquiry was to learn if Frank would survive. She didn't want to lose her husband; but at the same time, she knew he would not want to live if it meant he was helpless.

As tenderly as he could explain, the doctor told Judy that there was no brain mass left. The brain tissue had been totally destroyed and torn into pieces. Therefore, even if his heart and lungs continued to function, Frank would be considered in a "vegetated state" the rest of his life. For now the most they could do for Frank was to keep him hooked up to a heart/lung machine to keep those organs working. The doctor stated Frank was considered clinically dead at this point; but would remain on the machines until it was determined it was best to turn them off.

Judy was in shock. This was so much information at one time. Not that long ago she was at home reading a book, waiting for Frank to get home. He had called her earlier to say he was really tired and was going to bed as soon as he got home. Judy was just waiting for him to walk through the door. Instead she found herself sitting on a cold plastic hospital chair hearing that her husband was brain dead.

The doctor told her she didn't have to make a decision immediately regarding the life support machines. She needed to take her time and understand the whole process before deciding what to do. Jimmy agreed to stay with Judy so she wouldn't be alone. He offered to call her family for her so she could be surrounded by loved ones during this crisis. Judy gave Jimmy her cell phone so he could find all the phone numbers of everyone she wanted notified.

While Jimmy was making phone calls on her behalf, Judy asked the nurse if she could see Frank. Knowing his face was so destroyed, the nurse asked Judy to wait a few minutes before going in the room. The nurse entered the room to make sure Frank looked presentable and not so alarming. She also wanted to make sure the bandages weren't saturated with blood. Once the nurse was confident Frank looked as comfortable as possible, she escorted Judy in the room. The nurse quietly shut the door to give them privacy. Judy would need to say her final goodbyes before deciding to have the life support removed. Judy stayed with Frank until her family arrived. This gave her time to fully understand the magnitude of the decision she was facing. It also gave her time to think about what Frank would want if he had to decide his own fate.

Within thirty minutes Frank's two sons arrived at the hospital. They went straight to their mother's side, holding her tightly as she relayed what had happened. Kevin was the oldest. He continued to sit with Judy, holding her while she sobbed. Karl, the younger son, spoke to the doctor. After learning the details of his father's injuries, Karl understood it would take a miracle for Frank to survive. He rejoined his mother and brother on the couch, comforting each other. Kevin could tell by the look in his brother's eyes that the news was not good. No words were exchanged, but the silence said it all. The young men were gradually realizing their dad was not going to make it.

Judy knew in her heart that Frank would not want to be in a vegetated state, having people pity him. She knew he was a proud man. He was a handsome, robust individual; full of life. Frank would want her to let him go in peace. They had this discussion many times during their marriage; but hoped it was a decision neither would ever have to make. Now she had to listen to her heart and remember what was best for Frank.

Judy wanted each of her children to have the opportunity to spend time with their dad before requesting to have the machines turned off. After Kevin and Karl had an opportunity to have private time with their dad, they sat with their mother to discuss the options. They supported Judy's decision to have the life support machines removed. It was a unanimous decision, knowing this would be Frank's choice if he were here to make it.

As the sun began to rise the next morning, Judy was still sitting by Frank's side. She talked to him for hours, never certain if he could hear her or not. Judy wanted to tell him how much he was loved by her, his children, and all his friends. She felt the need to explain to Frank that she was giving the doctors permission to turn the machines off. For a brief second she thought Frank squeezed her hand. Judy felt comforted, believing this was Frank's way of letting her know it was okay to let him go. The doctor entered the room and wrote things on the chart as he unplugged each machine. Judy and her sons stayed in the room until Frank took his final breath.

Afterwards Judy and her family gathered together in the hallway. Jimmy didn't want to intrude on them, so he decided it was time for him to leave. Judy didn't need him right now. She had her family with her. They needed time alone to comfort each other. Besides, there was nothing more he could do for Frank or his family.

On his way home he had to pass the sheriff's office. Without warning, Jimmy began sobbing like a baby. He had to pull over to compose himself because he was unable to drive. The reality of what happened hit him hard as he looked at the sheriff's building. He would never see Frank again. What a horrible night it had been. He made a mental note to himself to call Judy later today, after she's had time to rest. He would check on her to make sure she's okay and offer to help with funeral arrangements or anything she needed.

As he slowly passed the sheriff's office, he noticed Butch standing on the parking lot talking to some men. Butch was laughing with the gentlemen. It looked like they were having a good ole time. How could Butch laugh at a time like this, he wondered? What could be so funny when your boss and supposedly good buddy just got killed? Jimmy was furious seeing this display of frolic right there at Frank's office, but knew there was nothing he could do about it. As he drove further away, Jimmy realized Butch might not even know about Frank's accident yet. After all, nobody else knew except for Judy, the officer, himself, and the killer. Everything had happened so quickly that it was possible Frank's murder wasn't known yet.

Jimmy wanted to call Charlie, but decided it would be better to tell him in person. A phone call was too impersonal to receive such devastating news. Charlie deserved better than that. Jimmy turned his car around and headed to Charlie's house to give them the sad news.

Reaching Charlie's house he realized the time. It was only five o'clock in the morning. Jimmy sat in the car trying to decide whether he should wake Charlie or wait till later. He knew if it was his best friend lying in that hospital he would want to know right away. With his mind made up he went to the door and knocked. As he stood there he tried to think of the best way to tell Charlie what happened. Someone turned the lights on and opened the door. Jimmy expected to see Charlie standing there at this time of the morning, but instead it was Susan.

She invited Jimmy in, asking if he needed to talk to Lois. Susan wondered if there was something wrong at the café. Jimmy just shook his head requesting to speak to Charlie. Susan went to wake Charlie realizing something wasn't right. In fact, at 5:00 in the morning it had to be bad. Before she could knock on the bedroom door Charlie was opening it wanting to know what was wrong. Susan explained that Jimmy was waiting to talk to him. Throwing his robe on he went to the living room to see what he could possibly want at this hour.

Entering the room he saw Jimmy pacing the floor. Charlie had never seen Jimmy act so nervous before. Concerned something was terribly wrong, Charlie suggested they both sit so Jimmy could calm down and tell him the problem. With that, Jimmy told him that he just left Judy at the hospital. He explained that Frank was shot late last night; and he died about an hour ago. Charlie sort of collapsed onto the couch. It looked as if someone had knocked the wind out of him. In a sense that is exactly what happened.

Susan poked her head around the corner asking if Lois and she could come in. Charlie nodded, telling them to sit down. They did as they were told, sitting on either side of Charlie. Jimmy repeated the story of how Frank was shot and died just a short time ago. Finally Charlie looked at Jimmy, asking where Frank was now and who did this terrible thing.

Susan just sat staring in disbelief. She felt it couldn't be true because Frank had just been sitting here only hours ago. He had been talking to them, laughing with them, and looking at photos together. What could have possibly happened, she wondered.

Lois just sat quietly next to Charlie. She seemed as if she were in shock as well. Lois didn't speak or really move. Instead, she just sat there clutching Charlie' arm; as if he were her only life line. After a few minutes of silence, Jimmy told them what happened from the beginning. He explained that he found Frank on the parking lot of the Sheriff's Office. Frank was seriously wounded, apparently from a gunshot wound to the face.

Jimmy also mentioned how he wanted to be the one to inform Judy, so the deputy stayed in the car when he went inside. From there he drove Judy to the hospital to be with Frank; and then left her with her family once the life support machines were turned off. Jimmy added that he thought Charlie would want to hear about this in person, so that's how it came about for him to be there now.

Standing up, Charlie said he was going to the hospital. Susan started to move to go with him, but Charlie told her no. He had wanted to go alone. While Charlie got dressed, Jimmy waited for him on the porch. Nothing seemed to be real to any of them at this point. Everything was happening but it was moving in slow motion. While Jimmy stood trying to compose himself; Charlie came out the door.

After some discussion, Charlie agreed to ride back to the hospital with Jimmy. Part of the reason he had agreed to ride with Jimmy was to get more information about what had really happened. Jimmy explained how he had found Frank and the series of events afterwards. Question after question shot out of Charlie's mouth. Unfortunately, Jimmy didn't have any answers. He was only on the scene after the shot, so he didn't know what happened prior.

Reaching the hospital, Charlie told Jimmy he wanted to see Frank by himself. Jimmy understood, telling him he'd wait in the cafeteria while Charlie went to Frank's room. Charlie promised he wouldn't be long. Charlie requested that he be allowed to go in by himself; Jimmy agreed to wait in the cafeteria. He just wanted to comfort Judy and be able to say his goodbyes to his longtime friend. Jimmy understood; and told Charlie to take his time. Entering the hospital lobby he found Judy surrounded by her family. She saw Charlie walking in and ran toward him.

He took her in his arms and held her while she cried softly. After a time she was able to compose herself enough to talk. She told Charlie that Frank had gone peacefully after the machines were turned off. She also asked if he wanted to go in to see him. He was grateful to have the opportunity to say his private good-byes to Frank. Judy escorted Charlie to the room where Frank lie peacefully.

Going into the room, it didn't even look like Frank. His friend's face was bandaged up to the point that all you could see was gauze and tape. Charlie sat down in the chair beside the bed, looking at his old friend. He then began to tell Frank how sorry he was this awful thing happened.

In his heart he feared this tragedy was somehow his son-in-laws fault. Too many things have happened recently; and it seemed like Frank was getting closer to putting the pieces of the puzzle together. Others realized that too, so somebody had reason to be afraid that Frank was getting too close to the answers. Charlie suspected it was all tied up some way with the robbery and other recent events. He sat for awhile longer holding Frank's hand. Just before leaving he made a promise to Frank that he would find out who had done this to him and his family.

Once Charlie had left the room he found Judy again. He told Judy he wanted to help her with anything she needed. She hugged him once again, saying she had always known it was possible for something like this to happen. They were aware of the risk being a police officer. It had been the topic of many conversations between Frank and her over the years. Of course, there was a part of her that never really believed it would happen. Especially in their small town. Frank dealt mostly with drunks and teenagers, not murderers. He was always the rescuer, not the victim.

Charlie saw Susan walking towards them. Somehow he wasn't surprised that Susan managed to show up. He let go of Judy so he could greet Susan. She wanted to make sure her grandpa was okay, so she dropped Lois off at work and came straight to the hospital. Susan thought Charlie might need a ride home anyway, so it made sense to be available for him. Susan saw Jimmy waiting in the cafeteria so she told him to go home and get some rest. She would driver her grandpa home later. Charlie told her he would be ready soon, he just needed a few more minutes with Judy before he left. Susan told him she would wait for him in the parking lot.

Walking over to Judy once more, he said he wanted to let her know he was leaving. Charlie offered to help her with anything she needed, telling her not to hesitate to call. He also told her he'd be calling her in a few days to make sure she was okay. Susan waited patiently for Charlie to come out. As she watched her grandpa walk over to her, she noticed he looked as if he had aged overnight. She started the car and drove to where he was waiting.

After getting in the car Charlie just sat there for a few moments. He was deep in thought when suddenly he perked up, asking Susan to take him to the police station. Susan didn't know why he wanted to go there, but she knew better than to question him. She simply turned the car around and headed for the station. Knowing her grandpa as she did, Susan was sure he must have a good reason for going there or he wouldn't have asked.

When they arrived they saw yards and yards of police tape strung across the parking lot. They had to park down the street a few blocks away; and then walk back to the station. When they entered, Butch was the first officer they saw. Charlie went straight to Butch, demanding to know everything that happened to Frank. He wanted to know what the police were doing to find Frank's killer. Butch played the objective cop role, telling Charlie to calm down. Butch explained they were actively working on the crime scene and gathering evidence. He was firm but kind as he spoke to Charlie. He knew Frank and Charlie were good friends; and he understood Charlie's anger.

Charlie settled down, realizing he was acting inappropriately. He listened to what Butch had to say, but wasn't satisfied with the response. Charlie asked if either of the Federal Agents were available because he'd like to speak to them as well. Butch seemed surprised that Charlie knew about the Federal Agents. He didn't realize Frank had taken Charlie into his confidence and kept him well informed of everything going on. Butch took Charlie to the office the agents were using. He introduced Charlie to them, explaining that Charlie was Frank's best friend. Agent Jones told Charlie they couldn't discuss the case right now, but they would be calling Charlie in a few days to gather some information from him. Charlie stated he would do anything to help the agents find Frank's murderer. Agent Jones added that they were taking over the entire investigation. It was now out of the local police department's hands, so they advised Charlie only speak to them from here on in.

Charlie told Susan he was going outside. He suddenly needed a breath of fresh air. Susan knew what he was going to do next. Going with him, they both walked over to the crime scene tape. There was an officer there telling them they had to leave. Charlie told the officer he wasn't leaving until he had seen where his friend had died. In his mind, none of this would seem real unless he actually saw the spot where Frank lost his life. The officer knew Charlie, so he agreed to let him look. Holding up the tape, Charlie ducked under, walking carefully in order not to disturb anything. Charlie walked over to the area where there was still a large pool of dried blood. He just stood there for awhile, then turned and thanked the officer. He then walked back over where Susan stood waiting for him.

On the silent ride home, Susan fiddled with the radio. She needed to hear a sound…any sound. She was ready to burst out of her skin and scream over the loss of Frank! For her grandpa's sake Susan was trying to be strong and supportive. Inside she was falling apart. She hurt so badly for her grandpa.

There was no doubt that his heart was breaking over the loss of his friend. Susan only wished she could do or say something to help. With that her cell phone rang. It was Lois calling to check on Charlie. Lois tried to call the house for several hours, but no answer. She was concerned when Charlie wasn't home yet. Susan explained how they went to the Sheriff's Office after the hospital and they were on their way home now. She would have Charlie call Lois back after they got home.

Charlie wanted to talk to Lois, but needed to lay down first. He was exhausted from being awakened so early with the terrible news about Frank. He asked Susan to call Lois back to let her know he was going to take a nap. He'd call her later when he wakes up. Susan did what he asked, then took a nap herself. They both needed to get some rest so they could think more clearly later.

When they woke up from their lengthy naps, Charlie poured a glass of wine for himself. If the circumstances weren't so sad, Susan would have laughed seeing her grandpa drinking liquor. He usually only did that during the holidays, but this was nothing to celebrate. Fixing herself a glass of iced-tea Susan wondered if her grandpa was hungry. As she recalled, they didn't have anything at all to eat today. She knew if she asked, he'd just say he wasn't hungry; so she scrambled some eggs and put a plateful in front of him. With hesitation he began eating. Realizing how hungry he was after the first few bites, he cleaned his plate entirely. That made Susan feel better because she knew he had to keep up his strength these next few days.

She reminded him to call Lois back while she was cleaning up the kitchen. While he talked to Lois, she took her time fussing with the dishes. Susan wondered if Frank learned anything from the photos he took with him. Charlie walked in the kitchen, telling Susan that Lois was on her way over. Lois informed Charlie that her boss gave her the rest of the week off, so she could keep Charlie company. He was glad to hear that. As much as he loved having his granddaughter with him, it was also nice to have Lois by his side.

15

Before Lois had a chance to get there, Agent Jones was at the front door. Susan let him and asked where the second Agent was. Agent Jones stated that they split up for the day so they could ask different people questions about the murder. They decided to sit at the kitchen table so Jones could take notes while they talked. As they were getting situated, Lois arrived. Agent Jones said he was glad Lois was there because she was next on his list of people to interview. Now he could talk to all of them at one time. Susan was comforted knowing they were all together for this inquisition.

Agent Jones told everyone this would be an informal interview. He was attempting to learn everyone's relationship to Frank; and to identify how the crime evidence Frank had gathered could possibly lead them to the killer. Charlie asked if the case Frank had been working on is related to his death. Jones agreed the case Frank was working on might have something to do with him getting killed. From the information they had to-date, it looked like Frank was on the verge of solving a crime and somebody was very nervous about his findings. Jones asked which one of them wanted to start talking about what they knew.

Charlie was the first to speak out. He told him about Susan coming to visit him, the history of Susan's father, what little he knew of Susan's boyfriend, Susan finding a dead body that turned out to be her own father, the photos they found, and the missing lock box keys. Agent Jones was writing rapidly, taking it all in. He didn't blink an eye as he wrote. He showed no emotion as he listened to Charlie's story. He just kept writing.

When he stopped writing, he looked over at Susan and Lois. Before he had a chance to ask which one wanted to talk first, Lois spoke up. She explained to Jones how she was previously married to Phil White. Jones held his hand up and asked what relevance Mr. White had to this case. Lois told the Agent to be patient and she would get to that part. She continued to tell Jones that they recently discovered Phil moved back to town recently; and is a neighbor of Charlie. Lois explained that Phil has a daughter and a son also. His daughter is the one who ran into Susan on the night Susan discovered a dead body in the woods.

Before she could say anymore, Agent Jones admitted he was getting totally confused about all the people she was talking about. He requested they try a new method. Jones wanted to make a list of all the people involved, based on what Lois was talking about. He thought listing them by name would be an easier way to sort things out. Next to each name he would write who they were, who they were related to, and who they knew in town. That would be the starting point of the interview, so as they answered his questions he could make a note by the person's name of their possible connection to this case.

It made sense this way. Jones wrote Frank's name first. They all had to choke back a tear seeing Frank's name written out. Yet, the three of them were determined to get past that. They would do whatever it took to help get this case solved. That was the least they could do for Frank. Getting past the sadness of seeing Frank's name written out, they each contributed their knowledge of what Frank knew up to the time he was killed.

Jones questioned the photos that were discussed in some of Frank's notes. Susan told Jones that Frank had the pictures in his possession; so he stated he would get them to review. Charlie told the Agent that he could identify some of the people in the photos; but he didn't know who everyone was. Jones scribbled his notes on the pad as Charlie gave names. Susan was next. She had the responsibility to describe her former boyfriend and his relationship to the White family. Agent Jones seemed shocked by that comment, but wrote it down with the others.

Jones' next question seemed odd to everyone. He let Susan know he was going to request her phone records; and she agreed. He wanted to check which cell phone towers were used during any conversations with Mike. He said it might be a long-shot, but at this point he wanted as much information as possible to get to the bottom of this. To everyone's surprise it was almost midnight when the interview ended. Charlie and Susan were grateful they had a nap earlier. Lois wasn't as fortunate so she was ready to fall over from the long day.

Agent Jones excused himself and told Charlie he would be in contact again soon. He let himself out while everyone stood up to stretch. Lois went straight to bed while Charlie picked up the coffee cups. Susan said she was going to shower and call it a night.

The next morning Charlie received a phone call from Judy. She wanted to give him the details of the funeral arrangements. Judy cried softly as she was telling Charlie the time for visitation at the funeral home. Charlie had to hold back the tears as Judy talked. It still seemed unreal. When they hung up he told Lois and Susan what the funeral plans were. They nodded quietly as they went about their business of getting dressed for the day. Lois was used to having to be at work by this time, but was glad she didn't have to for the next few days. She was going to need all the R&R she could muster so she could be strong for Charlie.

The three of them were feeling pretty sluggish this bright beautiful morning. It was as if the zip was taken out of them; and nobody knew how to get it back. Without warning, Susan's cell phone rang. Lo and behold, it was Mike at the other end. She almost dropped the phone when she saw his number on Caller ID. She didn't know what to do. For the moment she chose not to answer it. Susan felt she needed a cup of coffee to help get the cobwebs out of her head before speaking to Mike.

Charlie wanted to talk to Lois about what they were going to do today, but Lois spoke first, telling Charlie her plans. She started by telling him that she needed to pick up the rest of her clothes from her house. He stated it wasn't a problem; and he'd go with her. He reminded Lois that he didn't want to be gone long because he wasn't comfortable leaving Susan home alone right now. With everything happening, he didn't want to leave either woman alone very long. Lois agreed. It wouldn't take too long to gather her belongings.

Lois was really using the trip to her house as an excuse to be alone with Charlie. She wanted to talk to him privately, so it worked out perfectly that he was going with her to her house. They could have a little time to talk without other ears present. Right now his house was almost a revolving door. Crowds of people were everywhere in the house. It was a non-stop human traffic jam. Everyone wanted to talk to Charlie about Frank. What she needed to say to Charlie was going to require no interruptions from anyone.

Once they arrived at Lois's house it only took her a few minutes to pack the rest of her clothes and personal items. As they carried the items to the front door, Lois stopped. She asked Charlie to sit down a minute so they could talk about something on her mind. Without hesitation he sat down. Lois took a deep breath before she began speaking. She explained to Charlie that she had thought long and hard about this decision; but she had made up her mind to visit her husband, Mr. White. Charlie sat there waiting for her to continue. Lois reminded him that she was still legally married to Phil since there was never a divorce. When Phil took off, leaving her and the children behind, there had been no money for legal fees so she was unable to file for a divorce.

As the years passed it didn't seem to matter. Up until recently she had no idea where Phil was; so even if she filed for a divorce they wouldn't have been able to serve him the papers. Now that she knew where he was, she felt she had to see him. She needed answers that only he could provide. Lois also wanted to seek a divorce.

Charlie just sat there in a state of confusion. He knew Lois's last name was Lawson, but the man she was calling her husband went by the name of Mr. White. He asked her if she had taken back her maiden name when he left, but at the same time he already knew the answer. He remembered her children's last name was also Lawson, not White. Lois stated she had no idea why Phil changed his name to White. That was one of the questions she wanted to confront him about.

Now that she unloaded her thoughts to Charlie she wondered if he might change his mind about Lois staying at his house. She would understand if Charlie was disappointed in her for still being married, even though there hadn't been a real marriage in years. Charlie could almost read her mind, just by the sad look on Lois's face. He immediately stood up and held her in his arms. After a long hug, he told her it was getting late and they needed to get back home. With that, Lois sighed with relief. Charlie still loved her.

Even though Charlie understood why Lois needed to talk to Phil, he did not want her to go there alone. He didn't think this was the right moment to argue that point with her, but he was definitely going to tell her he'd prefer to go with her when she faces Phil. She probably won't like it, but he was feeling very strongly about the idea. If she didn't want him to go with her, maybe she'd accept the idea of having one of the deputies escort her there. This was something they could discuss tonight. He didn't want to dilly-dally any longer. Charlie didn't like leaving Susan home alone this long.

While Charlie carried her clothes to the car, Lois boxed up some food from the refrigerator. After getting everything loaded in the car, they headed back to Charlie's house. Glancing in the rear view mirror, Charlie noticed a dark colored car had pulled out on the road behind them. It wasn't a car he recognized. He didn't want to alarm Lois so he told her he had forgotten that Susan asked him to pick up some apples from the market. Charlie pulled into the parking lot of the market. The car behind him kept going.

Feeling kind of silly for being so paranoid, he laughed at himself for being overly cautious. He was justified in feeling this way with everything that has happened recently; but didn't like the feeling. He wondered if he was letting his imagination take over his logic always thinking there was a bad guy around every corner. He hurried in the store to pick up the bag of apples. His hope was to check out quickly so he wouldn't get stopped by anyone wanting to talk. Luck was with him. In just a few minutes he had the apples and was back in the car.

As he drove Charlie kept a constant lookout in the rearview mirror. To get his mind off his paranoia he decided to approach the subject of Lois visiting Mr. White. It was as good a time as any to discuss it. No matter what Charlie said, Lois was adamant about making the trip alone. She was determined to handle the situation on her own. As much as he dreaded her going by herself, he knew he wasn't going to change her mind. He didn't push the subject anymore except to let her know he would appreciate if she would at least let him know when she was doing this. Lois thought that was fair request, so she agreed to let him know.

Looking in the mirror again, he noticed that a car was behind them again. He debated if he should turn around or stop. Whatever his decision, he didn't want to frighten Lois. Since everyone knew where he lived he realized he couldn't hide even if he tried. Charlie chose to continue driving straight to his house and see if the car followed him. If the car follows them, at least they'll know who it is by the time they get home. He hoped Susan was near the telephone in case it was an unwelcomed visitor pulling in behind him.

As Charlie pulled into the driveway, the unknown vehicle behind him pulled in too. That answered his first question. Apparently they were following him. He could see two men in the vehicle. At this distance he couldn't make out who the gentlemen were. The strangers stepped out of their car and approached Charlie. They held out their hand to shake as Jones introduced his partner, Agent Adams. Charlie didn't recognize Agent Jones right away because during the interview last night, Jones had on a hat, dark suit and tie. Today both agents were dressed casually and looked much younger. Agent Jones said his partner wanted to sit in on the interview while they discussed a few more details. Jones asked if Susan was here also. About that time Susan came out the door.

Agent Adams started the interview by asking Susan the majority of questions. He wanted to know where she had met Mike, how long she had known him, and if she knew his recent whereabouts. Susan was able to answer most of the questions, but she told Adams that she had no idea where Mike was now or where he's been the last few days. She started feeling uncomfortable about the questioning. It made her nervous that so much focus was on Mike. Then she remembered he tried to call her on her grandpa's phone, but she didn't answer the call.

Agent Jones had taken her cell number to do some checking about incoming calls. He showed her the results he had. Apparently when Mike was calling Susan, he told her he was at his apartment in the city. But, in fact, he was actually calling her from somewhere in this town. The pings from the cell phone towers proved the cell phone he was using was in the same area her cell phone was when they talked to each other. In fact, oftentimes the pings were from the same tower…meaning Mike was very near Susan when they talked on the phone, not miles away as Mike led her to believe. Mike had been lying about where he was every time he talked to her. He was right here in town the whole time she's been here. Now she was truly baffled.

Going one step further, Agent Jones explained that Mike didn't even have his own cell phone plan. His cell phone was part of a family plan…with the White family. Phil White had four phones on his plan. Phil had one for himself, one for Paula, one for John, and one for Mike. The pings from the cell phone tower showed how the four of them spoke to each other often, all from somewhere in this town. Jones stated that they suspected, but haven't proven yet, the landline phone wires had been cut so Charlie wouldn't be able to call for help when his broken into. It was likely the other neighbor's line were cut so it wouldn't be obvious that Charlie was the target.

Jones and Adams had reviewed the original police report that identified the body Susan had fallen over the night she arrived in town. Later Susan was informed the body was actually her biological father. They apologized for having to bring that point up; but felt it was important that Susan understand the facts as they knew them. Jones further explained how Frank had this information early on, but wasn't at liberty to discuss it with anyone. Adams stated the same report also mentioned a key being found near the burned body. Apparently her father, Mark Williams, had the key hidden in his shoe at the time he was shot. The person responsible for shooting him was looking for the key, but didn't find it. The killer then carried the corpse to Susan's SUV; and set both on fire. The killer must have assumed the key was elsewhere, not knowing it was in Mark's shoe. That key matched the key found under the stool in Charlie's house. After checking the serial numbers on the keys, it was determined both keys fit the lock box from the bank. This was all the information Frank had, so they were aware he was getting close to solving the crime before he was killed.

Agent Jones went on to say that so far they had been unable to get a search warrant to enable them to check out the box. He said that they still wanted to go through Frank's files again because he felt like they were missing something. He was actually wondering if Frank had maybe managed to get access to the box and didn't tell anyone. If he had gotten it, it was possible Frank took it illegally. Of course it no longer mattered how Frank got it since he wasn't here to ask. Agent Adams asked Susan if Frank might have disclosed any of this information to her or Charlie. Susan replied that he did not.

Agent Jones hesitated. He looked at Agent Adams who nodded. With that, Jones said that they were going to take them into their confidence, even though it was highly irregular to do. Since Frank had trusted Charlie, Susan and Lois they would too. This was a highly unusual approach, but the Agents agreed it could prove to be beneficial. The agents requested that what they were going to say could go no farther than them. Everyone agreed. It was common tactic for agents to gain the trust of informants so they'd be more willing to tell everything they know about a case. As a lawyer, Susan recognized the tactic was being used on them, but she didn't mind. The agents believed Charlie and/or Susan had information about the case; so they were using their skills to get them to talk. The sad thing was that they would have gladly shared any information that would help them solve this case. They just didn't have any to share.

It was Agent Adams that began talking. He started by telling them the agency had reason to believe Mike purposely wanted to work for the FBI for the wrong reason. Mike had worked especially hard to get hired as an agent in the Illinois Territory so he would have first hand information on the armored car robbery and murder of his father. Adams stated they had evidence proving Mike had inside knowledge of this specific case. He shouldn't have because he wasn't directly involved with that investigation. Yet, he also had the information prior to getting hired with the FBI.

The agents were not at liberty to discuss how they knew that part. Since the robbery of an armory car was under federal jurisdiction, a city cop would have no reason to be checking into it. But Mike had been snooping around about the case long before he became an FBI agent.

This also gave Mike an inside channel to know when Mark Jones was going to be released. There is currently an internal investigation going on with the hope to learn how Mike was able to hide the fact the murdered guard was his own father. Mike's actual job in the agency had been to help track down drug lords and break up known drug rings. He would not have been assigned to an armored car robbery, much less murder. Yet, Agent Jones made some calls and it was discovered Mike had signed out some of the evidence on the armory car heist. He also gained access to the files regarding the case. The agents were sure Mike did not have permission to have this information.

Agent Adams added that they were not accusing Mike of any wrong doing at this point. They were concerned about Mike crossing a fine line by secretly taking evidence from another agent's case. They didn't have proof to-date, so they couldn't officially accuse him of any wrongdoing just yet. The agents advised Charlie and his family to be cautious when dealing with Mike. Before leaving, Agent Kennedy gave Charlie his cell phone number. He stated he could be reached any time, night or day.

Susan assessed what the agents had asked her about Mike. Their facts were clear regarding how shady Mike is. It was almost surreal, as if they had been talking about someone else. She didn't want to believe that she could be so naïve about Mike. Susan has always trusted her instincts; and for years she believed Mike was a good man. In a few short weeks she learned how far off she was in judging him. How could she have been so blind, she wondered? Were there signs she missed that would have unveiled the mask he wore? Maybe he wasn't a criminal; but he was certainly a skilled liar. Susan felt used and betrayed.

Lois could tell Susan was struggling with this new information about Mike. Knowing Susan, she'd probably wanted to talk to Charlie alone. Lois thought it would be a good time to slip away and make her move to visit Phil. If she weren't there Susan could have Charlie's undivided attention. At the same time, Lois could use this time to confront Phil by herself.

It didn't take Lois long to arrive at the White's house since it was less than a mile away from Charlie's house. Looking around as she got out of the car, Lois saw the jeep parked down by the barn. In the distance she could see a girl riding a horse across the field. Lois guessed that was Paula, Phil's daughter. She wondered if she would get to meet her during this visit. Lois was curious to meet her. After all, Paula is her own children's half-sister.

Lois knocked on the front door. She was nervous but determined to confront the man who walked out on her so long ago. When the door opened she was face to face with the husband she hadn't seen in years. It was a strange feeling, to say the least. She didn't know what to expect, but was taken aback to see him in a wheel chair. He looked very old and helpless sitting in this metal contraption. No one had warned her that he was handicapped. It made her wonder if his disability had anything to do with him leaving her those many years ago.

Phil didn't seem to be surprised that Lois was standing at his door. If anything, he looked as if he expected to see her. He invited her in, offering her a cold drink. She declined the drink but told him she did want to sit if that was okay. He pointed to the couch without saying anything. Taking a seat on the couch she told Phil that she had a few questions to ask him.

Before she could start asking her questions, Phil commented to her that he had known sooner or later she would show up on his door step. He didn't know when, but he was confident it would happen. Phil added he thought she'd find him one day and present him with divorce papers. Surprisingly, she never did. Lois didn't know whether to laugh or cry at that comment.

The first issue she wanted to discuss was why he abandoned her and the children. Lois felt she deserved an answer. She had waited a long time to get the opportunity to ask; and she wasn't leaving until she heard the answer. Lois wanted closure to her past so she could move forward with her future. She also wanted him to explain what she had done, if anything, causing him to leave. At that point Phil assured her he was ready and willing to answer any of her questions. In answer to why he left, Phil's only explanation was that he had to. It was never Lois's fault, nor did he mean to hurt her. He made a choice to leave for personal reasons that didn't involve her.

At best, his answer was vague. Phil obviously wasn't going to elaborate on what his personal reasons were for leaving her. At that moment Lois decided it was no longer important to know. She decided there were too many other important issues to discuss. Lois wanted to know why Phil had changed his name from Lawson to White. She was curious why he went to such great lengths to hide his identity. Phil explained he met someone named Brenda Arnold. When her husband died, she took her maiden name back, which was White. She had her name legally changed simply because she preferred her maiden name over her married name.

When he was dating Brenda he couldn't tell her he was married. Instead, he made up an entire story of how he was hiding out from an ex-wife that was trying to take every dime he had. Brenda suggested if he had his name changed legally it would be more difficult for his ex-wife to find him. Phil stated he went one step further. He asked Brenda to marry him and she agreed. Instead of Brenda changing her last name to his, he used the opportunity to change his name to hers. Hence, he became Phil White. He knew the marriage wasn't legal, but it had kept Brenda quiet and somewhat happy.

Lois's then asked him if he had ever loved her. The answer wasn't what she expected to hear, but she wanted the truth. Phil told her that they were too young at the time; and he felt they were more like two kids playing house. As he recalled, neither one was prepared to raise a family. Seeing the hurt look on Lois's face, Phil decided she deserved a better answer. He had already put her through hell once. Phil didn't want to lie anymore. It was time to redeem himself.

Taking a deep breath, he said the real truth was that he did love her. Phil went on to say he got himself into some trouble shortly after they were married. He didn't want Lois involved in his misdeeds, so the only way to avoid dragging her down with him was to leave. He believed Lois would be fine without him; and the kids would be better off too. Lois tried pressuring him to discuss the "trouble" he had gotten into; but he wouldn't say any more. With one more attempt, Lois asked if the "trouble" he had gotten into was the cause of disability. His non response told her the disability was connected to his misdeed, whatever it might have been.

Lois was getting frustrated with the partial answers he gave. She had never been one to pry, but she wanted to know the full truth. She hoped

Phil would open up to her. Lois needed him to tell everything so she could finally have closure to their relationship. When it became obvious he wasn't going to cooperate any further, Lois knew it was time for her to leave. Before walking out the door, she placed a packet of documents on his kitchen table. Lois requested that Phil read it carefully; and then sign at the bottom. Phil was sure the packet held the divorce papers he had expected long ago. He nodded in agreement and scribbled his shaky signature.

When Lois got back to Charlie's, Susan was in the process of fixing their evening meal. Lois didn't realize she had been gone so long. Susan told her that Grandpa had been pacing so much that he had just about worn the carpet out. Lois apologized for worrying them. She asked Susan if she knew anyone that could push a divorce through fast. Susan said that she probably could pull some favors and get it done fairly quickly. She would make some calls later to see what she could do. For now Lois needed to go to Charlie and settle him down. He was a nervous wreck waiting for Lois to return. He almost drove up to the White's house thinking he might need to rescue Lois from there.

While they were eating Charlie told them that Judy called. She informed him Frank's funeral was scheduled for the next day. There wouldn't be the standard viewing, just the funeral service. It made Susan reflect to the service they recently had for her dad. She didn't envy what Judy was going through right now. There was some comfort knowing Judy didn't have to go through this alone. She had wonderful children that would help her get through this very sad time.

Frank would have been pleased with the arrangements Judy made. It's the way Frank would have wanted it. He would want his friends to remember him for what he stood for in life; and how he had lived life to its fullest. He would not want to be gawked at and pitied. As they ate, Charlie talked about when he was single he had wanted to go out with Judy. Instead, Judy had her eye on Frank. Charlie couldn't compete with his friend so he started dating others. Then he met Nora. She became the love of his life. The four of them would double-date and all became best friends.

They talked more about Frank while they ate. Lois recalled how he had always been there to help her when her teenagers became more than she could handle. When they needed the guiding hand of a man, Frank was always there for them. After their dinner, Susan said she would clean the table so Charlie and Lois could sit on the porch swing. After she had finished putting dishes away, she fixed them all cups of hot cocoa. Susan felt like it was time to relax. It had been a very rough day.

Looking at the clock, Susan decided she should put off the call to one of her lawyer friends. There was a particular lawyer in her office that had a reputation for doing quick divorces. She would call her in the morning to see if she could help Lois with her divorce. She was taking their hot cocoa out to the porch but stopped before she opened the door. Fondly she looked on the porch and found Charlie's arm wrapped around Lois. The two of them were sound asleep. Taking the cups back to the kitchen Susan returned with an old throw. She covered them gently and let them enjoy their cozy bed on the swing. Susan then headed to her own bedroom, taking her cocoa with her.

16

The next morning Agent Jones called. He wanted to ask Charlie a few question in light of new information he received. Charlie told him to come over any time. They were just sitting around having a bite to eat. Jones stated he'd be there in about half hour. He requested a cup of coffee when he got there because he hadn't had any yet.

When Agent Jones arrived he looked like a kid in front of a candy store. He was smiling from ear to ear as he sat down at the kitchen table. Charlie noticed the happy face, hoping that meant Jones had some good news to give them. They sat around waiting patiently for Jones to start talking.

Jones first asked everyone how well they knew Butch, the deputy. Taking a moment to think about the question, Charlie spoke up first. He told Jones he remembers meeting Butch about two months ago. Charlie was visiting Frank at the office where he was introduced to the new deputy. Butch politely shook his hand, but left the room right afterwards. Charlie remembered commenting to Frank that his new deputy wasn't very friendly. Frank told Charlie he seemed like an okay fella, but agreed he didn't talk much.

Susan spoke up next. She said the first time she met Butch was when Frank came over to the house during the investigation. Butch took notes while Frank did all the talking. She had asked Frank how long he had worked for him and was told four years. Her recollection of Butch during that first meeting was he had tiny eyes that darted back and forth. At the time she was too distraught about all the drama going on, so she didn't think too much about Butch. In looking back, she would have labeled him as a little shady. He had the appearance of somebody who was sly and untrustworthy; yet she had no grounds to prove that. It was just a feeling on her part. Then she remembered the day Butch surprised her in her own house. She thought she was home alone and instead found Butch in her living room on his way out the door. His explanation for being there seemed logical at the time; but it was still creepy that he was inside, uninvited.

Lois said her first meeting with Butch was also the night he came to Charlie's during the investigation. He was a quiet man and stayed in the background most of the time. She saw him at the café a few times, but he never acknowledged that they knew each other. Lois found that very strange because everyone that comes to the café is extra friendly. She couldn't say that about Butch. If anything, he always seemed very distant. Lois described Butch and Frank as the "odd couple" because Butch was so different than Frank. They seemed like an unlikely pair of partners in her view.

After everyone described what they knew about Butch, Charlie asked Agent Jones why he wanted to know. Ignoring Charlie's question Jones mentioned that there was reason to believe Frank knew his killer. He went on to explain that any officer would avoid going directly up to a driver's side window unless they knew the person. Law enforcement staff is highly trained to approach a vehicle with caution, stepping toward the back of the driver's side...not right in the middle of the window. The FBI was aware that Frank was shot at close range, leaning into a vehicle's driver side window. The driver was the apparent shooter. Agent Jones knew Frank would have never stuck his head in the window like that unless he knew who the driver was. That was a Safety 101 Rule.

Secondly, when they took prints of the tires that were next to Frank's body, they learned the tires matched the truck that Butch drove. Butch drove a unique truck with very large tires. It was the kind of truck rarely seen in their small town. Butch was very proud of his truck and spent a lot of money fixing it up like a hotrod. It would make sense if Frank recognized his deputy and approached the vehicle without concern. If Butch was the driver, Frank wouldn't think twice about sticking his face inside the window to talk. Of course, there was always a chance that someone else was driving Butch's truck; but not likely. Butch never let anyone else drive it as far as they knew. He was very protective of his unique truck; and complained when people so much as touched it. For now, without proof, they couldn't say for sure that Butch was the driver. What they did know is the tire prints matched the tires on Butch's truck. What didn't make sense is *why* the driver would want to shoot Frank.

During their investigation Jones admitted they did a background check on everyone that knew Frank. This included doing background checks on Charlie, Susan, and Lois as well. They were surprised to learn this, but at the same time didn't mind being checked out. None of them had anything to hide.

At least the women had nothing to hide. However, they did discover that Charlie had been arrested many years ago. In his younger years he was a bit rowdy and took part in a painting spree. He and his friends were out drinking one night and found several unopened cans of spray paint. Being young and foolish, they took the cans of paint and began spraying cars up and down the main roads. Because they were eighteen years old, they were treated like adults and arrested.

Of course, Charlie was a model citizen after that escapade and never did anything illegal again. Susan teased her grandpa after learning about his "wild" days. He hadn't thought about that incident in years; so he was a little embarrassed to be reminded about it in front of his granddaughter. Susan assured him he was forgiven for his foolish behavior. Charlie just grinned.

In addition, they did a background check on Butch. At first they had a difficult time learning who he was or where he came from. When they ran Butch's social security number through their system, it came up as a deceased person's former number. Apparently Butch was using a dead person's identification to avoid being discovered. This prompted the agents to dig a little deeper. It was imperative they find Butch's real identity. They wanted no stone unturned. Although it isn't uncommon for a criminal to change his last name, they generally choose a new name that's very close to the original one. For example, someone named Richards might change their name to Richardson. It was easier for the person to remember their new name that way.

IMPENDING JUSTICE

The FBI decided to experiment with that method regarding Butch. He stated his last name was Millwood, but that name didn't match his social security number. They played around with other names close to Millwood. By doing this, they discovered the name Miller. The name Butch Miller matched his social security number in their data base. He was lucky enough to find a deceased person with a similar name to his, making it easier for him to remember his new identify. Butch Millwood didn't exist at all, even though that's the name Butch was using. The next step was to find why Butch found it necessary to hide his real identity and how he had managed to pull it off. If Frank were alive today he would be furious to learn this information about his deputy. Frank was a proud man and would have been devastated to know his own deputy pulled the wool over his eyes.

Oddly enough, it was the same name as Frank's. Frank's name was Miller also. The FBI felt it was too coincidental for both men to have the same last name under the circumstances. Miller is a common name, but given the situation, it was odd for the sheriff and deputy to have the same name. If Frank had known his deputy's real name was Miller, he would have questioned it. In such a small town, most people with the same last name are relatives. They wondered if there was a chance that Frank and Butch were related. Frank would have had no reason to keep that a secret, if he had known. This discovery put a lot of suspicion on Butch. What did he have to hide that he needed to change his name?

The next problem with this discovery was deciding on how to find out if Butch was related to Frank in any way. They were certain Frank wasn't aware of any biological relationship between him and Butch. And if Butch was related to Frank, why would he want Frank dead?

From the beginning the agents believed Frank's murder had something to do with all the evidence he'd discovered in his investigation of Mark's murder. It was clear to the FBI that Frank was getting very close to solving the case; so it was assumed his death was to prevent him from exposing his findings. Agent Jones said the timing of Frank's death made it appear it must have something to do with the case he had worked so hard on.

To their surprise, the FBI discovered that Butch had a far different connection with Frank. Through old records they found Butch was actually Frank's biological son. Although that didn't explain why Butch would want his father dead; it did give another aspect on the murder. With what the FBI knew to this point, it appeared Frank was unaware he had a son from someone other than his wife. Butch apparently didn't want Frank, or anyone else, to know he was Frank's son.

With further investigation they learned that Butch's mother was a one-night-stand for Frank. She meant nothing to him. They had a few drinks in a bar, and then went to a hotel for the night. When he woke the next day she was gone. He never looked back or thought about her again. Little did Frank know she had gotten pregnant from their one-night-stand. She never told him. Instead, she had her baby boy, and then attempted to commit suicide.

All this was unknown to Frank. This nameless woman was a blur in his memory. He had no idea she was pregnant. He didn't know she tried to commit suicide. He certainly didn't know this little baby boy was taken from her and placed in foster care. The State determined her to be an unfit parent, so she lost custody of her child. The baby was moved from foster home to foster home. He never had a stable life. In many of the homes he was abused and neglected. He grew up to be an angry child, then a crazed adult. He vowed to find the man who did this to his mother and ruined his life.

Butch paid his own way through school by working various odd jobs. He went to the library nightly so he could learn how to search for lost relatives. In a short time he discovered Frank was his father. Now Butch was ready to seek revenge. He thought the best way to get close to Frank without causing suspicion was to get a job at the sheriff's office. Working with Frank every day would give Butch a chance to earn Frank's trust and know his every move. While he was planning his revenge, he knew he needed to change his last name. Butch changed it to Millwood so no one would question him about having the same name as the sheriff.

Once his name was changed, he applied for a deputy position in Frank's office. He joined the sheriff's department which gave him the opportunity to learn Frank's every move. He would finally be able to seek revenge that he's waited so long for. Butch was confident he would know when it was the right moment to destroy Frank. He was determined to get revenge.

Charlie, Susan, and Lois were dumbfounded. They couldn't believe what they just heard. Poor Frank! He was one of the kindest, gentle persons they knew. If Frank had known there was a child of his out there, he would have been the first one to rescue him. Judy would have been a wonderful step-mother as well. If only Butch had realized, the scenario could have been so much different. Instead, Frank was gone, Butch was on the run, and Judy was alone. None of this needed to happen. It was truly a senseless murder.

While they absorbed that piece of news, Agent Jones mumbled he had more to tell. The sheriff's office received a call this morning from the White residence. Paula White called for an ambulance for her father. She found her dad lying unconscious, sprawled across his bed. Paula had taken her horse for a run earlier. When she got home she put the horse back in the barn and came in the house. She said she called out to her dad, but he didn't respond. His wheelchair was empty, so she assumed he was still in bed asleep. When she checked his bedroom, Paula noticed he was laying across his bed in an unusual manner. It wasn't a position Phil could accomplish on his on. She immediately got closer to the bed, finding his eyes open and his breathing was very shallow.

He was dead by the time the paramedics arrived. Agent Jones stated an autopsy was going to be performed. Although the coroner didn't suspect foul play, he wanted to identify the accurate cause of death. Jones added that Paula consented to an autopsy, even though she wasn't sure it was really necessary. She knew her father was in poor health, so it wasn't surprising that his body gave up.

Susan said that she would go see Paula later in the afternoon. As a neighbor, she wanted to offer her help. She knew Paula was very young, so she probably would be lost attempting to make funeral arrangements. At the same time, Susan didn't want to interfere. She knew it should be her brother and half-brother helping Paula. She decided it was best not to get involved with the funeral arrangements after all. If Paula needed her assistance, she would call. Susan didn't want to get caught up in any of Mike's family drama. She would be more than happy to help Paula; but she wanted to steer clear of Mike. Unfortunately, since Mike was Paula's sister, it was best just not to be in the middle. On the other hand, what kind of friend was she if she didn't reach out to Paula in her time of need? Susan decided to put her personal feelings aside and offer Paula help.

Agent Jones didn't seem to like the idea of Susan going there. He frowned when she told him she would help Paula. Jones suggested that Charlie and Lois go with her. Susan didn't understand why, but since Charlie and Lois were agreeable she wasn't going to argue about it. She would call Paula to let her know they were coming.

Later that afternoon, Susan and Lois fixed a casserole and a pie to take to the Whites. All three of them climbed into Susan's jeep, each holding a food dish on their lap. As they bounced down the drive Lois was trying to keep the casserole from being pitched all over the car. Charlie had the pie and expected it to end up on the floorboards if Susan didn't drive more carefully. He told Susan to take it easy on the craters she was driving through or they would all be wearing the pie. As she came down the final stretch of the drive, she saw the car that Mike had been driving when he had came by the house. She was glad that she had not come alone now. Susan was not ready to face Mike alone after everything she's learned recently.

Stopping the car they were all relieved to find all the food was still intact. As they were approaching the White's front door they heard what sounded like a shouting match going on inside. Susan recognized one of the voices as being Mike's. Another voice was Paula's, but she couldn't make out the third voice.

In spite of the yelling from inside, they decided to proceed with their plan to visit. Susan knocked on the door, unsure of what to expect next. Suddenly the screaming stopped. Silence was the only thing coming from the house now. Before they could change their mind and leave, the door opened. It was Mike standing there.

To break the silence, Lois spoke up first. She held out the casserole, telling Mike they came to help relieve Paula of the burden of having to fix meal during this time of mourning. He opened the door to let them pass, but as Susan walked through he whispered that he would like to talk to her privately. She didn't respond. Instead they all walked into the kitchen where Paula was standing. Paula thanked them for coming and bringing food. She looked like a lost puppy as she hustled in the kitchen putting the food out for everyone to eat.

Mike announced that he and Susan were going to take a short walk. Charlie looked at her with great concern. He didn't think it was a good idea for Susan to go anywhere with this man. She could tell what her grandpa was thinking, so she nodded her head saying they were just going outside on the front porch. Charlie felt relieved. He didn't feel safe being around Mike after everything they learned about him.

Mike asked Susan why she has been ignoring him. He also mentioned how many times he's tried to call her, but she never calls him back. Susan figured it was time to tell him her concerns after what she's learned about him.

Without hesitation, Susan blurted out she no longer trusted him. She confronted him directly. She told him she is aware of the times he has lied to her. Susan also mentioned Mike has been deceitful from the very day they met. She calmly told him she was no longer interested in maintaining any type relationship with him because he couldn't be trusted. Susan was proud of herself for verbalizing her pent up feelings. It felt good getting all of this off her chest; even though she didn't intend to do this at Paula's house. Even so, Susan felt like a thousand pounds had been lifted off her shoulders by confronting him finally.

Mike pretended to look hurt. He acted as if he couldn't understand what could possibly make her say all these things. Susan wasn't bluffed by his innocent reaction. Knowing how deceitful he's been all along, she recognized his pitiful response as just an act. She felt like she was looking at a perfect stranger because the Mike she thought she knew obviously never existed. Before he had a chance to reply, Susan's cell phone rang. The ringer volume was turned up high, so even though the phone was in her jeep, she could hear it. She walked away from Mike to get her phone from the car. Susan was glad to have an excuse to get away.

By the time she had gotten the door open and phone in hand it stopped ringing. There was a voice mail from a number she didn't recognize, so she dialed it out of curiosity. The phone number and message was from

Agent Jones. His message requested Susan or Charlie call him right away. She was ready to dial his number immediately, but saw Mike walking towards her. She quickly put her phone inside her pocket so Mike couldn't see the number that called her. Mike asked who the call was from. Even though it was none of his business, she told him it was Judy. At this point she would rather lie to him than let him know anything in her business. Susan told Mike that Judy needed them right away. She walked passed Mike to go back inside to tell her grandpa that they needed to leave. Mike told her to stop, that he just wanted to talk to her a few more minutes. Susan continued walking away, leaving Mike dumbfounded. He was so used to her doing whatever he asked that he had a difficult time accepting the "new" Susan. He wasn't used to her walking away from him while he was talking; but she was no longer allowing Mike to dictate her life. Susan was proud of herself for taking control. It had been a long time coming; and it felt pretty good.

Susan still wanted to talk to Paula for just a few minutes. She wanted to make certain Paula knew she could count on her and her grandpa if she needed anything. In spite of being Mike's sister; Susan would never abandon Paula if she needed help. Just because Mike was her half-brother, that didn't make Paula a bad person. There was something special about Paula; and Susan trusted her. In fact, Susan sometimes worried about Paula being related to Mike. She felt Paula was just an innocent kid; and probably didn't have a clue what her brother was really like. Susan hoped Mike would have sense enough not to involve young Paula in any of his activities; especially if they were illegal.

Susan told Paula to make sure to call if she needed anything. Paula appreciated the offer; and agreed to call. She wanted to introduce her brother to Susan before she left; but when she turned around he was walking out the back door. Paula would introduce them later, probably at the funeral home. Susan, Charlie, and Lois said their good-byes to Paula. They managed to get out the door without saying anything to Mike. When they got to the Jeep, Susan asked Charlie to drive so she could make a phone call. Charlie gave a little laugh saying that he would gladly drive instead of suffering from her driving! He felt confident they were safer with both his hands on the wheel rather than Susan driving with one hand on the wheel and one holding a phone! At least he would keep them from running into a ditch!

Climbing in the back seat she called the Agent back. As the phone rang she couldn't help wondering why he had called. If Jones would answer his phone soon, she could find out the purpose of his call. Instead, his phone went directly to voice mail. When the recording came on, Susan left him a message stating she was returning his earlier call. She added that he could call them back any time because they stayed up late. She ended the message by telling him it seemed as if they were playing phone tag.

Before they got home, Susan's cell phone rang. It was Agent Jones returning her call. Jones told her he had the autopsy report on Mr. White. The coroner detected foul play after all. Susan asked why they suspected foul play. Paula hadn't mentioned a bullet hole or strange bruises when she found her father semi-conscious. Jones explained that he wasn't at liberty to talk about the findings of the autopsy. All he could tell Susan was that White's death appeared to be suspicious. His words implied that White may have been killed rather than died of natural causes. If that was the case, Susan knew anyone involved with Mr. White would suddenly become potential suspects...including Paula, Mike, and their brother.

Jones stated he was only telling Susan about the findings because he knew her and Charlie intended on visiting the White's. He wanted to warn Susan and her family to be very careful if they still intended on visiting that family. Susan explained they were just returning from there. Now that Jones knew they had already been to the White's house, he decided it was safe to explain the autopsy results. He didn't want to discuss it over the phone; but knew he could trust Susan not to say anything to anyone else. The most important thing was he wanted to make sure Susan realized how serious the situation was and to make sure they didn't go back to the White's house.

Agent Jones explained Mr. White officially died from a heart attack. He further explained there was evidence to show his heart attack was brought on from an outside source. Even though Phil was already in poor health, he wasn't ready to die just yet. The autopsy revealed burn marks on Phil's chest, which appeared to be from an electrical source. With Phil being so fragile, it wouldn't take much effort to cause him to expire. Apparently somebody used a Tazer Gun on Phil, causing his heart to be over-stimulated. The excess stimulation caused his heart to give out, resulting in his death.

Phil's family assumed he died from an old bullet wound, where the bullet had remained lodged in his chest. Phil always claimed if that bullet ever moved, he would be a goner. Therefore, Paula thought the bullet must have moved for some reason, killing him. What she didn't know was that the bullet was still lodged in the same place it had always been. The coroner removed it during the autopsy. That old bullet had no affect on his heart or his death.

Being thorough in his job, the coroner had the bullet tested at the lab. The results proved the bullet came from the same gun that killed the guard during the old armored car robbery. The same guard Susan's father went to prison for killing. Once again, Susan couldn't believe all the coincidences from the old robbery and the death of her father. Before hanging up, Agent Jones told Susan to be very careful. As if that wasn't enough, Jones chose this opportunity to remind Susan that she and her family were also under a degree of suspicion. She didn't expect that comment at all! That statement really unnerved Susan, to say the least. With that they hung up. Susan told Lois and Charlie what he had said.

Poor Charlie came unglued hearing he could be under suspicion for Phil's death! "How dare them!" he yelled. Susan calmed her grandpa down, explaining that anyone that even remotely knew Phil was going to under suspicion until they sifted through the possibilities. She assured him he had no reason to be alarmed. Susan agreed it was an uncomfortable feeling; but not the end of the world. It seemed all their lives had been turned upside down recently; but Susan was confident they would get through this as long as they remained united.

When they got back to the house, Lois took her shower first. Susan fixed them a snack to eat before leaving for Frank's funeral. Charlie kept repeating he never thought he would have been a pallbearer for Frank's funeral. If anything, he thought it would be the other way around. Charlie was older than Frank, so it seemed logical he would die first. Nobody expected this.

Charlie was going to miss Frank deeply. He realized it was the nature of life to start losing friends as they got older, but Frank wasn't that old. Susan continued listening to her grandpa talk about Frank. She tried to distract him by placing a sandwich and pie in front of him. She hoped he would eat something before they had to leave. Just then Lois walked in announcing she was out of the shower. Someone else could take a turn while there was still hot water. Susan took the opportunity to shower next. Charlie was still chattering about Frank, so she let Lois attempt to console him for a while. Once they were all showered and dressed, they headed to the funeral home.

Susan was pleasantly surprised to see how many people were at the funeral home. For Judy's sake, she was glad to see so many people pay their respects. The bigger shock was seeing Mike standing in the parlor. He stood in the back with the two Federal Agents. Susan stayed with Lois hoping Mike wouldn't notice her. While she kept an eye on Mike, she also watched her grandpa. She was worried about him, knowing how hard it was to accept Frank's death. He did seem to be doing better in the funeral home than when he was home. Nevertheless, she wasn't going to maintain a tight vigil on him to make sure he was okay.

When the service was over, Charlie told Susan he and Lois were going to Judy's house for a while. They wanted to keep her company so she wouldn't have to go home alone. He asked Susan if she wanted to go with them, but she declined. Susan didn't feel she knew Judy very well; and thought it would be more comforting for her with just Charlie and Lois. Susan knew the reason for Charlie asking was because he didn't want her going back to the house by herself. She told Charlie not to worry she would be fine.

As she was about to leave the funeral home, John, the funeral director approached her. Susan didn't know why she was surprised to see him standing there. After all, this is where John worked. When he got closer to Susan he offered his condolences, asking if she was related to Frank. She explained how Frank was a long time friend of her grandfather, so she's known him since she was a little girl herself. They continued to make small talk; and then John got the courage to ask Susan what he had been wanting to ask her all along. John suggested they meet for coffee when he got off work. He told Susan that he'd like to get to know her better…providing it wasn't too soon after her father's death.

Susan was shocked, never expecting to be asked on a semi-date at a funeral parlor. Without hesitation though, she quickly answered that she'd love to have coffee with him. John told her he got off work at ten and he could come pick her up. She told him the time was fine, but she preferred driving herself. They agreed to meet at the same café where Lois worked. It was only seven o'clock now, so she had three hours to get ready. Susan decided to go home and rest for a while.

Susan was glad to be alone in her car for a while. With all the recent activity, she didn't have a moment of time to herself. Susan had so many things on her mind, including a date with a man she hardly knew. She found it difficult to focus on any one problem at a time. At least with all the negative problems surrounding her, she now had one positive thing to look forward to.

On the drive home she reflected on some of the recent events. One thing that nagged at her was Lois's lack of respond after hearing about Phil's death. Susan thought it was bizarre for Lois not to show any emotion at all. In fact, she felt like Charlie reacted more surprised than Lois did. Susan had to control herself to avoid jumping to conclusions. For a brief moment her lawyer role kicked in. Her first thought was realizing Lois could easily be a suspect in Phil's murder. She had every motive to want to see him dead…Lois just went to visit him yesterday; and today he's dead. Another bizarre coincidence. If Charlie thought he had something to worry about, he might want to reconsider and worry more about his girlfriend's situation. If anyone, she could be the prime suspect in Phil's death. The problems seemed to pile higher and higher as each hour passes.

Lois may have hated Phil White; but killing him seemed out of character for her. Lois would never harm a fly. Susan was sure of that. No matter what Phil had done to Lois previously, Susan knew Lois well enough to know she would never lower herself to murder. Thinking like a lawyer, Susan knew her imagination was just running wild for the moment. Susan was logical enough to know that just because Lois didn't react surprised at Phil's murder didn't mean she wasn't affected by his death. And it certainly didn't mean Lois was responsible for his murder either. Yet, Susan couldn't help wondering why Lois treated the news so lightly. The simplest answer had to be that, like Susan, Lois had too many other things on her mind.

Nobody was behaving like their normal self these days. Lois probably confided her feelings about Phil's death to Charlie. Susan would get an opportunity to talk to Lois about it later. For now she wanted to get home and put some sweat pants on. She wanted to relax and get all the ugly thoughts out of her head. Maybe she'd have a glass of wine and call her boss to see what's going on back at the office. That will help her get her mind off the chaos surrounding her here.

Nothing was new at her office. She was about to tell him some of what's been going on; but he already knew about the murders. Her boss reminded her that her grandpa's town has been the highlight of all the newspapers and TV stations. It was no secret that Susan's hometown has been turned upside down since his star attorney has arrived. Susan didn't know whether to laugh or cry at that comment. She chose to laugh. Otherwise she'd want to bury her head in the sand until this nightmare was over.

After the wine kicked in, Susan began feeling a little mellow. She covered herself with a warm, fuzzy blanket and fell asleep on the couch. The phone was ringing, but in her foggy state it sounded like the noise was very far away. She finally woke up, shaking the cobwebs from her mind. The answering machine turned on; and she could hear one of the Federal Agents leaving a message. With that she jumped up to answer the phone.

It was Agent Adams, telling her they arrested Butch Millwood. He was hiding out in a room behind the café, waiting for the Greyhound bus to swoop him away. Butch had several thousand dollars tucked in his suitcase when they found him. He broke down and told the agents he knew Frank had found one of the locked boxes; and was keeping it in his truck. After Frank was rushed to the hospital, Butch drove back to where Frank's truck was. He grabbed the locked box and took it back to his hotel room. Butch had made a copy of the key before submitting the key as evidence; so he was able to open the box and empty the contents.

Butch thought he had gotten away with his revenge to kill his biological dad; and get rich at the same time. Or so he thought.

Instead, he was caught red-handed; and will now be facing a prison sentence. In fact, he told the agents that he'd like Susan to represent him at trial. The agents just laughed at his request.

For one thing, Susan was a prosecutor. If anything, she would prosecute the case against Butch; not defend him. Secondly, even if Susan could represent Butch; it was not likely she would accept his case. She was far too close to Frank to be objective or kind to anyone involved in his murder. Butch was dreaming if he thought Susan would even consider representing him.

For some time now it was assumed that Butch killed Frank; and would then try to get out of town quickly. To prevent that from happening, the agents and local police ordered the airports, bus terminal, and taxicab companies to be on alert. These officers were not going to let Butch or anyone else get away with killing one of their finest law officers. The entire team was determined to catch Frank's killer as quickly as possible.

Although Butch was mentally unstable, he wasn't a typical criminal. He was so focused on getting revenge against the man that hurt his mother (and him); he didn't stop to think his greed in taking the money might slow down his escape. While he reveled in ending his father's life, he got sloppy with the rest of his plans of getting out of town. Butch forgot to use a false name when making his bus reservation. He bought a ticket for Butch Miller, forgetting to use the name Millwood. That mistake made it easy for the authorities to trace the bus ticket back to Butch. The agents were alerted from the bus attendant that someone matching Butch Miller's description had just purchased a bus ticket only moments before. The attendant stated that the man used the name Miller, but he wasn't sure it was the same man the Agents were searching for. The bus attendant explained that the bus was going to be leaving the station in an hour; so he warned the Agents to hurry. Butch would be boarding the bus in the next few minutes. The Agents hoped they could get to the bus station in time to take Butch off the bus and arrest him.

Luck was on their side. With only a few minutes to spare, they found Butch on the bus, clutching the box of money on his lap. He was arrested and booked, sitting in jail awaiting trial. The first phone call they made was to Susan. Jones wanted to make sure she was one of the first to know Butch was safely behind bars. Susan thanked the Agent for letting her know. It may not bring Frank back, but at least they could rest knowing his killer was behind bars. Even so, Susan had a difficult time accepting that Frank's own deputy turned out to be his killer. She was glad Frank didn't have to know Butch was his son.

Susan was anxious for Charlie to get home so she could tell him the news. She wondered if Judy knew yet. The Agents might not have told her yet, since they wouldn't want to disturb her at the funeral home. She decided to take Charlie up on his offer and meet them back at Judy's house after all. If the Agents haven't told her yet, then at least Susan could bring her some good news on this dreadful day.

Driving into town, Susan had a sudden chilling thought. Her mind drifted back on Mike. She wondered how Mike had gotten her cell phone number again. She was certain she requested it be unlisted. Susan knew the sheriff's department had her phone number; but she was certain they would have never given her number to Mike. Well, at least she didn't think they would. Susan thought Mike might have gotten from the federal agents without their knowledge. She was aware that Mike had retrieved other information without permission. It seemed if Mike wanted something, he didn't let anything stop him from getting it.

It was also possible some agents gave him permission to have her number. Since Mike has been working undercover, some agents may have assumed it was okay for Mike to have her number. Agent Jones and Adams wouldn't have done it; but maybe it was possible another agent shared the information unknowingly. Susan made a mental note to tell Agent Jones that Mike has her phone number again. He'll know what to do.

Susan pulled into Judy's drive, observing how many people were at the house. It looked like at least half the town showed up to pay their respects. Frank would be honored knowing how many people cared for him and Judy. Susan couldn't help but feel sorry for Judy right now. Poor woman just buried her husband and she probably wants to be alone to grieve right now. Instead she has to play hostess to the majority of the town folks in and out of her house. Of course, Susan realized all the people were there to give Judy moral support. Judy was probably in a daze and hasn't comprehended how many people were there. The reality of the situation would sink in later when Judy was alone. For now she was busy accepting everyone's well wishes and sympathy. Later she would need her private time to grieve. At that time Judy would begin coming to terms with what happened. Frank's death was so sudden that nobody was able to absorb the situation yet. Later Judy would have plenty of time to come to terms with her loss.

As she entered Judy's house, Susan started looking for her grandpa and Lois. She shuffled through the crowd of people in the living room; but wasn't able to find them. Looking into the kitchen, she found Charlie, Lois, Judy, Agent Adams, and Agent Jones sitting at the table. Charlie sat on one side of Judy while Lois sat on the other. As serious as everyone looked, Susan thought it best not to interrupt them. She assumed the agents were informing Judy who Frank's killer was; and that he is behind bars.

Susan was correct. The agents were telling Judy about Butch being the murderer. They also told her Butch's motive for killing him. There was no way to soften the details of Butch's determination to get revenge for his mother. Judy listened, but she had a glazed look in her eyes. To her, it wasn't important why Butch did what he did. What comforted Judy was the fact Frank's killer was behind bars. That's all that mattered to her. Nothing was going to bring Frank back.

Another reason the agents wanted to speak to Judy right away was to ask if Frank ever brought any case files home with him. They apologized for having to bother during this private time; but explained that it was vital to their investigation. Both agents disliked this part of their job. It was always difficult intruding on a funeral, even when it was necessary. It seemed so cold and uncaring; but neither agent fit that description. In fact, the opposite was true. Both officers cared so much for the victims and their families, that they wanted justice served as quickly as possible. They stressed to Judy how important the case files were to their investigation, hoping she would be able to tell them where he kept the files. Judy stated her husband never brought his work home. They had a longtime agreement that Frank would never bring work home.

Of course, that wasn't the answer they were hoping for. The agents looked at each other, shrugging their shoulders. They agreed there was no point bothering Frank's widow any further right now. If anyone, Judy would have known if he ever brought work files home with him. If she said he didn't bring work home, they would have to accept her answer and look elsewhere. Some of their officers were already checking out the sheriff's office for any evidence they might find. Jones and Adams decided they would make a thorough search of Frank's truck. Butch had mentioned previously that Frank had hidden the box of money in his truck. Maybe he kept files there as well.

In the meantime, Susan noticed all the empty paper plates and cups piling up throughout the house. She decided to make herself useful by gathering up all the trash and taking the bags outside to the dumpster. By the time she had things straightened up most of the visitors had left. Charlie came out of the kitchen to tell Susan that Lois was going to stay the rest of the evening and all night with Judy. He said that he would leave his car for Lois and ride home with Susan. She was glad to know Judy wouldn't have to be home alone tonight.

17

When they pulled up in the drive there was a car parked in their driveway. Susan didn't recognize the vehicle or who was sitting on their swing on the front porch. By the look on his face, Charlie seemed to know who it was. He told Susan it was Allen Lancaster, the same attorney who wrote his and Nora's Last Will and Testament. Charlie admitted he had no idea why Mr. Lancaster was at his house waiting for them to get home.

Allen was sitting in the swing, making himself right at home. As Charlie approached the house, Mr. Lancaster apologized for showing up unannounced. Charlie said he didn't mind the visit, but realized there had to be an underlying reason for him to drive all the way over. They all went inside, as it was getting chilly outdoors. Charlie motioned him to take a seat and let them know what the visit was all about. He didn't waste any time. Allen explained he had a letter in his possession that belonged to Susan. Mr. Phil White was one of his clients; and requested this letter be given to Susan upon his death. Susan was totally confused with this news. She asked Allen why Mr. White would write her a letter. His response was to tell her the letter was self-explanatory. Once she read it, she would understand why Mr. White wrote it.

Allen got up to leave but Charlie requested he stay until Susan read the letter. He thought the letter might bring up questions; so he preferred that Allen be there to answer them. Mr. Lancaster felt it was a reasonable request since they obviously had no idea what the letter was about. Even if he didn't have the answers, Allen could make inquiries regarding the contents since he was Mr. White's attorney. Susan sat down in her favorite chair to begin reading.

The letter was addressed to Susan Mitchell. Still surprised this letter was actually written to her, she continued reading. Mr. White wrote,

"*If you are reading this letter, it means I am gone. You won't be able to ask me any questions since I will already be dead when you read this. Therefore, I will do my best to make this letter as clear as possible. If you know anything about me, you already know I was never a trustworthy person. I have done many bad things in my lifetime and hurt many people along the way. Although I am not proud of my past, I can't change it. The one good thing I can do before I die is write this letter to you. I want you to know the truth about your father. You deserve to know what your dad was really like instead of remembering him as a thief. It's the least I can do; even though I realize it might be too late.*

When your mother was pregnant with you, your father and I lost our jobs. Neither of us could find jobs at the time. I had a friend that worked for as a security guard on an armored truck. My so-called friend had a plan to rob the local bank; and he was willing to split the profits. He promised it was a full-proof plan; and your dad and I were naïve enough to believe him. To pull it off, he said we needed one more person to drive the getaway van. I knew your dad was as desperate as I was, so I asked him to be our partner in the robbery.

I guess I should explain that my friend, the guard, was also Mike's father. The plan was to knock the other armored car guard out. My friend did knock him down, but the officer was still conscious. He woke up when Mike's dad and I were still unloading truck contents into the van. Your dad was sitting inside the van, ready to drive away. His part of the robbery was strictly to be the getaway driver. Nothing more, nothing less. We didn't know the bank officer had a gun. That wasn't in our plan. The officer grabbed for his gun and started shooting. This was unexpected so we panicked. My friend and I started shooting wildly. Then I took direct aim at the officer who was shooting at us. Just as I pulled the trigger, my friend, Mike's dad, stepped in front of him.

The bullet hit him in the chest. It all happened so fast I'm not sure what happened next. Mike's father came crashing down on top of me and my gun went off a second time. This caused me to end up shooting myself. Apparently the noise was the gunfire alerted your dad while he sat in the getaway van. When Mark saw me stagger out the door, he bravely came running to where I was.

Your father saved my life. He picked me up and carried me to the van. After putting me in the back of the van, he ran back to pick up the gun I dropped. Your father was worried some child or other passerby would pick the weapon up and accidentally hurt themselves or someone else. Mark couldn't let that happen. His good deed caused him to get his fingerprints on that gun. It was the same gun that shot Mike's dad. Even though I'm the one who shot my own friend, I had worn gloves so there wouldn't be any fingerprints on the weapon. Mark didn't wear gloves that day.

At this point we knew my friend was dead. Mike's dad would no longer be around to raise his son. The money he hoped to get out of the robbery lost all importance in that brief moment. It was never intended for your dad to get out of the van. Afterwards Mark didn't realize I was the one who shot my friend. Looking back, I guess I was a coward. I never told him. I was young and didn't see the sense in both of us getting arrested. I kept my mouth shut. I really believed Mark would be cleared and not serve any jail time once they knew he was just the getaway driver. But I was wrong. As you know, your dad ended up in prison.

The police assumed I got struck by stray bullets that day, so I never confessed that I participated in the robbery. What they didn't know didn't hurt them. At least that's how I justified it then. I was in the hospital a long time before coming home in the wheelchair. That was my prison and punishment. The doctors couldn't remove the bullet either. It was lodged too close to a vital organ; so I got to keep the bullet as a reminder of what we had done.

Mike's mother took me in after the "accident". We pretended to get married; and I even took her last name so we could put the past behind us. Eventually I was able to receive disability so we had a legitimate income. That way nobody would question how we were able to live so comfortably. We dabbled in the stolen money every so often, but knew we couldn't live luxuriously without raising suspicion.

By now you realize your dad wasn't a criminal. At least not in the same sense you could label me. He deserved to get some of that money after everything he went through. Not only did he go to prison, he almost lost his family over what they believed he had done. There's no way I can spend all the money we took, so it seems only right that you should have the rest.

I put your father's share in a locked deposit box that I keep under my bed. You will find the key sewn inside your stuffed animal. I know that saying I'm sorry won't change anything or bring your father back; but I am honestly sorry for what I have done. Your dad and I were both wrong to do what we did; and I know he always regretted it. I hope you read this letter and accept my apology; but more importantly, forgive your dad. He always loved you and your mother. That never changed.

Mike has been a problem through all this. He grew up an angry young man after learning his father was killed in the robbery. He has recently come back trying to find and claim his dad's portion of the robbery money. Mike sucked his own mother dry. I gave his mother one-third of the money, kept one-third, and put one-third in the locked box for your dad. Unfortunately, Mike has used all of his mother's money and now wants your father's share. He tried to con me out of my third by threatening to tell the Feds I'm the one who killed his dad. I let him know I didn't care what he did. My life has been over for a long time, so there was nothing he could do to hurt me.

With Mark out of the way, Mike figured he would be able to take his share for himself. He's had bits and pieces of clues to where the money was hidden, but not enough to find it yet. He bragged about getting to know you personally. He wanted to find out if you had the money; so he figured you might confide in him some day. Apparently that never happened, so he had to figure out a different way to find out where the money was. It was probably a good thing you didn't know about the money before or he might have conned you into turning it over to him.

Right or wrong, I feel like Mark's family deserves his share of the money after everything that's happened; just as my family deserves what money I have left. Mike spent his father's share long ago; and that's all he gets. We earned what we got, not Mike. I know you're a fancy lawyer and maybe don't even need the money like we did. That shouldn't matter. Take the money and use it however you see fit. Your dad gave up his life over this money; so it is rightfully yours.

Now I hope you understand why I wrote this letter. You might even hate me after reading it, but I don't care. It might be selfish but I wanted to clear my conscious before I died. In addition, I thought you should be warned about Mike. You need to be aware of his immoral intentions. He is an evil man and won't let anything stand in his way to get what he wants. In the process I also hope you can forgive your father. He loved you enough to be dumb enough to commit a robbery just to keep a roof over your head. He would want you to accept the money because it is rightly yours. At least that's my opinion.

Paula knows where the black box is; and she will turn it over to you when she knows you've read this letter. Please don't be mad at Paula either. She's an innocent *bystander in all this. I didn't even tell her what was in the box. She only knows she is supposed to give it to you when you show her this letter. I left her a letter as well, so she'll be expecting you to come get the box."*

When she finished reading the lengthy letter, she glanced up at Charlie. He was waiting patiently to find out what Mr. White could have possibly said in this letter. Susan handed Charlie the letter. She was at a loss for words after reading it, but asked Mr. Lancaster if he knew what the letter said.

Allen explained that Mr. White was his client, but did not disclose what he wrote in the letter. He only requested the letter be given to Susan upon his death. Lancaster added that he had a letter for Paula also. He gave her the letter before coming to Charlie's house. He didn't know what either of the letters said; but instructions were clear to give Paula her letter first, followed by giving Susan hers. That's all he knew. She asked if Allen could stay a little longer while Charlie had the opportunity to read it. He agreed to stay. He was in no hurry.

Susan suspected she might need an attorney's advice after learning about the illegal money she was about to inherit. Being a lawyer herself, she knew this letter would be used as evidence of criminal activity. It was a written confession of Mr. White's part in the robbery and shooting. He implied that Mike would do anything to obtain the rest of the illegal money. This letter needed to be given to the Federal Agents to help build their case against Mike and Mr. White.

To her surprise, Charlie laughed as he got toward the end of the letter. He apologized for the burst of laughter, but explained how happy he was to learn Susan's dad did not kill the guard. Charlie was comforted with the knowledge his son-in-law tried to save a life; and didn't take a life. That was the man he remembered. Susan would no longer have to hold her head in shame thinking her father was a murderer.

The rest of the letter was troubling though. Mr. White clarified Mike's reason for wanting the contents of the mysterious Lock Box. He also mentioned how Mike is willing to do anything to obtain the stolen money. Susan already knew he had been deceitful to her. She suspected he was the one who gave her grandpa the concussion during his search for the Lock Box key. What she didn't want to think about was if Mike had anything to do with the murders of her father or Mr. White. The more she learned of her father's past, the more she discovered how Mike was also involved. Never in her wildest dreams would she have guessed Mike was a part of all this evil.

While Lois was reading the letter, Susan was dialing the phone. She didn't want to waste any precious time waiting. The Federal Agents needed to see this letter. Agent Adams took the phone call. He requested that Susan wait for him to get to her house to talk. He was concerned her phone could be tapped. Mike has access to a lot of the law enforcement tools, including wire tapping equipment. Agent Adams didn't want Susan to say anything over the telephone that would alert Mike to what this letter might say. She agreed to wait for him to come to the house so they could talk privately.

By the time Susan hung up the phone, Lois had finished reading the letter. Charlie asked Mr. Lancaster if he wanted to read his client's confession. Allen stated he would like to read it, but thought he'd wait until the Agents had an opportunity to read it first.

While they waited for Agent Jones and Adams to arrive, they had a surprise visitor. Mike was at the door. Susan stood up to answer the door, but Charlie stopped her. He told her to get his rifle out of his bedroom while he answered the door. Susan did as she was told, her heart beating rapidly. While she was in his bedroom she called Agent Adams again. This time he didn't answer, but she left a message for him to hurry. Before hanging up the phone, she added that Mike was in the house.

18

Mike didn't try to hide his anger as he stepped inside. Charlie asked him what he wanted, but before Mike answered he pushed Charlie out of the way and demanded to talk to Susan. About that time Susan walked out of the bedroom, holding the rifle in her shaky hands. Boldly he walked right up to Susan and grabbed the rifle from her hands. She didn't try to fight back. She knew the best way to handle someone out of control was to back off. Softly Susan asked Mike what he wanted.

He lashed out angrily, yelling right in her face. Mike told her he would leave as soon as she gave him the key to the Lock Box and told him where Phil hid the box. He promised he would be out of her life as soon as he got the money he was owed for her father killing his father. Susan knew there was no point in trying to talk to him. Mike didn't really care who did what in the past. His only goal was to get what his father lost his life for. Mike wasn't going to let anything stand in his way. He came too far to walk out now.

With a smirk he told Susan she was an idiot not figuring out what was going on right under her nose. How dumb was she to think he ever loved her or wanted any part of this stupid little town. Mike continued degrading her; and then switched gears. He told Susan she was going with him to find the Box. Mike was convinced Susan could lead him directly to the money. He was determined to have a hostage in case anyone was fool enough to try to stop him. Charlie offered to go instead, but Mike only laughed. He didn't want an old man tagging along. He knew Susan would make a better shield to protect him.

Mike continued barking orders. He told Lois to get him a roll of heavy duty tape. His intention was to tie Charlie and Lois together so they wouldn't be free to contact the police. Mike told them how lucky they were he didn't just shoot them right on the spot. In his view, the couple was useless. He wasn't going to waste his time killing them. Mike just wanted to make sure they weren't free to get help for a long time. Frightened, Lois did was she was told. She ran into the kitchen to find the tape Charlie had in one of the drawers.

Mike pointed the gun at Charlie, telling him to throw all the old photos in a trash bag. He wanted to throw them in the fire pit outside to make sure any evidence was burned. Mike told Susan to hand over her wallet and credit cards because they were going to need money to survive on. With shaking hands, she placed her purse on her lap. Charlie and Susan were afraid to move. It was obvious Mike had gone over the edge; and his temper outweighed his logic. Susan could see Lois out of the corner of her eye. She was scrambling in the kitchen looking for the tape, but it appeared she had something else in her hand as well.

Susan wanted to distract Mike so he wouldn't look in the direction of the kitchen. She asked him why he thought she knew where the money was. He bragged about how he had her phone tapped. He could tell by her conversations with the Federal Agents that she knew something, but was smart enough not to divulge everything over the phone. Mike told her he was tired of waiting for Susan to slip up and tell everything she knew…so he decided to end the mystery today. As he babbled how he came up with the plan to kidnap her, she glanced over to see what Lois was doing.

Lois pointed toward the kitchen window. Susan didn't know what Lois was trying to tell her. She knew she had to stay focused on Mike, so she couldn't keep staring into the kitchen. Mike could see that Susan wasn't paying any attention to him. He turned toward the kitchen to see what she was looking at. Mike noticed Lois was trying to give Susan a signal of some kind. In a rage, he ran into the kitchen, knocking Lois to the floor. With that, Charlie and Susan ran behind him, tackling Mike to the floor. In the commotion, Lois picked up a kitchen chair and swiftly brought it down on Mike's head. As he lay sprawled on the floor, Charlie and Susan acted quickly.

They bound Mike's arms and legs with the tape while Lois ran to the front door. Too busy to see what Lois was doing, Charlie and Susan continued wrapping Mike in tape. Earlier Lois was trying to signal the Agent's car was pulling up in the driveway. Lois assumed he was there to rescue them; but when he didn't come in right away she grabbed a knife to ward Mike off. Not realizing Mike was in the house, Agent Jones didn't hurry inside. He was talking on his cell phone, still sitting in his car when Lois ran outside screaming for help.

Startled, Agent Jones looked up. He saw Lois hurrying towards him. Sensing there was a problem he quickly ended his call with his partner. Before hanging up, Jones told his partner to send help to Charlie's place fast! As he got out of the car he drew his gun. He told Lois to sit in the car and lock the doors. Jones ordered her not to get out of the vehicle until he came back. Lois did as she was told.

As he entered the house, Susan was just walking out of the kitchen. Behind Susan he could see Charlie standing over someone lying on the floor. At closer glance, he noticed the person's hands and feet were bound with tape. Jones realized it was Mike lying there. He appeared to be unconscious.

Charlie stood over Mike with a smirk on his face. He told Jones since it took him so long to get there; they took matters into their own hands. Because Jones took his sweet time arriving, Charlie explained how he and the women took charge to catch the perpetrator. Agent Jones was confused. He thought he was coming to Charlie's to read some letter. He never expected to find such disarray, much less find Mike bound in tape. Charlie suggested Agent Jones talk to Susan and Lois so they could explain what happened. In the meantime, he was getting pleasure out of guarding Mike.

From the front door, Jones waved to Lois to come back inside the house. Although she hesitated, Lois decided she better do as she was told; and hoped everything was under control. When she walked inside she could see that Mike was still bound with tape, lying on the kitchen floor. Charlie was standing over him, as if to guard Mike from going anywhere. Jones told the two women to stand together as he pulled a rumpled piece of paper out of his pocket. Lois and Susan had no idea what Jones was doing, but within a few seconds they found out.

Jones began reading them their rights. To everyone's surprise, Agent Jones then handcuffed the two women together. Too distraught, the women complied without uttering a sound. About that time Jones could hear Mike mumbling as he woke up. The Agent told both two women to sit on the couch while he went back to the kitchen. With the crumpled paper still in hand, Jones began reading Charlie his rights. In a very firm voice, he told Charlie to sit on the couch next to Lois. Jones intended to handcuff Charlie too, but couldn't. He had already used the only pair of handcuffs he had with him. He would handcuff Charlie after Agent Adams arrived with his set of cuffs.

By this time it was obvious that Mike was fully conscious. Mike had watched the Agent handcuff the two women; and he heard the agent read Charlie his Miranda rights. He started thinking to himself the Agent's actions might work in his favor. For the moment, it appeared Jones thought the other three were guilty of harming him instead of the other way around. Mike knew he had to take advantage of this any way he could.

While everyone waited to see what Agent Jones was going to do next, Agent Adams walked in. Adams had a total look of confusion on his face when he saw Susan and Lois handcuffed. He was even more perplexed when he saw Charlie sitting on the couch next to the women and Mike bound in tape in the kitchen. He had no idea what was going on. Adams looked over to his partner, expecting some sort of explanation. Jones responded to the look, telling Adams that he would explain later. For now, he requested that Adams take Susan and Lois to his car. He added that Charlie needed to be handcuffed also.

Adams was sure there was a logical explanation for this unlikely scene; but he couldn't imagine what it might be. While he took the women to the car and handcuffed Charlie, Jones was busy taking the electrical tape off of Mike. The most bizarre part of the entire situation was seeing the family handcuffed and Mike free. Adams would not have been as surprised if it had been reversed. He would have understood if

Mike had been the one in handcuffs. Mike has been a suspect for a while, so that would have made sense. Not the other way around.

Adams put the two women in his car; and Jones put Charlie in the back seat of his car. Agent Jones wanted to keep the women separated from Charlie temporarily. He didn't want them to discuss anything between them until the detectives had a chance to question each of them. Charlie wondered why he got stuck riding in the same car as Mike. He knew better than to question it; but he would have preferred to ride with Susan and Lois. He was too disgusted with Mike to have to sit in the same car with him.

Once everyone was settled into the cars, Agent Jones went back to have a word with his partner. The handcuffed threesome couldn't hear what Jones was relaying to Adams. They also didn't understand why Mike was being treated so nicely. It was as if the three of them woke up from a nightmare that turned out to be real. None of them could figure out what was going on; and the agents weren't telling them anything. With that, the Agents started their cars and headed back to town.

As they drove along, Agent Jones asked Mike what had happened. Mike immediately began telling a story of how he went to Charlie's house earlier, interrupting a conversation between the three others. While he stood on the porch he overheard the three of them discuss how they didn't mean to kill Mr. White. Mike stated the comment caught his attention, so he stayed on the porch to continue listening. Very dramatically, Mike described how the three of them spoke about the night they tortured Mr. White. He stated he overheard Charlie laughing as he described holding the Tazar over him as he threatened to use it if White didn't tell where the money was hidden. When White didn't cooperate, Charlie continued to torture the guy, zapping him with the Tazar Gun over and over. Mr. White was apparently too weak to fight him off. Mike stated he could also hear Susan in the background yelling for Charlie to "Zap Him Again!" Mike provided elaborate details of how the group tortured and killed poor Mr. White.

Charlie sat in the back seat listening to Mike's tell Agent Jones one lie after another. Charlie sat there in disbelief, not knowing whether to speak up or not. Jones and Mike acted as if he wasn't even in the car. They kept talking, knowing Charlie could hear every word that was being said. Charlie decided not to say anything. He would try to remember everything Mike was telling Jones; and hoped he had the opportunity later to dispute it.

Mike appeared sincere as he told Jones how shocked when he heard Susan talk about her participation in the killing. Then he mentioned hearing Lois saying something about how bad she felt that they killed Mr. White. Mike concluded that maybe nobody really wanted to kill Mr. White. They were just interested in finding out where the money was; and killing Mr. White was an afterthought.

As if that weren't enough, Mike added how Susan actually said she was entitled to that money. He admitted he was outside the door, so he couldn't see what the three of them were doing; but he could hear them loud and clear through the door. Mike said Susan was literally yelling at Mr. White that she deserved that money. Mike stated she justified the money was owed to her because her father paid his dues in prison and lost his share from the robbery. At that point, Mike faked a sob as he told Jones how sad he was learning how heartless his girlfriend was. Charlie prayed that Jones could see through Mike's fake façade. He felt it didn't take a genius to figure out that Mike was only acting. Everything Mike told Jones was a full-fledged lie.

Mike was on a roll, determined to convince Jones how Charlie and his family were killers. He stated it was clear how angry Susan was that Mr. White didn't go to prison like her father did. According to Mike, Susan wanted revenge on Mr. White for making her father pay for something he did. It was interesting that Mike had so much information to share with the Agents. Little did he realize he had talked way too much. Jones listened to every word Mike had to say. When he mentioned the group using a Tazar Gun on Mr. White, Jones radar was alerted. Jones was aware that Mr. White's cause of death had not been released. Only the coroner, the FBI, and sheriff's office knew about the burn marks caused from a Tazar. Even Mr. White's family hadn't been told to-date. The only other person that could know about the Tazar being used would be the killer himself.

Charlie just sat in the back seat listening. He couldn't believe what he was hearing. He was startled to hear someone actually used a Tazar gun on Mr. White. Charlie knew he didn't do such a thing; nor did Susan or Lois. For a second he wondered who would have done that to poor Mr. White. But worse than that, Charlie was worried that Agent Jones believed what Mike was saying. He hoped Jones recognized that Mike was lying and only spouted garbage from his mouth. He wondered if the Agent could be so naïve to believe anything that Mike was saying. Of course, Charlie realized how law enforcements agents had a special brotherhood; and always protected each other. If Jones was buying into what Mike was telling him, it would be one example of how the brotherhood of officers functioned. He hoped Agent Jones was professional enough to overlook the brotherhood bond in exchange for truth.

In Adam's car, the two women sat quietly. They were each in deep thought, wondering what the next step would be. Agent Adams assured them both he would soon get to the bottom of this mess. The ladies weren't feeling as optimistic as they sat with handcuffs on their wrists. Susan couldn't help but wonder what kind of crap Mike was feeding Agent Jones. It made her furious knowing the ease Mike had in fabricating a story. What kind of man was he, she wondered? Susan could only hope that Justice would prevail; and everything would be cleared up when they talked to the Judge. At least she hoped they would get the chance to talk to a Judge. The normal procedure would include giving them an opportunity to tell their side; but the way things have been handled were far from standard procedure.

Once they reached town they were each taken into a different room. Poor Lois was scared to death. Because of her history with Phil White, Lois was afraid the officers would believe she had the most motive to want him dead. The thought of being a suspect in a murder case was overwhelming, making her feel light-headed. Lois sat in the room alone, with all sorts of things running through her mind. Of course, she knew she wasn't guilty. No matter how she felt about the man, she would have never even considered murder. Plus, she knew she didn't do it. But, someone did kill Phil; and she had no idea who. Then she wondered if

Charlie could have possibly killed him. He was angry enough at how Phil had treated her; so was it possible he wanted to protect her? Lois reminded herself that she was letting her imagination go wild. She took a deep breath and waited for the detectives to question her.

Charlie paced alone in another room while Susan was being questioned. Agent Adams told Susan to explain exactly what happened tonight. At the same time, Mike walked into the interrogation room with them. Susan asked Adams if she could talk to him privately, without Mike. The agent asked her to pretend Mike wasn't in the room. Unsatisfied with that response, Susan stated if they didn't make Mike leave the room she would demand an attorney before she answered any questions. Mike interrupted then. He told Susan she could call an attorney shortly, but needed to answer a few questions first.

Susan was appalled that Mike was not only allowed to stay in the room; but given the authority to ask the questions. She was no dummy. She knew this entire set-up was unethical and wrong. For the moment Susan didn't understand why the Agent was allowing Mike to ask the questions. It didn't make any sense. With that, Agent Adams suggested she go ahead and answer Mike's questions. He promised she could have an attorney; but wanted her to at least provide a little background to the events that led up to her arrest.

As angry as she was to be put on the spot like this, Susan suspected that Adams had something up his sleeve that required her cooperation. With her female intuition signaling her to do as Adams ask, Susan agreed to answer a few questions. She began telling them exactly what had happened, but Mike stopped her in mid sentence. He turned to the Agent and accused Susan of lying. At that point, Susan hadn't even given him any vital information. When he abruptly stopped her from talking any further, it was clear that Mike didn't really want her to give her account of what had happened today. Instead, Mike wanted to tell his side of the story. He obviously didn't want the Agent to hear anything Susan might have to say. This was a huge mistake on his part. Once Mike started talking, he unconsciously revealed some things that only the real killer would know. He began revealing the same story to Adams that he had earlier told to Jones. Mike was so anxious to prove that Susan was the guilty person; he got carried away with his own version of the story, implicating himself. Mike told the agent what he had overheard earlier. He did his best to twist the story so the other three would look bad. Once again, Mike told Adams how Charlie and Susan killed Mr. White with a Tazar Gun; and he went to Susan's house to confront her. Before he was able to say anything, the three of them tackled him and knocked him unconscious. He blurted out how they probably would have killed him, like they did Mr. White, if Agent Jones hadn't shown up when he did.

Susan wasn't going to sit still while Mike accused her of murdering someone. She jumped out of the chair, practically lunging at Mike. Agent Adams grabbed her by the arms and made her sit back down. Adams tried to calm Susan down, but she was beside herself with anger and frustration. She demanded to have a lawyer present; and Adams reminded her that she could make a call to her lawyer later. As an attorney herself, Susan knew her rights. Looking Adams straight in the eye, she insisted on making that phone call immediately.

Knowing he couldn't stall Susan indefinitely, he gave Susan permission to place the call. She frantically called her boss, asking him to find a lawyer for her. Adams couldn't hear what Susan's boss was saying, but he assumed he wanted to know why she needed an attorney. She then whispered in the phone that she's been accused of murder; and needed a lawyer pronto!

With that, she scribbled some notes from what her boss was telling her; and hung up the phone. She looked back at Agent Adams and told him she was not saying another word until her lawyer arrived. He nodded his head in agreement; and looked over at Mike. Mike suggested Susan be taken to a lock-up area while she waited for her attorney; but Adams didn't agree. The only thing Adams was interested in was keeping Mike nearby.

By this time he wasn't concerned at all with Susan or what she might do. He knew it was more important to keep Mike calm so he wouldn't get suspicious of the Agent's scheme. Agent Adams recognized all the holes in Mike's story. He also knew Jones felt that Susan and her family were innocent. Jones wasn't specific; but when they were putting everyone in the patrol cars earlier, he told Adams to just go along with what he was doing. At the time Adams didn't know what Jones was up to; but he trusted his partner, so he agreed to go along with the plan. Adams was also told to handle the situation as if they knew Susan and her family were guilty; and act supportive toward Mike. Just the way he worded it, it was clear that Jones didn't believe Mike either. His partner was definitely up to something; and it would unfold soon. In the meantime, he had to continue the charade of arresting Susan; and act like Mike was innocent. Besides, Adams was confident Susan didn't have anything to do with the crimes. He couldn't say the same about Mike though.

In Mike's rush to incriminate Susan, he gave Agent Adams far too many details about Mr. White's torture and death. He mentioned details that only the murderer would know. The autopsy report wasn't public knowledge yet; so Mike couldn't have known those details unless he was involved in the murder himself.

19

Adams left the room briefly so he could get Jones to come in the room while Susan was being interrogated. Once Jones was in the room, Adams slipped out of the building. He went to the hotel where Mike had been staying so he could search the room. Adams was specifically looking for the Tazer that was used to torture Mr. White. Adams and Jones had planned this from the beginning. While Adams was doing the room search, Agent Jones would keep Mike occupied at the station. They would give Mike a false sense of hope, letting him believe he was helping them interrogate Susan. As long as Mike believed the Agents were going to arrest Susan, he could play the innocent victim, letting his guard down.

The Agents knew they had to act like they were on the verge of arresting Susan to make it seem serious. By detaining Susan, she was actually helping them pull off the scam to search Mike's room and belongings. As much as they hated putting Susan through this trauma, they felt confident it was a scheme that would pay off in the end. Agent Jones wanted to confide in Susan as to what they were doing; but felt it was better for now if she didn't know she was being used to zero in on Mike.

Neither Charlie nor Lois would be able to help pull this off because they didn't have the emotional ties to Mike like Susan did. Using Susan was easier because it was more believable; and they didn't want Mike to get suspicious in their tactics. They still had to interrogate Charlie and Lois to make their scam look legitimate. Agent Jones told Mike he wanted to talk to Charlie and Lois privately; and requested that Mike stand guard outside Susan's door so she wouldn't try to leave. Mike was convinced by now that they believed his story over Susan's. He maintained his confidence, thinking he got away with the murder of Mr. White. Mike laughed to himself thinking how dumb his partners were to believe Susan could actually kill someone.

Agent Jones went into the room where Charlie was being held. When the questioning began, Charlie held his hand up to stop Jones from talking. He demanded to have an attorney present; and his lawyer was his granddaughter. He insisted that Susan be in the room before he answered any questions. Smiling to himself, Agent Jones thought it was a great idea. The problem was they still had to pretend Susan was a suspect in the murder; so he wasn't sure what the protocol was to have an attorney that was also a suspect in the same case. Of course, Agent Jones didn't want to make a big deal out of the request since Susan really wasn't a suspect.

Jones told Charlie he was going to have to check with his supervisor before granting him his request to have Susan represent him. He stepped out of the room pretending to make a phone call to his supervisor. Mike approached him, wanting to know what was going on and to find out what Charlie was saying. Jones told him Charlie wanted Susan, his lawyer, to be in the room with him. Mike was furious hearing that. He didn't care what Charlie wanted! Mike didn't want Charlie and Susan being in the same room together at all. He didn't know what they might say to the Agents if they were together.

Finally Agent Adams returned. As he walked towards them, he nodded to Agent Jones. Mike observed the unspoken communication between the two agents. He sensed something was terribly wrong. Agent Jones told Mike to step into Frank's old office. With hesitation, Mike did as he was told. Once inside Jones began reading Mike his rights. He told him he was under arrest for the murder of Mr. White and the kidnapping of Susan. Jones let him know there would probably be additional charges against him as well.

Mike protested, stating they had it all wrong. How could they arrest him? He insisted he was innocent. At that point, Agent Adams showed him the Tazer Gun he found in Mike's room. Mike denied ever having a Tazer. He then tried to blame the Agents for putting evidence in his possession. With that, Agent Adams spoke up. He explained how the lab verified this particular Tazer was used on Mr. White, causing him to have burn marks, followed by a heart attack. It also had Mike's fingerprints on the handle. In addition, they had witnesses regarding Susan's attempted kidnapping.

There was nothing left for Mike to say or do. He realized he had been set up; and there was no turning back. Mike made one attempt to plead with them to let him walk out the door. He reminded them of the bond they had as law enforcers. They should back each other at all times, good or bad. Neither Jones nor Adams responded to the empty plea. Mike put his hands behind his back to be handcuffed, giving in to the inevitable. As Agent Adams approached him, Mike swirled around quickly. He pointed his service revolver at the Agents. Always prepared, Mike kept his extra gun in his back pocket.

Mike demanded they turn around and face the wall. He made up his mind he was not going to prison. If they wouldn't let him leave, none of them were leaving the room alive. With that, the door burst open. One of Frank's deputies had been listening to the entire conversation. When he realized Mike was about to shoot the Federal Agents, he threw open the door and shot Mike. Jones knelt down on the floor, checking Mike's vital signs. He was still alive, but unconscious.

Someone called an ambulance; and they whisked Mike away to the local hospital. When Charlie and Lois heard the gunshot, they bolted out of the room and searched for Susan. She was waiting in the hallway with the officers. Charlie held his granddaughter, not wanting to let her go. The Agents escorted them all to another room so they could discuss the investigation. They were relieved to learn that they were never really considered suspects. Jones explained that they had reason to believe Mike was somehow involved in Mr. White's death; and they needed to figure out a way to get him to confess.

As the investigation progressed, they learned more and more about Mike. Everything they knew about Mike indicated he might be at the bottom of the entire case. Their goal was to have enough evidence to prove it so they could arrest him; and the timing was ideal when they found him at Charlie's house bound with tape. It was the perfect opportunity to set Mike up, letting him believe he was off the hook. The agents were confident Mike would talk too much, implicating himself…which is exactly what he did. The plan unfolded when Mike acknowledged how Mr. White was killed. Adams apologized for using them to in this way; but Susan assured him she was glad as long as the end result was arresting Mike.

As relieved as they all were, Charlie still had a frown on his face. He let the agents know he wasn't too happy that they put them through hell and back. Susan sided with her grandpa, stating it was a tacky, underhanded plan; but at the same time she acknowledged that it was the cleverest plan that she was ever involved in. With that, everyone smiled. The agents offered to drive them all back to Charlie's house so they could regroup and relax.

They were all ready to go when Susan remembered she would have to call her boss and cancel the lawyer coming. Agent Jones laughed when she said that. They all looked at him like he had lost his mind. Adams explained that after she made the phone call to her boss, one of the deputies called her boss back and explained the scam. He assured Susan's boss that she was not under arrest, nor did she need an attorney. He did suggest she call her boss anyway, just so he could hear the good news from her own voice.

As they got ready to leave the building, Susan told Charlie and Lois that she would like to go to the hospital. Even though she was very angry at Mike, there was a part of her that wanted to see how he was doing. Agent Adams stated he would take her to the hospital; and Agent Jones could take Charlie and Lois home. Charlie offered to go with Susan if she needed him; but she wanted to do this alone. As Adams pulled up to the hospital door, he told Susan he'd come back to get her in a few minutes. He didn't want to leave her stranded at the hospital, so he would take her home after she visited Mike.

When Susan got to the room, it was empty. She walked over to the nurse's station, asking where Mike was. Susan thought maybe he had been taken to surgery or something. Instead, the nurse offered her condolences, stating Mike had died on the way to the hospital. Susan was numb. Even though she wasn't sure what she would have said to Mike, she felt it was important to see him one more time before he was sent to prison. She didn't expect that he wouldn't survive. As she walked away from the nurse's station, she bumped into John Fitzgerald. He was standing in the hallway, near Mike's room. Susan was speechless, never expecting to see John here.

John put his arms around her, guiding her to a chair. It was obvious that Susan was shaken and looked ready to faint. When they sat down, he asked if she was there to visit Mike. Wondering how he would know that, she just looked back at him without answering. John could see that she was surprised at what he asked. He reminded her that he was the only funeral director in town; therefore, he was the person to fill out the release forms for the hospital. The hospital was obligated to have a representative from the funeral home complete the forms before they could release the body; and John was the person obligated to perform that task.

Still wondering how John knew she would be here, Susan asked him why he thought she was there to see Mike. John explained that Agent Jones happened to be his Uncle; so he was well aware of the ongoing investigation involving Mike. He further explained that he overheard his Uncle mention Susan's name when he was talking to his partner Agent Adams about the investigation. From that conversation he learned that Susan was no longer romantically involved with Mike. Instead she was a victim in Mike's criminal activities.

Once he put two and two together, he realized that his Uncle had been talking about the same Susan he had met at the funeral home, the day she made arrangements for her father's service. John confessed it was a surprising coincidence; however, he was happy to learn that the Susan he was interested in was not in a relationship with anyone. At the same time, he was sorry to learn that Susan was a victim in one of his Uncle's investigations. Whatever the circumstances, John was more determined than ever to be part of Susan's life…whether it was now or later. From the first day he met her he knew she was someone he'd like to get to know better. Of course, he realized she would need time to grieve after her father's death; so he did not act on his feelings at that time. He was a patient man and would wait until she was ready.

She smiled up at John, thankful he happened to be here when she needed him most. Now she could close the chapter of her life that included Mike; and move forward to her life that included John. *Case closed.*